## PRAISE FOR *DROP DEAD ON RECALL*

"A smart first mystery. Fans of Laurien Berenson or Susan Conant will especially enjoy this pet-centered mystery."

—*Booklist*

"Boneham's debut will delight dog fanciers."

—*Kirkus Reviews*

"Boneham packs a punch."

—*RT Book Reviews*

"[A] delightful debut. Right up there with the likes of Sue Grafton (Kinsey Millhone novels) and Janet Evanovich (Stephanie Plum novels), without the profanity. An intriguing whodunit."

—*The Australian Shepherd Journal*

"With a sense of humor, a light touch of romance and a solid base of dog training experience under her collar, Sheila Boneham's first novel is worthy of honorable mention."

—*The Free Lance-Star* (Fredericksburg, VA)

"If I were a dog and not just a dog lover, my tail would have been wagging all through [*Drop Dead on Recall*]. As a typical whodunit-loving old English prof, I've loved the best—Sayers, Innes, Marsh, Allingham, et al.—and I'm impatiently awaiting the next Sheila Webster Boneham mystery."

—Lucia Robinson, Professor of English Emerita,
Northwest Florida State College

"A light-hearted read filled with amusing characters and lots of true-to-life info from the dog show world. Reminds me of Susan Conant's early work. Highly recommended!"

—Tracy Weber, author of *Murder Strikes a Pose*,
A Downward Dog Mystery

Named one of Petside.com's "Dog Books: The Best of 2012."

# Catwalk

## OTHER BOOKS BY SHEILA WEBSTER BONEHAM

# Catwalk

## SHEILA WEBSTER BONEHAM

MIDNIGHT INK
WOODBURY, MINNESOTA

FIRST EDITION
First Printing, 2014

Book design and format by Donna Burch-Brown
Cover design by Lisa Novak
Cover Illustration: Gary Hanna
Editing by Connie Hill

Midnight Ink, an imprint of Llewellyn Worldwide Ltd.

This is a work of fiction. Names, characters, places, and incidents are either the product of the author's imagination or are used fictitiously, and any resemblance to actual persons, living or dead, business establishments, events, or locales is entirely coincidental.

**Library of Congress Cataloging-in-Publication Data**

Boneham, Sheila Webster, 1952–
  Catwalk / by Sheila Webster Boneham. — First edition.
    pages cm. —  (An Animals in Focus Mystery ; # 3)
  ISBN 978-0-7387-3488-0 (alk. paper)
1. Photography of animals—Fiction. 2. Women photographers—Fiction.
3. Murder—Investigation—Fiction. 4. Mystery fiction.  I. Title.
  PS3602.O657155C38     2014
  813'.6—dc234                                          2014020778

Midnight Ink
Llewellyn Worldwide Ltd.
2143 Wooddale Drive
Woodbury, MN 55125-2989
www.midnightinkbooks.com

Printed in the United States of America

*For "the Margarets" who handed down the genes…*
*Peggy (my mom), Maggie (my grandma),*
*and Meg (my great-grandma).*
*I'm sure there were more.*

# ACKNOWLEDGMENTS

Writing a book can sometimes feel like herding cats, although I happen to think that writing is also as much fun as a basket of kittens. The truth is that everything depends on community—ideas, memories, feedback, support, and the occasional obstacle that says "try harder." So, in no particular order, my thanks to those—human and otherwise—who have fed my passions for writing and animals. I can't name everyone, but I will pick out a few special people who had their paws on this book, one way or another.

Because he usually isn't mentioned until the end, I'll start with my husband, Roger Boneham—thanks again for supporting my writing, for talking out (and offering) ideas, and for loving the animals. What's for supper?

Thanks also to my agent, Josh Getzler, for good-humored support, and to acquisitions editor Terri Bischoff, who believed in the Animals in Focus series enough to run with it. Special thanks to Lisa Novak, who designed the beautiful cover of this book; to illustrator Gary Hanna, who made the model Aussie look like my Jay; to Donna Burch-Brown, who not only designed the interior of the book, but who also rescued a Labrador Retriever named Cosmos while this book was in the works. Drake is proud! Brenna Spencer and Rhonda Calhoun Mullenix of Lumos PhoDOGraphy staged the "catwalk and body" photo from which Gary Hanna worked (brilliant!), and Doug Smith of Wysiwyg Photography took the photo of my friend Nita Gandara's Aussie in the perfect sniffing posture. Sharp-eyed, light-handed editor Connie Hill is always a pleasure to work with.

Special thanks to my brilliant early readers Linda Wagner and Nancy Gadzuk. Remaining booboos are mine, all mine! Although they didn't have a direct hand in this book, the members of the DogRead discussion list provided much useful feedback about the two preceeding books, and some story snippets that I have modified and used in Catwalk. Special thanks to Dana Mackonis and Patricia Tirrell for inviting me to sit in the author seat.

My profound thanks to the animals who enrich and inspire me in so many ways, and to the people who take animals seriously—the TNR community and other rescuers; the enthusiasts who share the joy of sports like agility with their animals; the serious, ethical breeders who pour love and knowledge into their animals from pre-birth through old age; the people who simply love their pets and care for them well and responsibly. Last, but far from least, my profound thanks to readers of all stripes, and to booksellers—especially the independents, and more especially, Kathleen Jewell and Pomegranate Books. You rock!

# ONE

THE VOICE CAME THROUGH as a half-squeal, but I managed to make out, "She's gone! They've kidnaped her! Oh, God, I hope they don't hurt her!" The caller's identity was blocked, but I was pretty sure I knew who it was.

"Alberta?"

"I know they did it to get back at me, but how could they? She's so little, she must be scared, terrified, oh God, we have to find her …" I heard a huge sob, then silence.

"Slow down and tell me what you're talking about."

"They've been after me for months but that was just my car and my house, you know, stuff, but this …" Another terrible ragged gasp.

Despite the sobbing, enough of the voice came through to assure me that it did indeed belong to Alberta Shofelter. I wouldn't say we were friends, but I had known her from dog shows for years, and had spent a weekend with her in Indianapolis a few months earlier. We were there on her dime to photograph her nationally

ranked Welsh Terrier, Indy, aka Champion Welsho's Start Your En-
gines, at the Indianapolis 500 Museum. While we were there, a little
boy went missing and my Australian Shepherd, Jay, found him
where he was hiding. Ever since then, Alberta has regarded Jay as
Superdog, and as Superdog's sidekick, I am now her photographer
of choice.

That's what I do, you see. I'm Janet MacPhail, and I take photos,
mostly of critters. It's so much fun that even after three decades of
being paid to play with my camera, I can barely think of it as work.
Truth is, though, that the publishers and animal lovers who buy my
photos enable me to pay my bills.

"Can you bring Jay? I know he can find her, I know he can." The
sobs gave way to a glimmer of hope. "Please, Janet, she's so small
and ..." Apparently Jay and I have also become Alberta's go-to finders
of lost creatures.

The clock on my microwave said 4:02. That meant we had a little more than an hour before sunset, and maybe another quarter
hour until full dark. "I can, but you'll have to pick me up. My car's
in the shop."

"I'll just grab my keys and ..." Alberta wheezed and grunted and
something clicked in my ear. "Tell me your address again ... GPS ... "
One of Alberta's dogs barked in the background.

The pile of bills and paperwork on my kitchen table seemed to
expand as I looked at it. I had hoped to whittle it down to nothing
before date night started, but how could I not help look for a lost
animal? At least I assumed it was an animal, since Alberta's kids
were grown and scattered across the country. I took a deep breath
and told Alberta to do the same. "And drive carefully. A ticket or

fender bender won't help." She wasn't the most cautious of drivers even without the agitation.

"Right, I will." Wheeze. "I'm fine. I'm on my way."

It takes *me* about half an hour to drive to Alberta's house, so I figured I had maybe twenty minutes until she arrived. "Jay, come on, Bubby. Work to do." He was sacked out on his big round bed in the kitchen, but at the sound of his name he rolled onto his feet in one smooth, muscular motion, ready for whatever I had in mind. I took him to the garage and grabbed his tracking harness from between leashes, long lines, collars, and assorted other training paraphernalia. When he saw the harness, Jay's rear end went into full Aussie wriggle, and he whined and snorted as if to say, "Yay! Tracking!"

Jay stepped into the harness and as I clipped the second of two fasteners, I said, "So, Bubby, here's the thing." He turned to look at me, his brown eyes wide, his expression saying, *Yes? Tell me!*

"I have no idea who we're looking for."

Jay cocked his head to the left.

"Alberta was so agitated, I never asked."

He swiveled his head the other way, and I hoped he wasn't thinking what I was. *What a dope.*

Once he was suited up, so to speak, I lifted the shorter of my two long lines from a hook. It's twenty feet of soft one-inch black nylon rope, shorter than a regulation tracking line, but a lot easier to manage than forty feet of potential tangles. I had no idea whether we would be working around traffic or pedestrians or other potential hazards, so I didn't want Jay too far ahead of me.

Jay followed me to the bedroom, where Leo was curled into an orange tabby knot between the pillows. I pulled on a pair of clean jeans, squatting a couple of times to loosen them up and promising that I really would lose those extra ten pounds I'd been carrying around for a decade. *Okay, fine. Twenty.* I stuffed the slacks and sweater I had been wearing, along with a pair of flats, my purse, and a pair of earrings, into a duffle bag. We had been having unseasonably warm weather, but the air had developed a chilly edge in the past hour, so I zipped my red Indiana Hurryin' Hoosiers hoody over my long-sleeved tee and tied on the waterproof running shoes I wear for tracking. Jay and I sat on the front steps and I called Tom to tell him what was happening.

I'm never sure how to refer to Tom. *Boyfriend* seems a bit silly at our age. We haven't made any long-term commitment and don't live together, so *partner* isn't right, but we're much more committed to everyday companiony things than *lover* seems to suggest. I rather like the sound of *paramour,* but can you imagine people's reactions if I used that? Mostly I just refer to him by name. When Tom nearly died a couple of months earlier, I thought I finally knew what I want out of our relationship. Since then, I had thought of all the reasons I liked being independent, if spending three or four nights a week together still counts.

"I'll come help," Tom said after I explained about Alberta's call. "Who are we looking for?"

*Good question.* "You know, she never said, but I assume it's one of her dogs."

"She lives near Times Corners, right? I can be there in half an hour."

"It might take a while." One thing about searching with a tracking dog—darkness is no obstacle to scent. As long as I could see to follow safely, we could search into the night if necessary. We agreed that I would call again when I knew more and had some sense of what the search might entail.

"My ride is here," I said as Alberta screeched to a stop in front of my driveway.

"Jay will find her, whoever she is."

# TWO

ALBERTA SCURRIED AROUND THE back of her SUV and opened the back passenger-side door. She glanced at me, her eyes feverish, then turned her attention to my dog. "If anyone can find her, Jay can," she said, leaning over to press her lips into the top of his muzzle. "You have to find…" Alberta choked, stood up, and turned wide, wet eyes my way. "She's pregnant, you know." I did not. After all, I didn't even know who *she* was. One of Alberta's dogs? She had a litter only about every five years, when she wanted a new puppy herself, and I was pretty sure her youngest terrier was only about two years old. Of course, the older I get, the faster time slips by, so I knew I could be wrong. I decided to wait until we were underway to ask who we were after, but I did have another question.

"What happened to your car?" The paint on the hood was pitted and crazed into a loose map of Australia.

Alberta didn't answer. She pointed to the open door and waited for Jay to jump in. I put my bag and long line on the floor and shut the door while Alberta climbed in behind the wheel. She really did have to climb. Alberta is maybe five feet tall in her sneakers. She has at least a dozen years on me, which puts her on the downslope to seventy, and she's even less athletic than I am. When we were both buckled in, she slammed the accelerator, raced to the end of my street, barely slowed for the corner, and ignored the thirty m.p.h. signs.

"You might want to watch your speed, Alberta," I said. "Our local speed trap is just behind those shrubs." We whizzed past the sprawl of unpruned forsythia and I swear I pulled three G's as we turned the corner onto Lake and shot toward downtown. Whoever set the Fort Wayne traffic lights years ago did a bang-up job because, as usual, once we got a green light on Washington, we had green all the way to Covington Road. We were through the business district and into the Westside historic before I talked my fingers into releasing the edge of my seat.

"So, Alberta, what's going on? Who are we looking for?"

"Gypsy! They've kidnaped her. Those ..." Her voice morphed into little heart-rending whimpers for a moment, and then anger restored its strength. "They did *that* a couple of weeks ago." She indicated the messed-up paint on the hood. "Egged it in my own driveway."

"But weren't quite a few cars vandalized out your way? I mean, Halloween..."

She cut me off. "And they sprayed 'crazy cat lady' across my garage door with red paint. Ruined the fiberglass. But those are just things, I can fix them, replace them. But this..." Her voice dissolved, then reassembled itself into a snarl. "If they've hurt her..."

I was starting to get a glimmer of clarity. "Gypsy is the cat you took in, right?" Alberta had told several of us at agility class the previous week that she had adopted one of the feral cats she fed in her neighborhood.

"Lovely little creature. Calico. I've always loved calicos. Not that it matters, really, what color they are. And she takes no nonsense from my dogs. They like her, well, all but Lola, and I keep her away from the cats. The rest of them like her, and I like her. I love her." Alberta karate chopped the steering wheel and then closed her fingers around it. I watched her knuckles blanche as she squeezed the leather cover.

"Could she have slipped out? I mean, she's been living on her own. Feral cats don't always like being confined."

"I just don't think she would." Alberta shook her head and spoke slowly, as if considering the possibility for the first time.

"Okay, let's just focus on finding her. Then we can worry about how she got out."

We drove the rest of the way in silence. Alberta turned into her subdivision, oddly named The Rapids of Aspen Grove. Sycamore or oak or maple or beech—those would make sense in northern Indiana. Perhaps the developer dreamed of Colorado. The subdivision was a place of sprawling homes, mature trees, and professionally maintained perennial borders radiating out from the centerpiece private golf course. The grandest of the homes are nearest the course, which seems counterintuitive to me. We pulled into the driveway of Alberta's 1990s take on the Craftsman. It was as stunning as I remembered, even in the bleakness of early November. The huge wreath of bittersweet on the double front door didn't hurt. If I remembered correctly from my only visit, the back of the house was virtually all windows, which looked straight at the club-house and the first tee.

"Alberta, aren't you afraid you'll get a golf ball through a window?"

She turned off the ignition and turned to me, eyes wide. "I suppose they might do that. I mean, they sprayed my door."

"No, I mean ..." I stopped, wondering for a split second whether this might all be a hallucination. "Your garage door looks fine."

"That's the new one."

She was out of the car before I could babble any more, so I hopped out and stood for a moment just inhaling the intoxicating fragrance of burning wood. The house to the north of Alberta's place was a sprawling ranch. To the south lay a field that sloped into a pond backed by a stand of bare-naked trees. A mixed assortment of waterfowl dotted the water's surface, and large stands of cattails hemmed the pond at ragged intervals. A truck was parked on the street in front of the pond, a small caterpillar chained to its trailer bed. A pile of bland white rocks, the sort used to shore up slopes on highways, filled two parking spaces in front of the trailer.

"What's that all about?" I indicated the construction equipment.

Alberta didn't even check what I was pointing at. "Bastards want to 'improve' the edge of the pond." She sneered the word *improve*. "They also want to put up condos."

"Where?" Other than the small field next door, I didn't see any available land.

She swept her arm to take in the pond and woods. "There. They want to cut down the trees and fill the wetland." A fire burned in her eyes. "We're trying to stop them."

That piqued my curiosity, but it could wait. The sun was low and hazy on the horizon, and we needed to get moving. I opened the back door for Jay. He waited, as he's been taught to do, and I snapped a leash to his collar, slipped the coiled long line onto my shoulder, and said, "Free."

A chorus of high-pitched barks sounded from inside the house, and Jay bounced around and wriggled his nubby tail, then looked at me and barkwhined. We followed Alberta onto the porch and waited while she punched numbers into a lock pad. Her hands were shaking and she had to try twice before the door opened. The barking got louder, but was coming from somewhere toward the back of the house.

"They're in the family room. I have the gate up. They're okay." She seemed to be trying to convince herself.

"Do you have something with Gypsy's scent?"

"Food bowl?" she asked. Then turning toward the uproar, she yelled, "Quiet!" Jay lay down with a thunk, I froze, and the barking all stopped. *Impressive*, I thought, although I'm not much for yelling at my dog. Then again, I don't have a house full of terriers.

Alberta was staring at me, and I realized she was waiting for an answer. "Something she's slept on maybe?"

"Perfect."

As I watched her hurry down a hallway and into a room, I felt my phone vibrate. It was a text message from Tom saying he wanted to help but needed an address. An odd blend of gratitude and annoyance whizzed through my mind. *We can manage this*, snarked Janet demon. *He knows that*, countered good Janet. *He wants to help, not take over.* I decided to give Jay a few minutes on the track and then call Tom and let him know what was happening.

Alberta returned, breathing hard. She set a pink-and-white striped cube with a pointed top on the floor in front of Jay. It looked

like a smaller version of one of those old-fashioned tents for changing clothes on the beach. The floor inside seemed to be a fleece-cov-
ered cushion. Jay shoved his head into the thing and, from the
sound of his sniffing, got a good schnozful of the cat's scent.

I checked my shoe laces, a tracking precaution I learned the
hard way, and zipped my sweatshirt up to my chin. "Are you going
to follow us, or wait here?" I ask.

"I'm coming with you!"

I knew she would, of course, but I worried about her tendency
to wheeze and gasp with minimal exertion. Still, it was her cat, or at
least she thought of her that way. Some feral cats don't settle into
domestic life easily, even if they like you, and I wondered whether
Gypsy had simply followed the siren call of freedom, despite its
hardships and dangers. I snapped the long line onto Jay's harness,
removed my leather leash, and handed it to Alberta. "Jay!" He looked
at me, back at the cat bed, and back at me, as if to say, "Yep, got it.
Let's go find her!"

# THREE

JAY HIT THE GROUND pulling, making me feel a bit cartoonish as I scrambled both to keep up and slow him down a notch. He was definitely on a trail, and I hoped it was Gypsy's. That's the thing with tracking—with our poor deficient noses, we must trust that our dogs are on the scent trail we want them to be on. It's a bit like asking someone to translate a page of writing in a script that we can't read. Trust. We have to trust the other guy. Jay had never let me down.

We angled across Alberta's leaf-strewn front lawn, the one next door, and the next. Jay's shoulders were well into the harness and I had to force myself to hold him to a speed I could manage at a faster-than-normal walk. Running may seem more efficient, but—another hard lesson learned—the small margin of time gained is offset by the high risk to middle-aged joints, bones, and skin trying to keep up with an engaged dog over rough ground. Sixty seconds into the search and I was already warming up inside my sweatshirt, but I couldn't stop to adjust my clothes. Alberta was still with us, but her breathing sounded a bit like my mother's old fireplace bellows.

"Gypsy never goes out anymore! Someone must have come in and grabbed her." I was surprised that Alberta could still talk between gasps. "They hate me, you know, because I feed the poor strays that live behind the club house." Maybe she was oxygen deprived, I thought. She was starting to repeat herself.

Jay veered toward the street, so I shortened the line and stopped him at the curb. Alberta bumped into me and clutched my arm. Her cheeks were so pink they glowed.

"Who hates you?" I asked. Jay turned to look at me. He whined something that sounded a lot like "Come on!" and bounced his front end impatiently. "Hang on, Bubby. Car." We could have crossed before the car reached us, but I thought Alberta could stand to catch her breath. Jay turned away from me, put his nose to the ground, pulled into the harness, and muttered again when I anchored him in place.

Alberta released my arm and put a hand to her chest. "But how can they hurt an animal? Especially one that's no threat?"

"Who?" I asked.

"Golfers for one. They claim the cats leave dead things on the greens." She snorted. "It's their damn kids out there with BB guns do the killing, you know, birds and squirrels and things, and they know I know it, too." She coughed and patted the notch of her collarbone. "They shoot the cats, too."

That I knew to be true. The paper had run several articles about Halloween violence aimed at animals in the area, including two elderly pet cats from Alberta's neighborhood that were shot with BBs at close range in their own backyard. One lost his eye. They still hadn't caught the shooter.

"Let's not get ahead of ourselves," I said. "Gypsy may have just slipped out. You said you had a plumber here this afternoon, right?"

Alberta looked past me. The red in her face spread and deepened and an artery in her temple puffed up and pulsed. I turned my head toward the street. A big white SUV slowed as it rolled by, but the occupants were invisible behind tinted windows. Jay startled me with a series of short, deep-throated barks and I took a step back from the curb, pulling him with me. "Jay," I said. He glanced at me, then back at the car. "Here," I said, and heard a bright edge in my voice. In a flash Jay was at my side, leaning into my calf, still alerting on the car. I had learned to pay attention when my dog seemed to find something amiss. I knelt and sank my fingers into Jay's dense fur and folded my fingers over the muscular curve of his shoulder.

"That's them." Alberta stepped into the street and screeched, "What have you done with my cat?" She swung the snap end of my leash at the car and missed. The driver's-side window opened a couple of inches and a chorus of male voices erupted within. Most of what they yelled was unintelligible, but I made out "crazy" and "cat" and "tree hugger." Then the window rolled up and the vehicle squealed away.

"Delinquent bastards," yelled Alberta.

Jay barked a parting insult, then went back to sniffing and whining. I gathered and re-coiled the loose end of the long line and let Jay haul me across the street. His posture told me that he was partly tracking scent on the ground, but also reading something in the air. He pulled me up a driveway and across a backyard. The dormant grass felt crisp under my feet, the ground level and safe. Jay's head came up and he leaped forward, shoulders strong against his harness. A small storage shed, salmon-pink with white gingerbread, huddled among bare-naked forsythias in the far back corner of the yard, and Jay raced toward it. He was no longer tracking. He seemed to know where he needed to be. Ankles be damned, I broke into a run and let him have his way.

"Go. Go." Alberta wheezed encouragement. "I'll catch up."

Jay went into a sniffing, whining frenzy at the door to the shed and pushed against it. A violet rocking chair sat on the brick patio that ran the length of the little building, and lace curtains waved gently behind a window that stood open a few inches. Jay started to dig at the threshold and the door swung open.

# FOUR

THE SHED TURNED OUT to be a little art studio, maybe ten by twelve feet. An easel stood next to a small wooden table that held a palette, a ceramic pot blooming with paint brushes, and a dozen or so tubes of paint lined up like colorful little soldiers. The interior smelled of linseed oil. The window let in a little light and revealed a chintz-covered armchair by the back wall. A cat was stretched across the upholstered seat, her back to us, tail hanging limp off the edge of the chair. I signed Jay to lie down, held my breath, stepped to the chair.

"Oh, no" I turned toward the sound and watched Alberta slide down the doorframe. I could barely hear her wheeze, "Is she...?"

Something in my chest folded in on itself and froze me in place for a moment, but I shook it off and forced myself to step to the chair and lean over. Gypsy tilted her head back and squinted at me. She opened her mouth in a silent meow and I felt my shoulders loosen and my chest reopen.

"She's fine." I sniffed, blinked hard, and started to laugh. "She's really fine." I ran the back of my finger along a tiny black back, then a tabby, then a calico marked just like her mama. All three were firmly attached to the food bar. Gypsy pushed her face against my hand, and I leaned in for a nose bump. "But we're going to need a carrier to get them all home, Grandma."

"What?" Alberta grabbed the doorframe and pulled herself upright. She smoothed her jacket down and crossed the space between us. "Oh."

Gypsy mewed at her.

"Oh, well done, my dear." Alberta's face looked the way I felt.

We stood in silence for a moment, and then Jay shifted and I felt as much as heard a barely audible growl. I turned around just as the little shed exploded in light and a voice boomed, "What the hell do you … You?"

"Charles!" Alberta stood up and looked at the figure in the doorway.

Jay leaned into my leg, filling the space in front of me and watching the man. The door frame was almost entirely filled by the body behind the big voice, but now he looked more perplexed than threatening. "What are you doing in my wife's studio?"

"Look." Alberta moved to the side and swept her hand toward the chair. One step and Charles was looking down at Gypsy and her brood.

"Oh, great, more of *them*," he growled.

Jay echoed him and I signaled my dog to lie down and stay.

The man pulled a plastic grocery bag from a shelf and moved a big hand toward the kittens. Gypsy and Alberta both hissed at him and I shoved my body between him and the chair. Everyone started yelling at once.

"What do you think you're doing?" said Alberta.

"Get out of the way," said Charles.

"Stop that!" said I.

Jay grumbled but stayed put.

Charles put a hand on my arm and started to push me. Apparently deciding that my "stay" command was now void, Jay stood and took a step toward Charles, the hair of his ruff and mane puffed out like a lion's and a hard glare fixed on the man's face. He barked once, then let a low growl roll from between curled lips. Charles pulled his hand away and retreated a step.

"Get out! Get off my property and take your damn dog with you!"

"Happy to, but you'll have to wait while we get a carrier for Gypsy and her kittens." I was pleased that my voice came out as steadily as it did, and I kept going. "Alberta, can you go get a small carrier?"

"Right, yes." She glowered at Charles and said, "Don't you dare touch those kittens, or my cat!"

"Or what? You'll get an injunction?" Charles sneered the final word. He pulled out a cell phone and punched it three times with a thick finger. "I'm calling the police. You're trespassing."

"Now, Charles, dear. I'm sure there's a misun … Alberta?" A tightly coiffed blonde worked her way past the big buffoon. The top of her bouffant might have reached his rib cage if she had been wearing heels instead of glowing pink ballet flats. She glanced from Alberta to the little family in the chair and squealed. "Ohmygoodness! How absolutely adorable! Aren't they adorable, dear?" She giggled at her husband but he seemed to be impervious to cute kittens or gushing wives.

"Louise, what are you doing out here? And how many times have I told you to close the window and lock the door?" To the phone he said, "Yes, I want to report a trespasser, you know, breaking and entering." He thrust the phone away from his face and said, "Now don't touch them, Louise. They're those wild ones. Carrying God knows what diseases and parasites." Then to the phone again, "Yes, they're here now ... No, I don't think we're in imminent danger but I want them to leave and they're refusing ... I don't think they're armed but they have a vicious dog ... How many?" He leaned forward and stared at the cats. "Five. No, seven. There are seven of them. Yes, I'll be careful."

Alberta looked at me and rolled her eyes. I shrugged back at her.

Louise knelt beside the chair and addressed Gypsy. "Oo have booteeful babies, yes oo do, yes oo do."

Charles shoved the phone back into his pocket. He wrapped a hammy fist around his wife's bicep, pulled her onto her feet, and guided her toward the door. "Stop that nonsense. Bad enough that dinner is late because of these people, and you're going to have to change clothes and scrub up before we can eat. Now go clean yourself up and put those clothes in the wash. They're contaminated."

My lower jaw nearly dislocated itself at that and I started to say something, but the plea in Louise's eyes stopped me. She turned to leave, her shoulders drooping and her face a crimson mask, and Alberta followed her out the door, calling back, "I'll get a crate." The two women could have been sisters, they were so well matched in size and age. They walked together toward the back of the house and, after a quick hug, separated at the steps to the long, multi-leveled deck that ran the length of the house. Alberta hightailed it back the way we came in. I watched Louise stalk up the steps to the back door and wondered what Alberta had said to her. The woman's shoulders no longer drooped. Her posture and movement were stiff, as if all her muscles had tightened into a knot of pure anger. I couldn't be certain at that distance, but her hands seemed to have balled into fists.

Not for the first time, I was happy to have Jay at my side for reasons beyond companionship. Like most Australian Shepherds, he tends to take his time assessing people he doesn't know, but occasionally he makes a snap judgment. The first time he met Tom, he turned himself into a pretzel—his way of saying *Hail fellow, well met!* Now he had his gaze fixed on the man with the big voice, and his expression was not friendly. No one who didn't know Aussies would have noticed that his hackles were up, but I knew that his coat doesn't usually stand away from his body that way. I also knew that he had made another snap judgment, and that gave me the freedom to ignore the ogre in favor of Gypsy and her mewling brood. Jay had my back.

As I knelt next to the chair to admire the little family, a whisper of regret blew through my mind. If I had taken Tom up on his offer to join us, I wouldn't be here almost alone with a belligerent boor. *Oh please.* Devilish Janet drowned out the whisper. *Who saved whom last August, eh, girlie?* That thought, too, was short-lived, because what mattered was not who did what, but that neither Tom nor I had been seriously hurt. But that was months earlier.

That line of thought led my mind to an article I'd read not long before on how to survive a back-country encounter with a large predator. They meant, of course, a mountain lion or bear, but some of the moves would probably work on human bullies. The memory was interrupted when Charles took a loud couple of steps across the plank floor behind me. Jay's hip was pressed into my back and his muscles were vibrating. I whispered "Down" and he oozed to the floor, his body still touching mine.

"You'll be sorry you ever got involved with that woman." The man's voice was pitched low, almost a snarl, and I fought the urge to stand and face him. In the silence, I recalled what I had read. *Face the animal. Expand,* the article advised. *Grow large. Raise your arms. If you have a jacket, raise it over your head like bat's wings. Yell.*

"You're trespassing and I intend to press charges. Police will be here soon. I have friends..."

*Keep your wits about you. Don't run, whatever you do. Don't run.* Even if I had wanted to run, I didn't have time.

# FIVE

"Sir, are you the homeowner?" The voice was one I knew. Jay knew it, too, and I felt him start to wriggle, although he stayed down as I'd told him to.

"Who the hell are *you* now?" Charles asked, then, "Whatever you're selling, get out!"

I turned in time to catch the look that flickered over Homer "Hutch" Hutchinson's face, and I smiled. Charles may have called the police, but luck seemed to be on my side. I had met Hutchinson before, when he and his then-partner, Jo Stevens, investigated some murders that were far too close for comfort. We'd gotten off to a less-than inspiring start, but Jay had brought the man around and I'd come to almost like him.

The studio's lighting showed a flush spreading across Hutchinson's fair skin, but other than a quick flicker of jaw muscles, he kept his feelings to himself. He lifted his badge holder toward Charles and said, "Hutchinson. We had a report of intruders. Woman at the house directed us back here." Two uniformed officers with flashlights were in the yard, one of them checking the shrubbery near the house, the other apparently watching the studio from a few yards back.

"About time you got here," said Charles.

Hutchinson pulled out a notebook and pen. "Your name, sir?"

"Rasmussen. Charles Rasmussen." He stepped to the side and turned toward me and the animals. "There, you see? I want you to arrest them."

Hutchinson's eyes went wide when he saw me kneeling by the chair. "Janet?" He looked at Jay, who lay watching Hutchinson with his nubby tail wriggling like a whirligig. "Jay?" Hutchinson paused as if he expected one of us to explain, but we both just grinned at him. "What's going on here?"

"Look for yourself," I said, gesturing to the chair.

Hutchinson stepped up, and the question written in the lines of his face morphed into a full-out grin. "How old are they?"

"Brand new," I said. "Alberta went to get a carrier so we can move them."

"Oh, wow!" Hutchinson bent for a closer look, then straightened as Charles started to yell again.

"For heaven's sake! Do something about this. They're trespassing and that, that," he hesitated as if searching for the right word, then continued, "that *woman* brought her vicious dog onto my property. I want them arrested."

Janet demon made me smile, whispering *That the best you can do? Woman?*

Hutchinson scratched Jay's chin and said, "Gooboy, gooboy." What is it about animals that turns big tough men into baby-talking mushballs? Hutchinson stood and turned back toward Charles. "Sir, if someone has gone for a carrier to take the cats, then maybe you can just be patient for a little longer?"

"Patient? First this filthy animal gets into my wife's studio and then these people come tramping in without even asking and bring that vicious dog..."

Jay cocked his head at the word *dog* as if to ask, "What? Vicious? Me?"

"Sir, this dog is a search dog. He has assisted the police in the past." Hutchinson was stretching the truth just a tad, but that was close enough for me. He gestured toward the window and said, "A screen or closed window would keep animals out of your building. In fact, sir, it's illegal to entice animals into a trap," but Rasmussen didn't seem to hear him.

"...and now my entire evening is ruined, dinner is late, my wife is upset..." He turned around and slammed the window down so hard that the glass rattled.

"I'm not upset." Louise stood in the doorway. The first thing I noticed was that she had not changed clothes despite her husband's earlier directive. The second thing I noticed was that her bubble hair had disappeared in favor of a neat little pixie, a much better match for her tiny frame. *That was a wig?* Had to be, unless she'd gone after herself with an electric hedge trimmer in the past quarter hour. "How are the kittens, Jane? It is Jane, isn't it?"

"Janet."

"Oh, yes, Janet." She walked past her husband and Hutchinson, but stopped short of Gypsy's chair. "Are they doing well?"

Before I could confirm that they were, Alberta burst in, which put the little studio just about at capacity. It was starting to get a bit stuffy. Alberta pushed past the men and set a small plastic pet carrier on the floor by the chair. "Sorry it took so long. I had to find some clean bedding. Just back from a dog show, you know, and I haven't washed the crate pads." She stopped to wheeze, then went on. "I found some fleece. I've been saving it to make some tug toys for the dogs. It makes a nice cozy bed for the little guys." She stroked Gypsy. "I just hope you'll go in without a fuss, my dear."

"Just get them the hell out of here." Charles's face had a purplish cast and I wondered whether he might be working himself up to a cardiovascular event. He turned and stepped toward the door.

Hutchinson looked at his notebook, then at the back of the man who had called him out here. "Sir, one question."

Charles wheeled around and said, "Yeah, what's that?"

"You said there were seven intruders."

"That's right."

Hutchinson looked at Alberta and me. I shrugged. "So where are the others? I only see two."

Charles fluttered a hand in our direction. "Two women, that dog, and those four cats. Seven." He started to turn away, but stopped and said, "Louise, I'm ready for dinner. Come on."

"But I want to help get the kitties loaded up." Louise's voice quavered, as if she were balancing on a fine line between self-determination and self-preservation. "Everything's ready. You can go ahead without me, dear."

For a few seconds, no one seemed to breathe, and then Charles spoke one word—"Louise!"—in a tone dark as a scab. Hutchinson stopped writing and looked at Charles. Alberta looked at Louise, then met my eye and shook her head. Louise hesitated, cast a last glance at the kittens, and followed her husband across the lawn and into the house.

Hutchinson broke the silence that gripped us all. "Won't be surprised if we're called out here again."

"Bastard," said Alberta, then followed up. "I mean him, not you, officer."

I thought Hutchinson might laugh at that, but he didn't. He just nodded and said, "Come on, let's pack these guys up and I'll help you get them home." He leaned over the chair for another look. "Cats don't like to get in those cages, do they? How we going to get the mommy in there?"

Alberta picked up the little tabby, kissed him, and placed him gently in the carrier. Gypsy craned her neck to watch, but she didn't get up. I picked up the black kitten and lifted him to my face so that I could smell him and feel him. His body was warm and still slightly damp. Jay nudged my leg, and I held the kitten in front of his muzzle. Gypsy sat up and watched the interaction, but she didn't seem to be agitated, so I let Jay get a good sniff. After all, he did find them.

As if she were reading my mind, Alberta said, "Who knows what might have happened if that lummox had found them first?" The thought made me queasy.

"You're a good boy," said Hutchinson, riffling Jay's fur.

I handed the black kitten to Alberta, and she set him next to the tabby in the crate. She picked up the calico and turned to Hutchinson. "Would you like to hold her?"

"Really?" You'd have thought he'd won the lottery from the look on his face, and when the kitten was nestled into his hands he whispered, "He's so warm." He looked at me and his eyes were wet. That did it. I was no longer on the fence about Hutchinson. I should have known he was a good guy at heart since Jay liked him.

Alberta said, "She."

"What?"

"She's a girl. Calicos are girls."

"Awww."

I think Hutchinson might have sat there all night holding that kitten if I hadn't said, "Maybe we should get these guys home to your house, Alberta."

She lifted the kitten from Hutchinson's hands and set her between her siblings. "Okay, mama cat, you want to ride with your kids or walk home?" Gypsy opened her mouth but nothing came out. She hopped off the chair, stepped into the carrier, and arranged herself carefully around her three kittens. Hutchinson closed the carrier, picked it up in both hands, and hugged it against his body. I pulled the door shut behind us, but I left the lights on. It was dark now, and someone had turned off the back porch lights. We needed the light from the studio, and I didn't much mind running up Charles's electric bill.

# SIX

Two hours later my taste buds were ecstatic. Tom and I were snuggled into a corner booth at the Bight of Bangkok washing down savory mouthfuls of *pad thai* with Singha beer. I had just wrapped up a fairly detailed account of the evening's happenings.

"I saw a photo of Charles Rasmussen not long ago," said Tom.

"Where? The post office?" Ill-tempered as the man was, it wouldn't surprise me if he were wanted for something.

"*Connectivity.*"

"The school newsletter?" The school I referred to is the Indiana-Purdue joint campus in Fort Wayne, where the two universities join forces. Tom teaches full-time in the anthropology department and I sporadically teach photography classes in their non-credit division. "Why was he in there?"

"Donor. I skimmed the article and it was a couple of weeks ago, but he gave the school a pile of money. Golf scholarships, if I remember correctly. There was some controversy. Apparently he's trying to develop in a wetland, and faculty and students in the environmental studies program objected to the university taking his money. I didn't read the whole article, so I don't know all the details."

I made a mental note to check the online edition of *Connectivity* for the article, but the little Janet demon who likes to poke her barbs into the left side of my brain whispered, *you will* not *remember to do that, and you know it.* She was right, of course, so I grabbed a pen and an old grocery receipt from the depths of my tote-bag-cum-purse and wrote myself a note. I looked across the table. Tom's lip was twitching. "What?"

He laughed. "Nothing."

"Not nothing."

"Okay, so you're going to stick that note in your bag and find it six months from now."

"Am not." *He's right, that's exactly what I'll do.* "I'm sticking it in my change purse where I'll be sure to see it."

"Why don't you write yourself a note on your phone?"

I just rolled my eyes. I'd be sure to forget about it there.

I told him about the pond and woods near Alberta's house, and told him what Alberta had said about condos. "I wonder if that's Rasmussen's development." We also talked briefly about Alberta's attempts to help the feral cats in her neighborhood, and about the kittens and how quickly Jay had done his job. I told Tom how the little calico seemed to put a spell on Hutchinson.

"Boy, he's like a new man since he met Jay and Leo, huh?"

By the time we left, the temperature had dropped and the wind had picked up enough to make the misty air prickly against my cheeks.

"Want to come over and play?" asked Tom as we fastened our seatbelts.

"Play what?" I turned around and stuck my hand into one of two large dog crates Tom kept in the back. Jay pushed the top of his head into my fingers.

"Backgammon?"

"I dunno ... Doesn't sound very exciting."

"Strip backgammon?"

I hadn't planned to be away for the night, and I don't like to leave Leo alone that long, so I made a counter offer. "How about my house? We can pick Drake up on the way."

"Perfect." Tom leaned over and kissed me, then turned to Jay. "Kittens all safe. Good job, my man! You're a hero again."

"Hard to believe that jerk Charles would give anything away." I was thinking again about his donation to the university. "You should have seen the way he humiliated his wife tonight. It was odd, though," I said, remembering how differently Louise carried herself when she came back out to the studio. "She was like a changed person the second time I saw her." I told him about the shift from bouffant wig to gamine-look pixie. "She was completely submissive, cringing almost, and then twenty minutes later she was almost defiant."

"Hunh."

"Don't you think that's weird?"

"Probably." He paused, then spoke again. "Maybe she had a pharmacological intervention in the meantime." Tom's professional interest in the cultural uses of plant-based products popped up at the oddest times and I half expected him to speculate on what exotic botanicals Louise kept in her cookie jar.

I started to say something, but let it go. I love Tom, but I found myself wishing I had Goldie or Peg or one of my other women friends to talk to. Even Alberta. We weren't exactly friends, but she had seen the events of the evening and she knew the Rasmussens at least a little. She might have had another take on Louise's transformation.

Tom changed the subject. "Why don't you call Goldie when we get home."

*He's doing it again*, whispered a voice in my head. *Stop reading my mind.*

"It's not that late. We could have some hot chocolate. I haven't seen her in ages." Tom and Goldie had some sort of strange anthropologist-to-shaman connection that I didn't fully understand.

"I don't think I have any milk."

He pulled into his driveway and turned off the engine. "Be right back."

I undid my seatbelt and turned toward Jay, letting my fingers slide through the bars of the crate again. "What did you think of that guy Charles, Bubby?"

Jay rocked his head to the side and slapped the bottom of the crate with his paw. It was probably a comment on sitting in front of Tom and Drake's house, but I chose my own interpretation.

"Yeah, me neither." The memory of Charles grabbing that grocery bag and reaching toward the kittens made the Singha bubble in my stomach, and I forced myself to think of other things. The look on Hutchinson's face when he saw the kittens was a good counter balance. When we got the little family back to Alberta's house and set up in the spare bedroom, where they would have privacy from the dogs, Hutchinson had told us that he'd never seen newborn anythings before. He hadn't known they would be so small. I think he'd still be there gazing at them if he hadn't gotten another call. I hit Goldie's quick-dial number and issued the invitation.

"Oh, lovely! I've just baked scones. New recipe." Goldie was always trying new flavorings, usually edibles from her own garden, in her baked goods. "You can be my guinea pigs."

The back hatch of the van beeped and opened and Tom let Drake into his crate, where his Labrador tail whammed the side like a sledgehammer. Jay's nub was too short for whacking things, but he made up for it by bouncing and wiggling. They'd be wild men when we got them home, I thought.

"All set. Why don't you call Goldie?"

"Done. We need to stop for milk if you want hot chocolate."

"Done."

*Of course it was.* Tom's kitchen was always well-stocked and much tidier than mine. But then he *liked* to cook.

"I've been thinking about that oaf Rasmussen," I said. "I wonder if he's the one who wants to put in a new development by the pond next to Alberta's house."

"Seems likely," said Tom. "The development that has the environmental students up in arms is somewhere southeast of town."

"He's quite a guy," I said. "Alberta said he's the one who has riled up a bunch of their neighbors about the TNR program."

"The what?" Tom glanced at me.

"You know. Trap, neuter, release. The feral cats."

"Okay."

Tom is a cat-person-in-progress. In fact, my Leo is the first cat he's ever really gotten to know, but since he met the orange guy, he's been smitten. He didn't seem to know squat about programs that work with feral and free-ranging cats, though, much less the politics surrounding them.

He asked, "Alberta is doing this? Catching cats and having them neutered?"

"Yes. Apparently they have quite a little colony hanging around the club house at the golf course out there where she lives."

"And then she finds them homes, right? How can anyone ob—"

"Some of them. Some of them don't want to be anybody's pet, though." I told Tom about a stray cat my mother had tried to bring in when I was a kid. "She had her spayed, and that night the cat practically took down the walls in the bathroom where Mom put her to recover. She screamed like a banshee, and tried to dig her way out the door."

"So what did you do?"

"Me? I cried. Mom and Dad decided the cat would be better off outside where she didn't feel trapped. She'd been holing up under the back porch, so Dad put a box and blanket under there to keep her warm, and my mom cleared a path and sort of guided her to the door while Bill and I watched from the dining room."

"I can't picture you cowering in the dining room."

"I was really upset."

"Afraid of the cat?"

I snorted. "No! Afraid she'd hurt herself." I started to laugh. "Speaking of hot chocolate, Bill and I both needed hot chocolate therapy after things quieted down."

Tom took my hand and we drove in silence until we stopped for the light at State and Lahmeier. Then he spoke.

"So they spay and neuter all of the cats and then turn the really wild ones loose?"

I wasn't entirely sure how the process worked, so I said, "I think they get at least a basic exam first, probably depending on the resources available to the group. And I'm sure they must be vaccinated, for rabies if nothing else."

Tom flicked on the turn signal for my street and both dogs jumped up in their crates, Drake's tail providing the bass counterpoint to the rat-a-tat-tat of their paws on the plastic flooring.

"So why would anyone object? It's not as if cats run around in packs like feral dogs do."

"Later," I said, gesturing toward the house next door. Goldie was headed our way. The light from her porch left her face in shadow but created a silvery aura around her caftan. Her long silver hair was out of its usual braid and wild on the rising wind. She held a plate in front of her like an offering, and my own heart beat a little faster in gratitude that she was still with us in body as well as spirit.

Tom sighed. "She really is magical."

# SEVEN

Tom raced out the door a bit later in the morning than he had planned. Neither one of us ever says it out loud, but the fact is we don't greet mornings after nights before quite so bright-eyed as we did two decades ago. Not that we had such a wild night, but Goldie stayed until just after midnight, and we were awake another hour or so after that. Most days Tom takes Drake with him to his office, but the doggy boys were having such a good time chasing each other around the backyard that I suggested he just pick Drake up later.

I try not to put too much on my Monday schedule, but this one seemed to have filled itself nevertheless. Unlike Tom, though, I insist on a nice cup of coffee with my critters to start the day. One of Goldie's lemon balm scones, left over from the previous night, would be a bonus.

Leo was waiting for me in the kitchen. "What are you doing on the table, you?" I asked. He shoved his head into the hand I held out, and I bent to bonk noses with him. Our pets meet us more than half way in respect to life style and communication, so I figure I can at least make an effort to say hello in feline, albeit with a heavy accent.

I started the coffee and then addressed Leo again. "Your big weekend is coming up, Mister. So how about we practice this morning for a while?"

He squinted at me and twitched the tip of his tail.

"Okay, we'll think about it. First let's have some breakfast. By *we* I mean *me*, because you've had yours." I lifted him off the table and set him in a chair, then checked Jay and Drake. They were sprawled, panting and grinning, in the grass, so I called them in. When I turned back to Leo, he had his back paws on the chair, front paws on the table, and nose at the brim of my mug. "Hey!"

*Mrrrrrlllll.* He sat back down on the chair and blinked at me.

"You don't like coffee. You know that."

*Mrrr mrrr.*

I pulled my cardigan closed and wrapped my hands around my mug. "Chilly this morning, eh?" I looked at the dogs. "Not that you two would notice."

Drake beat his tail against the floor in agreement.

"So, my boys, here's the plan..." The little demon on my shoulder seemed to be in a mood, because I heard something like *as if they care* coming from her direction. Okay, I know they don't care what's on the agenda as long as they have fun and get fed, and I know that they don't share all my enthusiasms and probably have some things they'd like to do if I'd give them a bit more autonomy. Still, they seem to enjoy being included in the conversation. At least I like to think so, because I enjoy including them.

"Leo and I need to train a bit, so we'll do that while you guys," I looked at the dogs, "have a snooze." They wouldn't snooze, I knew.

They'd paste nose glue all over the sliding door while they watched us in the backyard. "Then I need to return some calls. Got to make a living, you know." Jay tilted his head as if considering that one. "And then I need to go see Mom." I try to visit my mother at least three days a week, but the visits are becoming ever more difficult. I just never know what I'm going to walk into. "I hope she's having a good day," I told Jay. I took another bite and then said, "Or at least not a bad day." Mostly I hoped she knew who I was.

My house phone rang, but I decided to let the machine answer. My friends all use my cell number, so land line calls are mostly business, and I prefer to hear the message, line up my ducks, and call back. The next voice I heard after my own, though, was Alberta's.

"Janet! Are you there?" Pause. Wheeze. "It's me. Alberta." Pause. "Alberta Shofelter." *Right.* I waited, and after a few seconds she spoke again. "I'm so angry. Has anyone been to your house today?"

*Now that's odd*, I thought.

"Okay, I guess you're out. Maybe I'll try your cell. If I have the number." I assumed she did, since she had called it the day before. "Well, maybe they haven't been there yet."

*Who*, I wondered. But I knew that if I picked up the phone, I'd be on it for an hour.

"That bastard, Rasmussen," She coughed. "He's filed charges. Another lawsuit."

The machine cut her off. I sat perfectly still for a moment, trying to process the call. Did she mean that I was named in a lawsuit? How could I be? Then again, anything's possible in the world of courts and lawyers, or so says my brother-in-law Norm, and he would know. For about two seconds I considered calling Alberta back, but

I really did have things to do. I decided it wasn't life threatening. It could wait.

Ten minutes later I went out, checked that the agility obstacles were set the way I wanted, and then went back for Leo and my training equipment. I fastened my treat pouch around my waist, clipped my retractable clicker holder to the belt, and slipped a half-used tube of fish paste into a plastic bag in the main compartment. Both dogs had globs of drool dangling from their chops, and Leo was mashing his cheeks into my calf and chirping.

"Okay, Leo *mio*, let's do it." Leo shot out the back door when I opened it. I turned to the dogs and tossed them each a treat from the bag. "Not as yummy as ground up fish, I know, but something at least, boys."

Leo knew what was coming. He was waiting for me on the bottom of one sloped board of the dog walk, or, for the moment, cat-walk. As I looked at him, at the eagerness in his posture and round, whiskered face, I wondered what could make a person hate an animal, a whole species. It had to be something more, something deeper, I thought. What had gone wrong in Charles Rasmussen's genes or life to make him hate kittens and threaten to throw their lives away like so much trash? I shook that memory loose and made myself focus on Leo, waiting now with one paw raised.

Training on the canine equipment isn't exactly regulation feline agility, but a few months earlier the little orange guy had decided to stop watching from the sidelines. He started following Jay over the dog walk and the A-frame, through the tunnel, onto the pause table. At first he scooted under the jump bars, but I encouraged him to go over, and he never looked back. I could imagine him singing, "Anything dogs can do, I can do better."

Although I hadn't yet competed with Leo in a cat agility trial, I did know that the obstacles, rules, and training methods were different from what we were doing. But Leo didn't seem to mind working like a dog, as it were, especially when there was fish paste in the offing for a job well done. One of my regular clients is president of the local cat club, and when I mentioned Leo's performance prowess, she suggested that I help them put on a demo at the upcoming canine agility trial. The trial was being held at Dog Dayz, where I train Jay. Marietta Santini, the owner, has five lively Abyssinians, so she was an easy sell once we figured out the safety protocols. The planning all started months ago, and here we were, just five days from the big event. Even more exciting, it was all happening a week before another big event—the Tri-State Cat Show and Feline Agility Trial.

I squeezed out a wee dab of fish paste, called Leo to me, and let him lick the oh-so-fishy reward from the end of the tube. "Holy mackerel, Catman, that stuff smells worse than Limburger cheese!" Leo gave me his Foolish Human stare and licked his lips, so I said, "Okay, let's get started."

# EIGHT

WE HAD JUST FINISHED running the second course when I heard a voice say, "Who's that, the Border Collie of cats?"

I sat down on the ground to give Leo a jackpot squeeze of fish paste and called over my shoulder, "Nah, he's better than that. He could do it in the dark."

Goldie came through the gate. "Isn't it cold and damp down there?" she asked.

"No, not too bad."

She joined me on the grass. "You could do it in the dark, couldn't you, Mister Leo?" Her face had lost some of the gauntness it had just a few weeks earlier, and a warm sense of reprieve enveloped me as I watched her. Goldie was in remission, and I was beyond grateful.

"You look perky this morning," I said, withdrawing the fishy tube and twisting the cap on tight.

"Perky is as perky does," she said, holding the back of her hand out to my cat. He pushed his cheek into it, said *mmrrwwwlll,* and set about cleaning his muzzle with his paw.

We sat and chatted for a few minutes, and then Goldie got up and brushed off her pants. "Too chilly on the grass. Let me go grab a blanket to sit on."

"No, I need to get moving anyway."

Goldie turned and looked at me, squinting into my face. "I've been thinking about that Ratcatcher guy from last night."

"Rasmussen."

"Whoever." She adjusted a bobby pin in her upswept hair. "I think he's the guy my birding group is talking about. He's a developer, right?"

"More like an investor, I think. What were they saying?"

"If it's the same guy, he's part of a consortium of some sort that wants to put up some apartments or houses or..."

"Condos."

She gave me a look. "You know about this."

"They want to put up condos on a small wetlands next to Alberta's house."

"Be careful, Janet. From what I hear, he likes to get his way. And if your hunch is right about his wife, he's not averse to hurting women."

"Oh, come on. I'll be fine. I don't even expect to have any more dealings with the guy." I tried to ignore the nagging memory of Alberta's message.

Goldie gave me a look very like the one my mother used when I tried to hide things from her as a kid.

"You're right, though. Anyone my dog doesn't like is someone to keep at a distance."

"Exactly," said Goldie, and then let the subject go. "So what kind of trouble *are* you into today?"

"None at all. I have a very routine day ahead of me."

The words were no sooner out of my mouth than my Janet-angel began to tut-tut and Janet-demon sing-songed, *You'll be sorry you said that.*

I took Leo inside and let the dogs out for a short game of tennis ball. I couldn't shake the image of the pond, wetland, and woods. I had seen the place in summer, had seen wild roses dancing at the edge of the woods and heard the trills of the red-winged blackbirds that nested in the cattails. A rough estimate put the whole semi-wild area—water and woods—at eight or so acres. I had thought about walking the area when I was there in the summer, but had never followed up. Small places can be vast treasures. I kicked myself briefly, and decided it was time to call Alberta and go take a look.

It was my turn to leave a message, so I told Alberta's voice mail, "I want to take some photos of the pond, and the light is good this morning, so I'm heading over to your place." I started to hang up, then added, "If you get back before I leave, I could take a few photos of the kittens, too, if you like."

Ten minutes later I was on my way. The only sign of life at Alberta's house was a cacophony of terriers brought on by the doorbell, so I grabbed my camera and walked down the closely mowed slope to the pond. I spent about half an hour taking photos. You might think there's not much to see in the browns of late autumn, but you would be wrong. I found a dozen abandoned nests hanging from cattails, and managed to spot several cocoons. From Alberta's driveway, I had thought the pond ended before the woods, but in fact the more open water merged into perhaps a half-acre strip of marsh that extended into the woods, where a mix of sycamore, beech, and oak were, for now, standing in water.

I had just turned to walk back up the slope to my car when something caught my eye in the eastern sky. At first it was indefinite, just a suggestion against the glare of morning. But then a small flock of ducks became clear. There were only a handful of them, closing fast, but I had time to get set, and clicked off a long series of shots as they came in low over the cattails and settled into the pond. I was thrilled when I zoomed in to see not the ubiquitous mallard, but a half dozen green-winged teal. The males' heads gleamed like bronze where the sun caught them. One of the drakes started to whistle and chitter, and the duck closest to him let out a series of quacks. She sounded like Daffy Duck.

I lowered the camera and scanned the sky. A movement in my peripheral vision caught my attention, and I turned to see a figure watching from the far side of the street. That wouldn't have been unusual in itself. People are often fascinated by my long lenses. But something about this person gave me the creeps. I couldn't be sure whether it was a man or woman—or boy or girl, for that matter. Any measure of identity was obscured by jeans, gym shoes, and a dark hoody. I waved, but whoever it was never moved. *Fine*, I thought, and turned my gaze back to the water.

I snapped my lens cap on and spoke to the ducks. "They can't fill this. It's a wetland." As I drove home, I had an idea. One of my former students was a reporter for the Fort Wayne newspapers. She was always looking for good stories. I emailed her about the pond as a stopover for migratory waterfowl as soon as I got home, then decided to let it go for a while. The muscles in my neck were so tight they ached, so I thought it was time for a little self care. I took a hot shower, wrapped up in cozy old sweats, and made a pot of blackberry sage tea. The fragrance alone always calms me.

43

Rarely do I get to spend a whole afternoon catching up with all the small jobs and pleasures that pile up around the house in busy times, but that's how the rest of the day unfolded. I was beginning to think my angelic and demonic voices had been wrong this time—I really could have a routine day and stay out of trouble. I sat down and started to read the latest issue of *National Wildlife* with Leo on my lap, Jay snoring, and Drake sleep-running on the floor. When the phone rang, I looked up and was surprised to see that it was nearly dark outside.

# NINE

"Hᴙ ʏᴏᴜ." Iᴛ ᴡᴀs Tom.

"Hi yourself." That had become our telephone greeting ritual since … I couldn't remember when we started that. Funny how little things—a word or two here, a common memory there—stitch people together. "What time is it?"

"You still haven't found your watch?" Tom sounded more concerned than I thought a ten-dollar watch deserved and I bristled, waiting for him to say something snarky.

"It's around somewhere." *It's gone, and you know it.*

"It's a quarter to six. I got held up. The meeting took longer than it should have."

*Don't they all,* I thought, thankful once again that I work for myself.

Tom interrupted my thoughts. "I'm leaving now." I heard a door close and a lock snap to. "I need to run home before class tonight," he said, meaning obedience practice at Dog Dayz, "so I'll stop and get my boy. And you, too, if you need a ride."

"Thanks, but they dropped my van off at noon."

He never mentioned my watch again, and I heard a little scold in my head say, *Yeah, that was the ex who never let things go, remember?* After we hung up, I toured the house and found I was a little surprised at what I'd accomplished. Laundry done and put away—sheets, towels, clothes. I couldn't remember the last time all the dirties were dealt with at the same time. The dishwasher was empty. The floors were vacuumed. The pile of bills and correspondence on my desk was a fifth its usual size, and all my invoices were sent. I had even tidied the pile of magazines and books on the dining room table. Leo and the dogs followed me from room to room.

"So what do you guys think? Too organized?"

As soon as I said the word "organized," I realized what had been bothering me about Louise Rasmussen's painting studio. Well, other than her bully of a husband. *It was too neat.* There must be a completely organized neat-freak of a painter somewhere, but none of my creative friends are that tidy. I closed my eyes and pictured the space. There was an easel, I remembered, with a blank canvas on it. Surely I was just too distracted to notice whatever mess there must have been? I didn't think so. I don't have a photographic memory, but I do have a photographer's eye. I tend to frame scenes, and to notice and remember details and arrangements. I couldn't recall any of the things I would expect to be there—works in progress or newly completed, sketches and studies, pencils, half-empty paint tubes lying around waiting to be squeezed into service. As I recalled, everything in the studio had seemed regimented.

Drake made a gurgling noise that brought me back to the moment. He might have been agreeing with me. It was hard to tell since he had a tennis ball and a chew toy in his mouth and was banging the metal filing cabinet with his tail. Jay wriggled at me, and Leo watched from a bookcase.

"It won't last." I scratched a dog ear with each hand. "We'll have it all messed up again in no time." Leo meowed for equal attention.

Tom was there a few minutes later and left with Drake. I gave Jay a quick once-over with a brush, then ran it through my own hair. My brother Bill saw me do that once and was appalled, but really, I'd rather share grooming equipment with my dog than with most people. I clipped Jay's leash to his collar and grabbed my training duffle and keys and started for the door. *Phone!* I looked around, then remembered that I'd stuck it in my pocket.

When I had Jay safely in his crate and myself belted in behind the wheel, I wrestled my phone out of my jeans to check the charge. I'd become paranoid about failed batteries after having a series of them at critical moments and I checked my bars several times a day. When I opened the cover, the message light was flashing. I backed into the driveway while Voice Mail Woman retrieved the missed call, but shifted back into park as I listened to Alberta Shofelter's voice, running at warp speed.

"Janet, are you there? Are you there? Are you coming, I hope you're coming to training tonight. I'm so angry! I have to talk to you, you'll probably be getting one, oh, I just got served…" The message timed out and I closed the phone.

*What in the world?* What did she mean, she just got served? Was she in a restaurant? I flipped the phone open, intending to play the message again, but saw that I had a new one. From Alberta. I listened. She still spoke fast, her voice pitched high and punctuated now with wheezing every few seconds. "That man! What kind of … Oh, never mind, I'll see you, you're probably on your way there … I'd like to just knock him …" and the message cut off again.

For half a second I considered calling her back, but I don't talk while I'm driving and I didn't relish being stuck in my driveway while Alberta ranted for an hour. Besides, she sounded like she planned to be at Dog Dayz. That was a bit unusual, since it was obedience training night and she didn't compete in obedience with her Welsh Terriers. But she knew that Tom and I are both involved in the sport, so apparently she was making a special trip to see me.

I set the phone on the console, started the van again, hit the button for Northeast Indiana Public Radio, shifted into reverse, twisted around to see behind me as we started to roll, and slammed the brakes hard enough to launch my phone into the back of the van.

"What the … ?" I blurted. A black car was parked on the street smack behind my driveway. My street is dark—too dark—because a few hold-outs keep the neighborhood association from putting in street lights. I couldn't see much except that the car's headlights were on. "If this doesn't just …," I said, putting my van in park and undoing my seatbelt. As I reached to kill the engine, I heard a tapping and realized that a man was standing outside my door. A big man.

# TEN

THE MAN STANDING BESIDE my car window stepped back and made a whirligig of his index finger, so I rolled down my window.

"Hutchinson! What are you doing here?"

"Hi, Ms. MacPhail." Officer Hutchinson bent toward me and rocked mildly from foot to foot.

"Janet."

"Right. Janet." He held a cheap pen in one hand and was twisting the cap with the other. He didn't say anything.

*This can't be good*, I thought. "So, Hutchinson, what's up?"

"I just want to give you a heads up." A twitch tugged at his left cheek, then stopped. "That guy, that Rasmussen, he came by the station this afternoon."

I turned off the engine and stepped out of the van so Hutchinson wouldn't have to keep leaning over. "Okay." A half-dozen thoughts were spinning like dervishes in my brain, and I couldn't get any of them to slow down enough to come into focus. "And I'm guessing that had something to do with what happened last night?"

Hutchinson cleared his throat. "Right. He lodged a couple of complaints. Against me, first. And you."

"For…?"

"For not arresting you and Ms. Shofelter for trespassing." Half of his mouth smiled at me. "My lieutenant told him not to waste his time." The smile faded. "But I think the guy has some juice downtown." He shrugged and said, "Whatever."

"Wow, I'm so sorry. Such a big fuss over four little cats."

Hutchinson's smile was back with bells on. "Aren't they great? Ms. Shofelter says I can come see the kitties whenever I want to. Aren't they just the cutest little things?"

Every so often something like this—this lonely hulk of a man who had fallen for three newborn kittens—restores my hope for our species.

"Definitely the cutest little things, Hutchinson," I agreed. I paused for a moment, then decided that I might as well reinforce Hutchinson's position as an ally. "He wanted to kill them, you know."

Hutchinson's hands stopped moving and a deep furrow formed between his eyes. "Who?"

"Rasmussen. He wanted to kill the kittens."

At first I thought Jay had gotten out of the van somehow, but then I realized that the growl was coming from Officer Hutchinson. It was hard to tell in the light coming from the porch and headlights, but his face seemed to have changed color, and his breath was coming out in audible puffs. Then there was a loud *snap*, and half of Hutchinson's pen spun skyward, hit the hood of my van, and landed with a faint clatter.

I put my hand on Hutchinson's jacketed forearm and said, "It's okay. They're safe now."

He cleared his throat with what appeared to be some effort, then called Rasmussen a couple of spectacular names before he went on. "There's more. He said he was reporting Jay to Animal Control as a vicious dog, and was considering a civil action."

"Vicious dog?" The accusation was baseless, but I had been involved with dogs long enough to know that such an allegation can take on a life of its own. "Jay was nowhere near the guy."

"Yeah, I know. But he said Jay growled at him."

My heart was picking up speed. "Yeah, he did, when Rasmussen pushed me."

Hutchinson's face brightened. "He pushed you?"

"A little. He started to, and that's when Jay growled at him."

"Did he actually touch you?"

"Yes," I said, and reflexively grabbed my own arm where Rasmussen had laid his hand.

"Okay. That's good, actually," said Hutchinson. "I mean, … He didn't hurt you, did he?" I shook my head. "Good. But the touching is a good reason for your dog to defend you. Legal weight and all."

"Okay," I said.

"Look, I'm going to have someone get a statement from you in the next couple of days, just in case he tries to do something rotten. I don't know that any of this will go anywhere, but as I said, the man has some friends in high places. Better to be ready for him."

Something gurgled just beneath my sternum. "You mentioned complaints against me. Is there more, besides Jay?" I asked.

"I'm not sure exactly. Trespassing. Breaking and entering. Like that."

"Oh, come on!" *Now you've done it*, whispered my prissy little Janet angel, while her alter ego hooted *how stupid is that?* Just stupid enough to be a royal pain in the patoot, I thought. "The door was open."

"Unlocked. Right. It's in my report, along with the open window."

"No, I mean it was open. Unlatched. It opened when Jay pushed at the bottom."

Hutchinson pulled out his ever-present pocket notebook, wrote something down, and said, "I'll amend my report. I didn't know the door was open."

We stood in the quiet for a moment, and then Hutchinson picked up the fallen half of his pen and said, "Well, better go. I just wanted to let you know."

"Thanks, Hutchinson. I appreciate it, and I hope you're not in trouble."

"Yeah. I mean no, I don't think so." He turned to go, then turned back. "Hey, Janet, don't, you know, I mean, I don't talk about the kitties, you know…"

That broke right through all my little fears and I started to laugh. "Oh, big tough cops don't go squishy with itty bitty kitties?" I play punched him. "Don't worry, your secret is safe with me."

The basic pet obedience class was just finishing up and the members who come for more advanced training just starting to arrive when I got to Dog Dayz. I walked Jay around the exercise area for a few minutes and used one of my own poop bags to pick up after some dog-owner who was apparently too busy or fastidious or just plain rude to do it. As Jay sniffed every square inch of the grass and marked over nine or ten other "messages," I scanned the parking lot. Tom's van wasn't there yet, but Alberta's SUV was parked near the back door. A blue minivan with bumper stickers that said "Parents of twins do it twice" and "I ❤ Cocker Spaniels" sat next to it. I smiled at that. I was having a lovely time watching the Eckhorn twins, Meggie and Lizzie, grow from babies into girls, and their mom, Sylvia, was something special.

I grabbed my training bag from the van, flicked the locks, and had Jay heel beside me as we entered through the back door and headed for the ring at the far front of the building. The pet owners were clumped together at one side of the back-most ring, their dogs sitting or lying or spinning in circles beside them while the instructor gave them their marching orders for the week. As I walked by, I heard her say, "You can't expect your dog to be trained with one hour of class a week. So reinforce good behavior whenever you have the opportunity." I've always thought that it's too bad we can't follow pet owners around and hand them cookies when they are good people and help their dogs learn.

Sylvia waved at me from the front ring, where she was working with Tippy, her sweet parti-colored Cocker. The puppy that Sylvia had kept from her spring litter was shaking the stuffing out of a toy in an exercise pen set near the wall. I staked out one of the folding metal chairs to use as home base for the evening, told Jay to lie down and stay, and started fishing around in my bag for his dumbbell, thinking we could warm up and get in a few retrieves before the group practice session started.

A teenaged boy slouched a few seats down fiddling with a cell phone. Texting or playing a game, I guessed. He glanced at me when my training bag thunked onto the metal chair and I said hello. He grunted and returned to his gadget. I was sure I had seen him before, but I couldn't think where.

"Janet! Oh my! I'm so glad you're here!"

The voice made me jump, not so much for its presence as its panicky tone. I looked up and said, "Alberta. What's wrong?"

"Janet, I'm so worried." She laid a hand on her chest. "About Louise. You know, Louise Rasmussen."

I assumed her concern wasn't based strictly on events of the night before. "Why? What's happened?"

"Oh, my. I'm just so … Louise walks every morning. I always see her. Always. Even in bad weather. And I didn't see her this morning, and I haven't seen her all day."

"Did you try to call her, or go over there?"

She shook her head. "Charles was home, at least his car was. And that was just weird. He's never home on a week day."

She stopped to wheeze, and I took advantage of the opening to reorient the conversation. "Do you know who that young man behind me is?"

Alberta peered around me and said, "Rudy. Rudy Sweetwater."

"Candace's son?" I asked. Candace Sweetwater was in the practice ring with her Papillon, Butch. I didn't know her well, but I loved that she had not given her dainty little dog a dainty little name.

"The very one." Alberta's tone caught me up short, and I looked a question at her. "He was probably one of the little snots in that car last night," she said. "And I can't prove it, but I think he egged my car and defaced my garage door."

I wondered whether he might have been the creepy figure who watched me at the pond.

Alberta's voice broke into my thoughts. "I think he's done something to her. Again."

"What?" I thought she was still talking about Rudy Sweetwater.

"Charles. I think he's done something to Louise."

I remembered the frightened look in Louise's eye the night before, and wondered again about the change in her when she came back to the studio later. That looked like a change for the good, but I couldn't help wondering if she had done something later to bring the wrath of her husband upon herself.

"Do you know her number?" I asked. "Let's just call her now."

Alberta frowned. "No. And I didn't bring my cell," she said, patting all her pockets. When she hit the side pocket of her jacket, she gasped and pulled out an open envelope and waved it in my face. "And this! This is wrong! That man, I could just kill him." Figure of speech or not, her phrasing turned a few heads our way.

"Who?" I asked. *Who are you kidding, Janet? You know who she means.* Still, I had to ask. "What are you talking about?"

"Charles! Charles Rasmussen, that's who!" She shook folds from the paper and wheezed. "Just look at this!"

So I did. I didn't read it closely, just scanned it, but that was enough to make my whole body go cold.

# ELEVEN

TUESDAY MORNING FOUND ME cranky. Before I could get up, I had to unwind the sheet that had me swaddled into my bed, and Leo and Jay didn't make the task any easier. Jay thought it was all a great new game and flopped on top of me to add to the fun while Leo grabbed my toes through the covers. "Oww! Get off!" Sadly for me, I couldn't help laughing at the pair of them, which made Jay wriggle and Leo pounce all the more. "Come on, you big oaf! Let me up! I need to go! Oww, my toes!" When that didn't work, I forced my voice into command mode and said, "Off!" Leo leaped from the bed and raced out the door. Jay stilled himself and looked at me as if he couldn't believe I wanted to stop all the fun. I looked into his eyes, trying to make myself all alpha bitch, but he knows better and slurped my face. I hate to made my dog feel bad, but I *really* needed to get to the bathroom. I softened my voice and said, "Come on, Bubby. Please get off."

He hopped off the bed.

I freed myself, stumble-slid over a couple of magazines I'd dropped off the side of the bed as I finished them, and staggered out of the bedroom. My watch said eight-twenty. I hadn't slept that late in months, maybe years. Not that I wouldn't love to sleep late most days, but between Jay and Leo, and friends who call at obscene hours (because hey, don't photographers get up to catch the early light?), it rarely happens. Even so, I hadn't slept more than a couple of hours. Alberta's letter and Hutchinson's warning kept me tossing until the late wee hours, and then they infiltrated my dreams. I couldn't decide whether the queasiness I felt was prompted by apprehension or last night's leftovers.

I glanced in the mirror and restored a modicum of sanity to my hair with a jaw clip. I decided to load up on caffeine before I attempted any other repairs, and felt even grumpier as I reached for the doorknob. A movement near my feet made me look down.

When I replaced the carpet in the hallway with pet-friendly vinyl, the bathroom door was left with a two-inch clearance. I looked down at the toes of two white paws poked into the bathroom and a smaller orange paw and forearm feeling around the tile floor. Leave it to the critters to make me feel better.

My cell phone played the Beatles' "From Me To You" just as I started the morning kitchen routine. I decided this was a full-pot morning and set the coffee maker to work, fed Jay, fed Leo, let Jay out, toasted a bagel, let Jay in, and picked up the message. Tom said he was going to take Drake to Twisted Lake for a run and swim after his morning classes and offered to pick me and Jay up if we wanted to go along. According to the microwave clock, I might just catch him before his nine thirty class. I did, and declined.

"Come on. You'll feel better if you get out in the gray November light."

"I would, but I really have to go see Mom. I'm not likely to get there Friday, and Thursday's iffy." I didn't have to add that I didn't like to let too much time go between visits for fear that I would miss what was left of my mother's cognitive presence. Every visit was different and I never knew what I might walk into. Sometimes she knew me and Bill and even Tom. She was always happy to see Jay when I took him along, although more often than not she called him Laddie, the dog of her young heart. But there were more and more of the other days now, and I was terrified that soon there would be none of the good ones.

We agreed that there was no reason for Jay to miss the fun of a lake visit, so Tom said he'd drop by my house, pick him up, and bring him back later in the afternoon.

"And, Janet, don't worry about that jerk what's-his-name. No one's going to take him seriously."

I wasn't so sure, especially if Hutchinson was right and Rasmussen really did have friends in high places. I sat staring at my bagel crumbs while I considered my next move. The letter Alberta showed me the night before mentioned my name, sort of. It said "Jane McFall," but they would correct that boo-boo if Rasmussen went through with his threat. He couldn't get the police to arrest Alberta and me for criminal trespass, so he had already filed in civil court, citing "civil trespass." I didn't even know there was such a thing. I considered whether to call my lawyer, meaning my brother-in-law, Norm, now or after I was served. That might not even happen, I reminded myself, and I decided that the call could wait, at least until I'd had my shower.

Two hours later I sat at a sun-drenched table across from my mother, who had been paging through *Fine Gardening* when I arrived. She was fully present, at least for the moment, and was gushing and blushing by turns about one Anthony Marconi.

*Tony Marconi?* whispered Janet Demon. *Really?* But Mom was so buoyantly smitten with the guy that I held my tongue.

Mom leaned across the table and lowered her voice. "He's so sexy!" The corners of her lips, her eyebrows, and her shoulders all flicked up and back down in unison.

"So when do I get to meet him, Mom?" *And exactly when did these tables get turned?* I was thrilled to see my mother so happy, but a little concerned that Anthony Marconi might not be entirely real for anyone but her.

"Right now." She was looking past me and smiling. A dapper elderly man stepped up to the table, took her hand in his, and kissed it, sending her into a giggling fit. Still bending toward her, he smiled into my mother's face and her eyes glowed with a light I hadn't seen in them since my father got sick.

Marconi turned to me and bowed slightly. "You must be Janet." Although he appeared to be in his mid-eighties, his skin was smooth except for a looseness along the jowl. His eyes were a warm blue ringed with laugh lines, and his salt-and-pepper hair was thick and curly. "I've heard all about you and that lovely dog of yours. Jay, if I'm not mistaken?"

I looked at my mother. She hadn't remembered Jay's name in at least a year. Not within my hearing, at any rate. She didn't remember *my* name half the time. That's why she was living here in the first place. I wondered if Anthony Marconi had flipped some switch in her brain that would hold off the evil force of dementia a bit longer.

Marconi pulled up a chair and the three of us talked for another half hour or so. Somewhere around the ten-minute mark I realized that Mom and Marconi were holding hands. Twenty minutes in, I noticed something in their body language that bespoke an intimacy beyond casual acquaintance. When I left, I glanced back at them from the exit and knew it for sure.

*Fine by me*, I thought, and smiled all the way home.

# TWELVE

I HAD JUST LINKED my camera to my laptop when Leo strolled in, scratched his ear, hopped onto the table, and sprawled across my keyboard.

"Leo *mio*," I said, slipping the backs of my fingers across his cheek and down the length of his silky orange back. "Quiet around here, huh, buddy?" I glanced at the clock on my laptop. "They'll be back any time now."

Leo narrowed his eyes and chirp-meowed at me.

"Really, they will, although I hate to tell you, they'll smell of lake water."

Leo yawned and turned belly up, rolling several commands onto the keys and sending my photo management program into flashing seizures. I gently but quickly scooped his orange furry highness off the keyboard and onto the floor, where he feigned indifference, swiping a paw twice with his tongue and then strolling off with his tail crooked like an orange candy cane. The images on my computer screen were still dancing when I looked at it. They quickly ran through all the commands Leo had rolled out and I let out a long breath as the screen went still. Everything is backed up, but I still didn't relish having to redo my newly edited files.

"Okay, then," I said to the image on the screen. Leo's rollover had opened a new file, and I was looking at a stunning rooster, his feathers shimmery blue-black, his comb a proud scarlet. It was one of many photos I had taken in July at the county fair. I smiled at the handsome bird and was closing the file when the phone rang, the kitchen door banged open, and Jay and Drake rushed me, all wriggle and wag, doggy grins and damp fur.

"Whoa, guys!" I pleaded as my chair rolled backward across my dining-room-cum-office. It came to rest against the wall and Jay popped his paws onto my shoulders and stared into my eyes, his whole being vibrating from his two-inch tail to his grinning face. Drake wormed his head into the space between me and Jay and *wham wham whammed* his tail against the wall. I lifted Jay's paws off my shoulders, pushed him back, and let him down gently. "Come on, boys, give me a break! Off!" I tried to sound stern, but was laughing too hard to make it work. Still, both dogs obeyed and kept their feet on the floor. Leo watched from a corner of the counter, eyes half closed, nose and tail both twitching.

"Looks like boys' afternoon out was a success," I said.

Tom grinned at me from the kitchen doorway.

"We had a great time." Tom peeled off his faded navy University of Michigan sweatshirt and ran a hand through his graying hair. "Nothing like a good game of fetch and a bracing dip in the lake when it's forty degrees out." He mock shivered.

"It's not! I was out in just this," I said, indicating my long-sleeved T, "and wasn't cold."

"Sorry I missed that," said Tom.

"Funny guy."

"Temp has dropped a bit, and the wind is coming up," he said, then glanced at his watch. "I need to go home and get some dry clothes. Can I interest you in some dinner in, say, two hours?"

"Hmm. Depends. What do you have to offer?"

He raised his eyebrows and grinned at me. "Well ..." He dragged the word out. "But first, for dinner, how about linguini with clam sauce?"

"Sold."

"Boy, this commuter relationship is complicated," he said.

It wasn't the first time he'd broached the subject, and if I were honest about it, the idea of consolidating our resources had more than a little appeal. But giving up my autonomy scared me. I didn't want to get into it right then, so I ignored his comment.

"I'll bring the salad." Meaning I would stop at the Scott's salad bar on my way there. "Should I bring Leo?" I didn't like to leave Leo home alone, so if I was staying away for the night, the orange guy either came along or stayed next door with Goldie.

When Tom and Drake had gone, I took Jay to his grooming table in the garage. I pulled a few burrs from his fur, worked rinse-free shampoo into his coat, and blew him dry. I'll never win a house-keeper-of-the-year award, but even I don't want my bed, couch, and carpet to reek of wet, muddy dog. When Jay was cleaned up, I took a quick shower, pulled on clean jeans and a light-weight sweater, and sat down to read emails for a few minutes. Tom and the promise of a quiet, cozy evening with him and Leo and the dogs kept creeping into my thoughts, though, and I decided it was time to hit the road.

Tom was right, it had cooled down a few degrees since the last time I was outdoors. I loaded the boys into the van and went back in to grab a warmer jacket. My laptop screen caught my eye as I scurried past the kitchen. I'd forgotten to shut it down. My inbox was open and before I closed my email program, I cast a quick eye over the new messages. Several newsletters, a couple of ads that should have gone to the spam file, and a couple of emails from actual people. The most recent was from Giselle Swann and carried her usual subject line—"i need to talk to you, giselle." She never capitalized her name or pronoun, which was right in line with her level of self-esteem. *Now, now*, whispered Good Janet. *She's working on it and she has come a long way.*

It was true. Giselle had responded to major emotional trauma by losing weight and gaining a sense of personal hygiene and style. She had also enrolled in the nursing program at the IPFW campus, and that seemed to suit her. On the other hand, she was still putting pastel bows in her male dog's topknot, and making him look like a Shih-tzu instead of a Maltese. *Like you're so perfect*, I thought, glimpsing my wild hair in the screen reflection.

Right below Giselle's email was another with no subject line. I knew the screen name. AltaWelshies. That was Alberta, invoking herself and her Welsh Terriers. I thought about opening it, but closed the program and shut down my computer instead. They both could wait.

# THIRTEEN

A PICKUP TRUCK I didn't recognize sat in front of Tom's driveway. My headlights revealed that someone was behind the wheel. *Probably checking directions or something*, I thought as I pulled in behind it. I got Jay out of his crate, slung my purse over my shoulder, picked up Leo's carrier and the bag with the salad, and struck out across the grass toward the front door. A car door slammed behind us and Jay and I whirled around.

"Janet MacPhail?" The voice had a Southern edge to it. Its owner had an edge of her own. She was nearly six feet tall, boney thin, and a tad stooped, as if she had carried one too many heavy loads.

That article about predators popped into my head again, and I almost said *no, not me* as she strode toward us. Even as I fessed up, the obvious question skittered through my mind—*how does she know who I am, and more to the point, where to find me?* She wasn't exactly threatening, but she didn't smile, either. Still, Jay seemed alert but unconcerned, so I figured I wasn't in immediate danger. As soon as I confirmed my identity, the woman reached into her fringed buckskin jacket and withdrew an envelope from the inside pocket, pushed it into my hand, and said, "You've been served."

The truck pulled away, and Tom stepped through the front door to find me gaping at the letter in my hand. I could just read it by the street light and felt a stew of nausea and anger bubble up in my belly.

"Come on, let's do this inside." Tom picked up Leo's carrier, draped his other arm around my shoulders, and steered me toward the house.

When everyone was settled inside, Tom handed me a glass of wine and looked the question at me. I was too angry to say anything suitable for polite company, so I emptied the glass and handed it back to him. When the refill was in my hand, Tom said, "So, what's that all about?"

I was being sued for civil trespass, vandalism, and a few other violations of Charles Rasmussen's property and person. I set the glass down and said, "Next time I see that guy, I'm inclined to commit a few more violations on his person."

"That's my girl." Tom took the letter out of my hand and went on. "Don't get too worked up. This stuff won't go anywhere. It's too ridiculous. The police already refused to arrest you, right? That's what Hutchinson said?"

"More or less."

"Well, there you go." He paused for a moment, then said, "Call Norm after dinner and make an appointment. He'll know what to do."

"An appointment? He's my brother-in-law." I was still getting used to saying that, but it was true. My brother, Bill, had married

Norm in New York, and even though Indiana doesn't recognize the marriage legally, everyone who mattered to their lives does.

"Exactly why you don't clutter up his evening with business. But you'll feel better if you let him know something's up, and make the appointment. So do that much."

Smart man, that Tom. I took a deep breath and felt the oozy heat of the alcohol wind around me. I stared at the glass in my hand and sank into my own little emotional world. The last time I was served with legal papers, that simple act was the start of months of nastiness as my unemployed cheating soon-to-be-ex husband dragged me through a vicious property settlement over shockingly little property. And he didn't have Rasmussen's resources to play with.

Suddenly I felt I was being watched and looked around. Tom was gazing at me from the edge of his recliner, his expression concerned but patient. Leo had assumed a Bast-like pose on top of the bookcase, tail wrapped around his front feet and half-closed eyes fixed on my face. Jay and Drake lay side-by-side, sphinx-like and focused, eyes wide and worried and kind.

I sipped a little more wine and said, "Right. You're right. Let's eat."

Everyone jumped up at once. Tom let the dogs out and turned the heat up under the water and the clam sauce. I went to the bathroom and splashed cold water on my face.

"Do I have time to call Norm before we eat?" I asked when I came back to the kitchen.

"If you can do it in under ten minutes."

I opened my phone to make the call and saw that I had three new messages. I debated for a moment, then called Norm and told him the basics. I declined his offer to look at the letter right away and suggested we meet for breakfast near his office the next day. I glanced again at the message notice. *Good girl*, whispered Janet Angel as I dropped my phone into my tote bag. It's so hard these days to disconnect from the e-world and i-world that I was trying very hard to wrest control of my time from all the gadgets in my life. It was a small victory, but I ignored the messages for the moment. I'd see what they were after dinner.

Have I mentioned that Tom is a terrific cook? It's true. I can barely boil water, mostly because I don't care to do much more than that. If I can't eat it as is or nuke it to readiness in a few minutes, I'll go out for it, thank you. The salad I had assembled for us at the carry-out salad bar was about as creative as I get in the kitchen.

Tom had also been right about my state of mind. I felt much calmer since I'd spoken to Norm.

And then the phone rang. Not mine. Tom's. But he held it toward me and said, "For you."

"What?"

He waggled it at me. "I'll make coffee."

I scowled at the phone but took it.

"Janet, I guess you didn't get my messages. It's terrible! That man is a monster!" I heard a wheeze, then, "She's here with me and I told her not to go back over there, but I don't know that she's really safe here either. Do you know who we can call?" Wheeze. "I thought maybe that cop, er, police officer friend of yours, the woman, you know a woman cop, don't you? I think a woman would be better."

"Alberta, slow down. What are you talking about?" Of course, I already knew the answer to my next question. "*Who* are you talking about?"

"Louise. Louise Rasmussen." She lowered her voice to a stage whisper. "She's going to have a shiner and she won't show me but I think he hurt her arm, and she's limping and her lip is split." Alberta paused for a few seconds. "But this time I think she's had enough. She's been frightened and hurt before, but I think she's finally angry."

The image of Louise after we tracked Gypsy and her kittens came to me. Something in her posture had changed as Alberta walked with her from the studio to the house. When she came back to the studio that night, she was like a different person. I wondered why she hadn't left right then, before her husband hurt her again. *Why didn't she just leave*, I wondered. But I knew it wasn't that simple.

"Oh, man." I felt my fist double up. I did know a woman cop— Jo Stevens was Hutchinson's former partner—and I thought about some of the domestic incidents she had told me about. "Alberta, are all your doors locked? And your alarm system on?"

"Yes, yes, of course." Her voice was muffled as I heard her say, "I don't think you should take a shower until after the police see you, dear," and then, to me, "She said she fell down the stairs, but I got the truth out of her." She wheezed and coughed. "Someone should shove *him* down the stairs."

"Alberta, I think you need to get her out of there. Get her to a safe place away from there."

"The police are on their way."

"Will she press charges?"

There was a long silence, and then she said, "I don't know. I hope so." Alberta's dogs started to bark, and she said, "They're here." And she was gone.

# FOURTEEN

"IS THERE A NO-TRESPASSING sign?" Norm had a legal pad and the document that had ruined my previous evening laid out on the table next to his *huevos rancheros* and was switching back and forth between his fork and his pen. I wondered how long it would be before he stuck the nib of his eight-hundred dollar Montegrappa into his eggs. That would be tragic. Norm loved that pen.

"Where?" We had been talking about Thanksgiving plans, so the question caught me off guard.

"Rasmussen's place. You sure you don't want to eat?"

The whole lawsuit thing had made me queasy, and I shook my head. "Not that I noticed. It was dark. I'd be surprised if there was, though, in that neighborhood."

"Did Mrs. Rasmussen ask you to leave?"

"No. In fact, she wanted to help us with the kittens." I told him how Rasmussen the husband had reacted to that.

Norm made a note and took a bite, all with the proper implements. "Okay, if she is joint owner of the property, you're in the clear. I'll check." He switched implements and smiled at me. "How did you get into the shed?"

"Studio."

"Whatever."

"It was open. Jay just nudged the door a bit wider. The window was open, too. That's how Gypsy got in, I suppose." I studied my mental snapshots of the place. "Something was weird, though. Have you ever seen a tidy artist's space?"

Norm caught the server's eye and pointed at our coffee mugs. "Everett Bannister is pretty neat."

I knew the name and had seen Bannister's paintings, but I'd never met him. "Is he? Still, this studio seemed like a prop. The only painting I remember was a finished one, framed and hung. There were no works-in-progress, no sketches or studies, none of the usual chaos my artsy friends all create when they work."

Norm raised an eyebrow at me.

"Right. I don't know what it means, either," I said. After the server refilled our coffees and took the dirty dishes away, I asked, "What about his threat to report Jay as a vicious dog?"

"I'll check some cases, but I don't think it will go anywhere." He made another note. "Can you pull together copies of his certificates, therapy dog and whatever, and also get statements from experts who know him? Maybe the police in Indy from when he found that kid?"

"Sure. I have the newspaper clipping from that."

"If Rasmussen put his hand on you uninvited and in a threatening manner, your dog has a right to growl." Norm reached across the table and took my hand. "And, Janet, he didn't bite the guy."

"So this is all just smoke and mirrors? He can't really do anything?"

"He can make you spend some money, but I can't imagine the court ruling in his favor. And if he insists on proceeding, we'll fight back."

"That odious man. I'd like to …"

"Shhh." Norm shook his head slightly. "I'd like to, too, but until this is settled, stifle yourself. Make no threats, call him no names, say nothing that you don't want repeated in court, if it goes there."

"But I'm talking to you."

"In a public place." He leaned across the table and lowered his voice. "Janet, Charles Rasmussen has a lot of friends in high places, and a lot of money, so as your attorney, I advise discretion." He leaned back and picked up his water glass, then said, "As your loving brother-in-law, I say a pox on him."

"That I'd like to see," I said, and started to laugh as an image of Rasmussen covered in spots formed in my mind. Then I asked, "How?"

"How what?"

"How will we fight back?"

"Ah. Well, for one thing, we can call Neighborhood Code Enforcement and see if they will cite him for leaving his building open to entice pet cats into danger."

That made me laugh, but not for long. "But what danger?"

"Didn't you say he threatened the kittens?" Norm shrugged and went on. "It was a trap. He would have grabbed them and killed them if you hadn't stopped him. And I have friends in NCE. One thing, though. Alberta needs to be sure all her pet licenses are in order and all her pets are up to date on rabies vaccinations." He paused. "I'd recommend that you and Tom do the same."

"Already done. Mine, anyway." *Oh, sure, maybe three years ago,* whispered the prissy little angel on my shoulder. "The vaccinations, at least. I'll check the licenses." I would have, too, if I'd remembered.

We spent another few minutes on more pleasant subjects. Norm and Bill had moved into my mother's old house, the house Bill and I grew up in, and were putting the final touches on a complete kitchen update. "Bill is more relaxed since we moved than I've ever seen him. Sometimes I think he loves that old house more than he loves me." I knew from the crinkles around his eyes that Norm knew better, and that he spoke from a place of deep happiness.

"You guys should come to the agility trial this weekend. Come watch the boys," which was Norm's term for Jay and Drake and Leo. "Did I tell you we're putting on a feline agility demonstration? So even Leo gets to go this time."

"I'll be there. Bill leaves Friday for Europe."

My cell rang just as Norm was signing the credit card receipt and my heart did a little sidestep when I saw the number.

"What's wrong?" Norm was watching my face.

"It's Shadetree," I said, meaning the retirement center. "Hello?"

I expected to hear the calm contralto of Jade Templeton, the facility's director, but the voice on the other end was pitched at frantic and the only words I could make out were *die* and *love* and *next week*.

"Mom, slow down. I don't know what you're telling me."

Norm mouthed, "Okay?" and I signaled him to go. He had mentioned another appointment, and I figured if Mom was ambulatory and talking, I could manage whatever was going on. We left the café together and I got into my van while I tried to make sense of my mother's hysteria.

"Mom, are you sick?"

The sobs that answered tore a hole in my heart.

"Mom, please tell me what's wrong. I'm on my way, but tell me..."

The phone went quiet, and then Jade Templeton spoke. "Janet. It's Jade. We have a bit of a situation here."

# FIFTEEN

Tom and I talked as we walked the dogs around the field behind Dog Dayz. I had raced to Shadetree after the call from Mom, spent about an hour there, and then raced off again to take photos for several new associates in one of the big real estate firms. They wanted location shots as well as conventional mug shots, so the whole thing took almost four hours—half an hour taking photos, three-and-a-half driving to the locations. It paid well, but when I made the appointment I hadn't planned on squeezing those hours in between a heart-broken mother, a pending lawsuit, and agility practice. I felt frazzled and could only speculate on how I looked since I refused to look in a mirror. I also felt slightly dyspeptic from the blend of anger and sadness roiling inside me.

"You know the really weird thing?" I asked Tom, more or less rhetorically. "I almost wanted her to slide into that other dimension so that maybe she wouldn't hurt so much."

Tom shook his head. "So, someone who works at Shadetree called this Tony guy's son and..."

"Son-in-law."

"Okay, they called his son-in-law and tattled on Tony for sleeping with your mom?"

"That seems to be the gist of it. And he goes by Anthony."

Tom's jaw muscles tightened and twitched, and he said, "How is it anyone's business other than To…Anthony's and your mother's?"

I didn't answer.

"And why does the son-in-law have anything to say about it?"

"Apparently he's paying the bills, and he's worried about his reputation, if you can believe that. Some sort of wheeler dealer." *What's with all these belligerent rich guys who think they should run other people's lives*, I wondered. First Rasmussen, now Marconi's son-in-law. "As if anyone cares what two elderly people are up to anyway."

"Who is he? Anyone we've heard of?"

I shrugged. "Jade didn't mention his name." A few more people and dogs had come out to the exercise area, so I lowered my voice and said, "You should have seen their faces, Tom. They were both devastated. It was like Romeo and Juliet for octogenarians."

Tom gave me a look that dropped an iceberg into my stomach. "Oh, no, I don't think… Mom's not sui… They wouldn't, she wouldn't… I mean, why…" I let the thought trail away. We were almost to the back door, but I gestured for Tom to go in without me. "I'll be there in a minute." Jay trotted by my side to a more private spot, and went back to sniffing while I made the call. Jade had left for the day, but Jerry Warner, her assistant, was there.

"You know about my mother and Mr. Marconi, right?"

"Well, yeah, I think everyone does."

Everyone did not know about their impending separation, though, including Jerry. I filled him in and said, "Look, they seem pretty, I don't know, desperate. Sad. I'd really appreciate it if someone could check on them, you know, not to keep them from ... Look, I'm worried they might ..." I couldn't make myself say the words, as if saying them might give them power.

Jerry got it. He assured me that he himself would keep an eye on my mother.

"What about Mr. Marconi? Or the two of them together?"

"Marconi lives in the assisted section. Has an apartment there." I had wondered when I met him why he was in a nursing home. That explained it. He had privacy, but also maid service, prepared meals, and access to entertainment and companionship. "But I don't think he's here anyway."

"What do you mean?"

"I think his family already took him away. They were getting into a car when I got here. I thought it was for the weekend, but ..." A computer beeped in the background, and then Jerry said, "Yeah, here it is. His son-in-law checked him out. Doesn't say for how long."

*Talk about the morality police*, whispered my little voices in chorus. I told Jerry I would call back in a couple of hours to be sure Mom was okay, grabbed my training bag from my van, and stepped into the warm, rich dogginess of Dog Dayz.

Tom had already removed Drake's collar and leash and had a slip-lead on him. Rhonda Lake was on the course with her sweet Golden Retriever, Eleanor, and several other dogs in the same size group were waiting ringside. I noticed Candace Sweetwater near the spectator chairs. Her little dog was snuggled into her arms and her sullen son was slumped in a chair, legs flung out in front of him and head drooping toward the e-gadget in his hand.

I added my name to the wait list for the next group, found an empty chair, set down my bag, and got Jay ready to run. As I was heeling him to warm up, Giselle Swann waved from the next ring where she and her Maltese, Precious, were practicing the weave poles. They emerged from a series of weaves and Giselle called, "I need to talk to you, Janet."

"Let me get one run in, okay? I'm after the next dog," I gestured toward the course-practice ring. "There are only two of us at this height," meaning I couldn't switch with anyone because they would be changing the jump heights after my run. Giselle nodded and started her little dog back through the weave poles. Precious may hit nine inches at the shoulder and seven pounds dripping wet right after a meal, but he's a big dog on the agility course. I stopped to watch him rip through the weaves. His tail wagged the whole way and as he tore past the last pole he let out three sharp "Yippee" yaps.

Jay also had a happy run when his turn came. A little too happy. He held his stay at the start line, but the instant I signaled him to run he switched to I-have-a-better-idea mode. Like many lightning-fast, shockingly smart dogs, he likes to make up his own challenges if the human is too slow with the next directive. I had positioned myself at the third obstacle, the chute, so was able to signal the first three obstacles easily enough—bar jump, tire jump, chute—but after that I played a game of catchup and redo. If we had been competing, we'd have scored a nonqualifying run when Jay flew up and over an unscheduled A-frame. After that, I was late arriving at another bar jump, so my goofy dog jumped it, jumped back toward me, spun around, and jumped it again. He also took an extra trip through the tunnel and an unplanned on-and-off at the pause table. When we left the ring I was panting, Jay was bouncing and grinning, and everyone else was laughing.

Almost everyone. Peter Birdwhistle, a recent transplant to Fort Wayne, spoke as we passed him, "You need to discipline that dog and tighten up your run. I can help you if you like."

*Yeah, right*, I thought. Peter's Golden Retriever was a nervous wreck. Obedient, yes, and fast and accurate. But he lacked the joy we see in most Goldens and most agility dogs.

"Or I could run him for you sometime."

That made me turn around and ask, "Why would I want you to do that?" *Because I'm too old and fat and, wow, treat this dog-sport thing like a great way to have fun with my dog, win or lose?*

"Well, you know, to get the best scores..."

"Peter, I know you're pretty new here, so let me put your mind at ease. I don't do this to win. I don't do it for scores. And I don't have a dog so that someone else can play with him."

Peter's head tilted back ever-so-slightly and his eyes narrowed. "Suit yourself. Shame, though, a dog like that..."

Sylvia Eckhorn walked up, wrapped an arm around my shoulder, and said, "Janet, that was great! I love watching you and Jay. He's such a spectacularly happy dog!" She squeezed me, let go, and made a quarter-turn away from me. "Oh, hi. Peter, is it?" She smiled. "Janet and Jay have *such* a great relationship."

Peter excused himself.

She looked at me and shook a wild blonde curl out of her eyes. "What a dweeb."

Giselle joined us, Precious wrapped firmly in her arms. "That guy is too serious."

I bent down and kissed the top of Jay's head. "Whatever. It's his problem, not ours, right, Bubby?" Jay sneezed.

"So, Janet?" Giselle had lost about thirty pounds, gotten some style, and gone back to school in the past six months, but she still spoke as if every statement were a question. "I really need to talk to you, but," she glanced at her watch, "I have study group in half an hour? Can I, you know, talk to you tomorrow?"

We made plans to meet at the Firefly for coffee. It was close for me, and Giselle could get there easily between classes at the university. Then I found Tom and told him I was going to go on home and call again to check on my mother. He had an early class and I had a morning photo shoot for a local cat rescue group, so I declined an invitation to follow him home. It seemed like the right plan under the fluorescent lights of Dog Dayz, but a blanket of pure loneliness draped itself over me as I settled into my dark van. *You know,* whispered a voice as I started the ignition and turned on the lights, *you could do something about this.* I drowned her out with the oldies station.

# SIXTEEN

SATURDAY PROMISED TO BE crazy busy, so Tom and I were up before six. Indian summer had rolled back in and the forecast was for unusually warm and sunny fifties all weekend. That was odd weather for November in northern Indiana, but a relief for everyone involved with the agility trial, because we were hoping to run outdoors. The sponsoring club had lost their usual indoor facility due to a late-summer storm that had damaged the roof. They hadn't had time to find another, so the trial was being held at Dog Dayz. Marietta Santini, the owner, was prepared to make it work indoors if we had freezing rain or other seasonal unpleasantness, but we would have been jammed in tight. It seemed we had lucked out.

Tom and I also lucked out with a great parking place about thirty feet from the agility course so we decided to leave the dogs' crates in the van and set our chairs up right there. Leo was fine in his crates on the back seat. I had clipped two small wire crates together and put his bed and water in one and a disposable litter box in the other. I stuck my fingers through the wires to scratch his cheek and then went inside to be sure everything was set up for the demonstration during the break.

Alberta was already there setting up a display about feline TNR—Trap, Neuter, Release—as a way of managing feral populations. She had the money to back an informative, high-tech display, and she had used it to create a video, informational brochures, and a gallery of cat photos, many of which I had taken.

"Oh, Janet! There you are!" Her face was flushed and she was wheezing, but that was normal for Alberta. She pointed at the feline agility area that we had set up in the middle of the building. "That's going to be so much fun!"

"I hope so. We've been practicing, but Leo has never performed anywhere but home."

"But the other cats have, yes? So even if you mess up, the others will be great."

*Gee, thanks for the vote of confidence,* I thought. My inner demon didn't take it so mildly, though, and I felt her heat up and whisper, *Leo will show you! Jay's not the only furry hero in the family!* I did imagine Leo having a perfect run around the course that would wow the crowd, many of whom probably thought that cat training was an oxymoron, but mostly I hoped he wouldn't be frightened by the whole crazy thing.

Alberta emerged from behind her display table and, her arm looping around my waist, pulled me toward the open center of the room. I wondered why, since we were the only ones there. Then she spoke so softly I could barely hear her even at short range. "Janet, you'll never guess what happened." She waited as if she thought I should try.

"You're right. I'll never guess. What happened?"

"Louise came by last evening. She was roaring mad and said she's hired an attorney!"

Alberta still had her arm around my middle and it was making me uncomfortable. I squirmed free as politely as I could while she continued in a more normal voice. "Louise said that Charles threatened her father and that was the final straw." Alberta made a sound remarkably like *harumph* and went on. "Not enough that he bullied her for the past twenty years, I guess. Her and everyone else he could boss around."

People were starting to drift into the building to set up displays, so I wanted to cut this conversation short. I'm not paranoid, but Norm's warning echoed in my mind, so I checked that no one was close enough to listen in before I asked, "He threatened her father? What do you mean?"

"She said that Charles was having him moved from his assisted living place to a different one, which would take him away from his friends."

Cymbals started to clang in my brain. What were the odds? "Do you know his last name maybe?" I asked. "You know, her maiden name?"

Alberta gave me a funny look, then searched the ceiling. "Martini? Martoni?"

"Marconi?"

"Could be. Something like that. Why?"

Three women pushed a cart holding a big plastic container and two wire cat cages to the table next to Alberta's. A big gray Persian stared at us from one of the cages, and two short-haired kittens, one black and one black-and-white, curled up and clung together in the other.

I gave Alberta what I hoped was a conspiratorial look and said, "Tell you later."

"Okay." I turned to leave but Alberta called, "Oh, Janet, wait! Hang this on the door, will you?" She handed me two signs and a nearly empty roll of tape. One said "PLEASE—NO DOGS" in big red letters. The other announced "Agility—it isn't just for dogs! Feline Agility Demo after the morning competition."

I spotted lots of people I knew either by name or, in a shocking number of cases, by their dogs' names. There was Rhonda Lake and her Golden Retriever Eleanor, and Josie the Border Collie's dad, and Candace Sweetwater with her perky Papillon and sullen teenager. I wondered why she was dragging him around with her when he so clearly didn't want to be there. It couldn't have been fun for her, either.

An hour later I was on deck to run Jay in the twenty-inch jumpers class. Tom and Drake had already qualified in the twenty-four inch class. Tom was hoping for another Q, or qualifying run, on Sunday to finish Drake's AXJ—Agility Excellent Jumpers—title. Jay and I were just starting to compete in excellent, which everyone assured me was a giant step beyond the open classes.

They were right. It was a tight course with lots of quick turns. Jay ran perfectly. Me? Not so much. I got in his way on the second turn and accidentally sent him over the wrong jump right after he nailed the weave poles. But here's the thing with dogs. Just when my mental demon started to call me a bumbling idjit and worse, Jay raced to me and bounced up and down as if to say, "Wasn't that great? We played together and we ran and jumped and had fun and I'm so *happy* and I love you so much!" I caught him in my arms on the next bounce, buried my face in his coat for a couple of heartbeats, and let him down to put his leash back. We left the ring laughing and walked to the far end of the field.

"Can't stay out here long, Bubby," I told him. "Leo gets to run today, too." Jay's upper lip was caught on his tooth when he looked at me, giving him a "say what?" expression. "Yep, Catman is going to show 'em how it's done. And you're going to rest for a bit."

We ran into Jorge Gomez, Marietta's groundskeeper, about half-way back to the van. "*Hola, Jorge. ¿Cómo está?*" That's about all I remember from high school Spanish, but Jorge seems to get a kick out of my feeble effort.

"*Hola*, Señora Janet." He pronounces my name with a soft, breathy "j". "Haff you seen a cat here?"

I thought he was asking whether I had brought a cat. "Yes, my cat is here. You should come watch him do agility after the dog classes finish this morning. Will you be here?"

"Oh, yes, *bueno*. But did you see a cat here? The little colored cat?" He gestured with one hand along the tree-lined fence that defined the limits of the Dog Dayz's property. "Little cat, many *colores*?" Jay wriggled up to him, nose lifted and sniffing like a shop vac. Jorge raised the other hand out of the dog's reach and made a clucking sound at him. "Oh, no, Mister Jay. You no get the little cat's lunch."

I had Jay lie down and mind his manners, and asked Jorge, "Is it your cat, Jorge?"

"No, no my cat, but I feed. I think she have *gatitos* somewhere."

"Oh, my." I thought of Gypsy and her kittens, and how much harder it was to raise them outside than in the safety of a house. "I'll watch for her, Jorge. You said she has many colors?"

"Yes, many colors, like *arcoiris*." He saw that he had passed my vocabulary limits. "Like, you know," he made a wide up-and-down motion with his arm, "like *rainboo*." He grinned at me. "Yes, she is little rainboo."

# SEVENTEEN

THE OTHER THREE AGILITY cats had arrived with their people by the time I carried Leo into the building in his travel carrier. I knew Sue and Dave O'Brien and their Abyssinians, Dessie and Jimma, from photo shoots I had done at several cat shows. They introduced me to Jared Spencer, eleven years old, his mother, Dawn, and his well-named Maine Coon, Moose.

The demonstration would take place inside a portable enclosure that the local cat club owned. The sides were made of eight-foot-square PVC frames with netting stretched across them linked four to each side to form a square. Long strips of netting were stretched at the top edges of the panels and extended about eighteen inches toward the center to block any cat who tried to climb out. Heavy blue fabric hung along the bottom three feet to block the cats'-eye view of people's feet outside the ring. For extra security, Marietta had set up a portable kennel as a sort of foyer at the enclosure's entrance. We kept our cats in their carriers until we were inside the closed kennel and then got them out one at a time. No one wanted a loose cat running out the door.

The others seemed to have decided the running order earlier, and Leo and I were first. No one said so, but I had the distinct feeling they all expected Team Janet to botch the thing. I looked at Leo, and felt my throat thicken with pride when I saw how calmly he was taking the whole weird situation. Marietta appeared outside the kennel-cum-staging area.

"Classes are finished, so we're spreading the word about the demo. Dave, you'll say something by way of introduction?" Dave nodded, and Marietta checked her watch. "Good. Let's start in ten minutes."

I checked that I had my tube of stinky fish paste in my training pouch and then set the pouch on top of Leo's carrier. The O'Briens looked a bit surprised at my gear, and Sue wrinkled her nose when I opened the fish-paste tube. "It's pretty stinky, I know, but Leo loves the stuff," I said as I unzipped the carrier and lifted Leo to my face. He pushed his cheek into my chin and *mmmrrrowwllled*. "No fish paste until after you run, Leo *mio*."

Tom caught my eye and waved from behind the growing group of spectators and pointed at Norm, who also waved. We had agreed that they should stay out of Leo's sight until after the performance.

"Where's your teaser?" asked Dave. His voice had a worried edge.

"My what?"

"Your teaser. To lure him over the obstacles?"

"I don't use one," I said. "I trained him with a clicker and, well, the stinky fish paste."

Sue and Dave exchanged a look, and Dave said, "So you've trained him like a dog."

I started to respond, but when I looked at Dave I saw Jared standing behind him with a big grin on his face and a clicker held up in one hand. He gave me a thumbs up with the other. I smiled back and said nothing.

At the appointed hour, Dave introduced himself as vice-president of the Fast Cat Feline Agility Club and explained the basics of the sport. He directed those who wanted more information to the club's display and promised to be there to answer questions after the demo.

"Okay, Catman, we're up next," I whispered to Leo. "You know what to do, and remember, you run for the random-bred cats of the world."

I stepped to the arena entrance and Leo went rigid when he saw the obstacles. He squirmed and let out a loud *Mmrrrowwlll!* A soft laugh rippled through the spectators outside the enclosure and I heard a voice say, "He's ready."

I set him down at the start line and said, "Stay." More laughter, but it quickly morphed into an appreciative murmur when people saw that Leo stayed put and watched me while I got into position. Then I pointed to the first obstacle, the stairs, and said, "Leo, stairs!" He scurried up the three steps and down the other side. From there I signaled him over the one-bar and two-bar hurdles, around a left turn, through the tunnel and then a hoop. "Easy, easy," I said, signaling him with my palm to slow down as he approached the weave poles. "Weave, weave," I said out of habit, but he didn't need me to tell him. From there he shot forward over the three- and four-bar jumps, through the second tunnel, and through the final hoop. "Leo *mio!*" I squealed. He turned toward my voice and launched himself, and I caught him in my arms. He draped himself over my shoulder and let out a loud "Mmrrowwwllll," which I understood to mean "Fish paste now!"

People started to clap and cheer, and I heard "Wow! That was amazing" and other comments, and then Alberta asking people to hold down the volume because it might make the cats nervous. Leo didn't seem bothered by the racket, and I carried him back to the kennel and squeezed out a jackpot stretch of fish paste for him.

"You guys totally rocked it!" said Jared, his grin even bigger than the one he'd flashed in support of clicker training. "You gotta compete with him!"

"He's entered next week," I said, grinning, and then I kneeled to put Leo in his carrier with another smear of fishy nomness.

"Nicely done, Janet," said Dave.

"Outstanding!" came a familiar voice, and I turned to see Tom grinning like a Cheshire cat. "I had no idea he would run like that!"

"That was so exciting!" said Norm. "I wish Bill were here."

I couldn't stop smiling.

Sue didn't say a word, but she was busy getting Dessie ready for her turn. She picked up the lithe little cat in one hand, a feather teaser in the other, and went to the course enclosure. Dessie started out fine, but when she exited the first tunnel, she leapt into the air and spun around as if something had startled her, then streaked to the far side of the course and straight up the netting to the top of the panel. She hung there, eyes wide and tail flicking, until Marietta brought a ladder into the enclosure and Dave climbed it and brought her down. Sue's face was crimson when she came back to the staging area.

I scanned the audience while the O'Briens put one cat away and got the other out. Alberta had her back to me and seemed to be hugging someone. When she let her loose and turned around, I saw that it was Louise Rasmussen. She had sunglasses on, which seemed odd until I remembered that Alberta thought the woman's husband had given her the makings of a black eye. As I watched, Louise appeared to introduce a man to Alberta. Her father, I guessed. He was turned sideways to me and I couldn't get a proper view of his face. Marconi? I'd soon know.

Dave and Jimma had a nice run. Jimma did all the obstacles and got a few extra leaps in as he tried to catch the odd creature dangling from Dave's teaser wand. I got a look at it when they finished, and confirmed that it was indeed a feathered mouse. I decided that an afternoon stroll through the vendor stalls would be in order. Leo would enjoy a mouse with feathers.

As soon as Dave had Jimma back in his carrier, Jared brought Moose out. He was big even for a Maine Coon, and I was sure he must outweigh Leo, Dessie, and Jimma together. Stretched full length he was probably as tall as Jared. He was a brown tabby with yellow-green eyes, and he wore the fur around his head and neck like a king's mantle. Long tufts of fur stood out beyond the tips of his ears, giving him a wild look that belied his gentle demeanor. Jared lugged him into the course enclosure and set him down. The big cat flicked his left front paw, then the right, for all the world like a sprinter loosening up at the starting blocks. Moose held his long tail high in the air and fluffed out wide as my forearm. He was not a cat you'd want to cross. Jared said, "Moose, go!" and they were off. The boy and his cat were a team, and my eyes went wet as I watched them run.

"Stunning," said a low voice behind me. Tom smiled when I turned my head, and the lump in my throat got bigger when I saw that his eyes were moist, too. Was it Saint-Exupery who said, "Love does not consist in gazing at each other, but in looking outward together in the same direction"? I thought so. And there was no denying that we saw animals, and good bonds between animals and people, in the same light.

Beyond Tom I saw that Alberta was still talking to Louise Rasmussen. The man with Louise was now in full view, and I saw that we'd already met. It was indeed Anthony Marconi, my mother's new love, Louise Rasmussen's father, and that odious Charles Rasmussen's father-in-law.

# EIGHTEEN

THE EUPHORIA I FELT after Leo's spectacular agility performance stayed with me through most of the afternoon. I served as leash runner for half of Tom's class, moving leashes from the start gate to the end gate for competitors to collect on their way out. Drake had an all-but-flawless run in the excellent class. He lost a few seconds when he sat up part-way through the down-stay on the pause table, but otherwise ran clean and true. Tom did a little victory jig on their way out, garnering a wolf whistle from somewhere in the stands. Rhonda Lake and her lovely Eleanor had a clean run that finished Eleanor's AX—Agility Excellent—title.

Jay's class was next and, not to be outdone by Leo, he ran fast but with a close eye on my directions and earned his first AX leg with third place. I dished out a half dozen quarter-size hunks of roasted chicken from the container in my ice chest and played a nice game of tug-the-bungee-duck, to Jay's growly delight. I took him for a short walk, then put him in his crate with a new marrow bone and fresh water inside and two bright new ribbons hanging on the door. I spent another three-quarters of an hour helping in the ring, and then Ray Williams, the chief ring steward, said he had plenty of people if I wanted to take a breather. *Time to shop*, Janet demon whispered. I checked Jay and Drake and Leo, then shoved a couple of twenties and my credit card into my pocket, locked my billfold in the van's console, and closed the door.

Something rustled in the tall grass across from my van and I stood still to see what was there. Nothing for a moment, and then a pair of bright yellow-orange eyes appeared among the dry brown stalks. "Hello," I said, and knelt. "You must be Jorge's little rainbow girl." The cat stepped toward me and made a meow-face, though I didn't hear anything. "Would you like something to eat?"

I rinsed out a plastic coffee-cup lid and filled it from the container of cat food I'd brought with us. "Here you go," I said, moving slowly toward the cat. Her coat was, as I'd been told, a glorious mix of colors—black and orange and gray and white—all swirling and mingling in wild patterns. She mouthed another silent comment and watched me but didn't move away, and as soon as I backed off, she sniffed the food and took a bite. I left her in peace and set out to find Jorge, among other things I needed to do.

It was just after three, but we still had a nice crowd of spectators outside watching the final canine runs and inside looking at the various felicentric exhibits and, of course, the vendors. Alberta had five or six people at her table so I moseyed down to the local cat fanciers' table where a handsome Birman sprawled across a variety of handouts on everything from litter and scratching posts to cat training to health issues and care. A little girl just tall enough to reach comfortably across the table stood with her hand resting on the Birman's shoulder, fingers wedged in under the strap of his harness, eyes fixed on the cat's beautiful face. I swear he was smiling back at her, and I could hear him purring from the other end of the table.

My favorite vendor's booth featured gorgeous dog collars, leashes, harnesses, and show leads bedecked with ribbons, fabric, and, in a few cases, charms and glittery stones. I didn't see anything I needed for my guys, but a navy-blue fabric collar embroidered with ducks —five different species—caught my eye. It would look great on Drake. *Yeah, until it soaks in lake water or snags a gezillion burrs,* whispered the voice of caution. I smiled at the booth's owner. "I'll think about it," I said, and headed for the exit, amazed that I'd spent a mere six dollars for a catnip mouse and two homemade ginger dog biscuits that smelled good enough to eat.

I was halfway back to my van when raised voices near the ring caught my attention. The sun was hanging just above the tops of the naked trees clustered along the edge of the property, and I raised a hand to shield my eyes and squinted to see what was going on. Alberta and Louise stood shoulder-to-shoulder, and both seemed to be talking at once, but a low-slung blue spruce blocked my view of the rest of the players. Candace and Rudy Sweetwater walked over from their car. Candace stood beside Louise, Rudy off to the side. His habitual sullen disinterest had been replaced by a fixed glare and clenched jaw, but I couldn't see who had inspired his change in demeanor.

A man's voice broke through the ambient sounds of people talking and leaves stirring in the wind. An angry voice. I had heard it before and knew its owner even before I rounded the spruce and saw Charles Rasmussen reach past Candace Sweetwater, making her recoil, and grab his wife by the arm.

"Stop this nonsense! You're coming with me," he pulled Louise two stumbling steps forward and I caught sight of Anthony Marconi. Rasmussen shook a finger in the older man's face and shouted, "And you are moving to St. Agnes's Home tonight. It's all arranged."

Louise tried to pull away and Rasmussen shook her by the arm. Then everything seemed to happen at once.

Alberta shouted something incomprehensible and shoved with both hands against Rasmussen's midriff.

Candace shoved Rasmussen's shoulder with both hands. He called her a stupid bitch, and Rudy howled and flew at Rasmussen, both arms swinging. Rudy's mother grabbed him around the waist and pulled him away from Rasmussen.

Marconi threw a punch that missed Rasmussen's chin and glanced off his shoulder.

Jorge appeared, waving a water jug and yelling in Spanglish. All I could make out was "not wetback" and "little cat."

Rasmussen shoved Marconi, who took a dozen stutter-steps backward before he found his balance.

Louise flailed her free arm at her husband and screamed, "Let me go! You're not doing this to me again! Not ever!"

Tom ran in from somewhere and tried to pull Rasmussen away, saying, "Okay, calm down everyone, let's ta ..." He was cut short by the back of the bigger man's hand to his cheek.

I ran toward the fray, wondering vaguely how much clobber power two medium dog biscuits in a plastic bag might wield if I swung really hard.

Rasmussen took a step toward the parking lot, dragging Louise by the arm. She stumbled and lost one of her shoes.

Tom came back at Rasmussen, a look in his eye that I hope never to see again. Tom's shoulder dropped back and I knew he was winding up a punch, so I was ready when Tom snarled, "Coward." Rasmussen's upper body swiveled toward Tom, but his feet were still moving in his original direction. Rasmussen still had hold of Louise, but he swung his free arm at Tom. Alberta brought her cross-body purse around at the end of the shoulder strap and caught Rasmussen in the ear. Marconi took a one-handed swing at Rasmussen with his fancy walking stick but came up short and knocked his own hat off. Tom's arm shot toward Rasmussen's face, but I ducked in close and kicked my foot into the oaf's line of travel and the two men never connected. Rasmussen's foot sent a burst of bright pain up my shin and his body seemed to rise off the ground, and then he fell, hard and heavy. Louise went down, too, but Rasmussen lost his grip on her and she rolled away from him. Her father and Alberta helped get her up and out of the way. Candace Sweetwater had a death grip on her wild-eyed son.

"The police are on their way!" Marietta Santini arrived at a run and I half expected her to pin Rasmussen to the ground with a chair as she might an aggressive dog. Instead she pointed at him and snarled, "What's your name?"

He struggled to his feet, his eyes narrowed into a piggish squint and his breathing choppy and loud.

"I'm Charles Rasmussen." His face was a shade somewhere between cranberry juice and grape jelly and his remaining hair stood away from his scalp at an odd angle. "You're all going to be sorry!" He squared off with Marietta. "And who the hell are you?"

Marietta snorted. "I'm the woman who's going to swear out as many complaints against you as I can. Now get off my property."

Rasmussen swayed a little, though whether from fury or pain I couldn't tell. He cracked his neck to the side and brushed a leaf off his sweater. "You people are pathetic. You," he glared at Tom. "I know who you are. I have friends at the university, you know." Rasmussen looked at each of us in turn. "I have friends everywhere. Even," he nodded toward the driveway, where Homer Hutchinson had just emerged from his unmarked car, "among the police." He sputtered something incoherent at me, then turned his venom on Alberta. "I've taken care of those damned cats of yours. Filthy things. Cats and rats at one blow." Rasmussen let out what might have been a laugh. He pivoted toward the parking lot, but turned back and shouted at his wife and father-in-law. "You'll get nothing. Nothing. And you, old man. Just wait." He climbed into his luxury SUV and sent gravel flying as he gunned it onto the road.

Everyone stood in a stunned little cluster assessing the damage until Alberta broke the silence. "What has he done? What did he mean?"

We all looked at her and I asked, "What are you talking about?"

"He said he'd 'taken care of' the cats." Her hair seemed to be standing on end, and she turned wide eyes toward Louise. "Dear God, what has he done?"

Louise was a bit quicker on the uptake than I was, maybe because she knew the jerk so well. She fished her phone from her purse and handed it to Alberta. "Call Sally Foster. Number 4 on my speed dial. Have her get some others to start looking."

Alberta's eyes went wide, and she murmured "Oh no oh no oh no" as she waited for someone to answer. Then she spoke quickly. "Sally, please please. I'm on the other side of town. Please get some people and go check all the places the cats hang out. I think ..." She made a strangling sound and burst into tears.

Louise grabbed the phone and spoke into it. "Sally, it's Louise. I think Charles may have put poison out for the cats. Please get some people out right now and check." She looked at Alberta and listened, then ended the call. "Her book club is there. They're all going out to check everywhere. She'll call me back."

"Oh no oh no." Alberta's eyes were red. "I have to go ..."

But Hutchinson wouldn't let any of us leave until he got statements from us. "I think we should have a paper trail with this guy," he said. He interviewed Alberta first and she was about to leave when Louise's phone rang.

Louise listened, then told us, "They've looked everywhere they could think of, even under the shrubs around the golf course. No sign of anything." Louise patted Alberta's shoulder and went on. "They picked up all the food that was out, and they've even emptied the storage containers. Sally's husband is cleaning them, and Chris Schneider is off to get more food to replace what they've tossed."

Alberta blew her nose and said, "Oh, they're all so, so ... Why would he do such a thing?"

"Chris is a chemist. He's going to check a sample of the cat food, at least that's what Sally said. They'll dispose of it all just in case, but they want to know whether Charles actually put anything in it." Louise pulled herself up straighter, and said, "That's Charles for you. I doubt he really did anything. There was hell to pay last year when Beryl Reese's husband put rat poison in his shed and the neighbor's dog ate some. Charles wouldn't risk the lawsuit. He just thought of it and said it to scare you. To hurt you." She laid a hand on Alberta's arm.

"Sally said they'll all take turns checking on the cats this evening, just in case. But believe me, Charles is just plain full of it."

"I wouldn't put anything past him," said Candace. She hugged Alberta and Louise and said, "It's going to be okay. He'll get his one of these days." She put an arm over Rudy's shoulder. As they walked away, I heard Rudy say, in a tone that made the hair on my arms tingle, "I hate him."

Hutchinson took the rest of our statements. He also asked around and took the names and emails of five people who had gotten some or all of the incident on video. When he was gone and the day's events were officially a wrap, Alberta, Louise and her father, and a few others decided to order a pizza and invited us to join them, but Tom and I were ready to go home. I started to get into the van, but passed the keys across the front seat and said I had something to tell Marietta.

I found her setting up the last of the obstacles for the next morning's class. "Don't look around or make a production of it, but be sure you lock everything up." I nodded toward the empty restaurant across the street. Dog Dayz was well lighted, inside and out, but dusk was coming on fast and it was hard to see beyond the perimeter of lights.

"That's him? The car over there?"

"He came back about ten minutes ago. He's been there ever since."

# NINETEEN

THE SMALLEST DOGS RAN first on Sunday morning. Roman Markoff's Toy Poodle, Monet, was on fire over the first three jumps, the dog walk, the tire jump, the weaves. Then he dashed into the tunnel, had a barkfest inside, and finally shot out the other end to finish the course just in time to qualify. He was followed by several Pomeranians, a Toy Poodle, Giselle Swann and her Maltese, Precious, and a long-haired Chihuahua.

"Do they seem slow through the tunnel to you?" Tom stood beside me, arms crossed and baseball cap pulled low against the sun.

"A little," I said. The tunnel was set up with a ninety-degree bend in the middle, half of it running parallel to the dog walk, and the other part passing beneath the elevated horizontal board. "Maybe the light inside is funny?"

The last dog of the eight-inch class skipped the tunnel entirely, so didn't qualify. Tom and I ran onto the course at Marietta's signal to reset the jumps to twelve inches for dogs eleven to fourteen inches tall.

The first dog on course was a Pembroke Welsh Corgi. I didn't know her, so assumed she was from out of town. She came in barking and earned an NQ—a non-qualify score—at the first jump, which she by-passed entirely. From there on, though, she ran as fast her as her short legs would carry her until she reached the tunnel. She entered it at a good clip but shot right back out the end she'd gone in, provoking pockets of laughter outside the ring. Her handler tried to send her back in, but no dice. They finished the rest of the course and left the ring.

Next up was Tess, a Cavalier King Charles Spaniel from South Bend. I knew her and her owner, Joan something, from trials around the state. Tess ran at a steady pace, tail wagging the whole way. She seemed to take a long time through the tunnel, but at least she came out the correct end and finished her run within the time limit.

I was beginning to think there really was something wrong with the obstacle. Most dogs love the tunnel once they learn to run through it. A lot of agility people swear there's a suction effect because so many dogs add an extra tunnel or two to their runs. Then again, light, wind, and setting can make familiar objects look strange, for dogs as for us.

The twelve-inch class wrapped up ten minutes behind schedule. Two more dogs, a Dachshund and a Miniature Schnauzer, negotiated the tunnel, and five others skipped it one way or another. I thought about taking a peek inside as we reset the jumps, but the judge seemed impatient to keep things rolling, so I let it go.

The first dog in the sixteen-inch class was Caper, a little red-tri Aussie from Toledo. I needed to get Jay ready for the next height group, but decided to watch Caper run first. Her owner, Bud Monroe, was a fire fighter. He was also a member of a wilderness search-

and-rescue team, and Caper was his SAR dog as well as his agility teammate. I had photographed them during a training exercise a few months earlier, and I knew that Caper had recently found a missing four-year-old who wandered away from a campsite near Lake Erie.

Caper waited at the start line with her front end down, fanny in the air, nubby tail wagging. Her whole body quivered and she let out a series of staccato barks. Bud gave the signal and she was off, her red coat flashing like sparks in the wind. She cleared the first three jumps, sped over the dog walk, sailed through the tire jump, whipped through the weave poles, and shot into the tunnel. And then she backed out the way she had entered, lay down, and started to bark.

Bud, who was sprinting to the next obstacle, spun around and stared at his dog. The judge muttered something I couldn't make out, and a collective sigh of regret rose from the spectators. If it had been any other dog, I would have seen just a performance slip-up, but I knew what Caper's behavior meant in other contexts. I felt a little chill and thought, *this can't be good.*

"What's she doing?" Giselle had come up beside me.

Tom and I answered in unison, "Indicating."

"What?"

Bud ran toward Caper. She stopped barking but held her position, flicking her gaze from the tunnel to Bud and back. Marietta Santini stood across the ring from me, one hand across her mouth.

I spoke just above a whisper. "She's indicating a find. There's something in the tunnel."

"What do you mean?" asked Giselle.

"She's an SAR dog," said Tom. "There's something in the tunnel."

*No*, I thought. *Not something.*

*Someone.*

Bud signaled Caper to stay and knelt at the opening to the tunnel. He said something I couldn't make out and disappeared into the vinyl tube. Marietta climbed over the rope that defined the ring and ran to the tunnel. Tom did the same. Marietta bent to look inside, then straightened, patted her pockets, and shouted something at the judge, then at whoever might be listening.

"Phone! We need a phone!"

My first thought was that an animal was in the tunnel, injured or dead. It was possible, I supposed, since the equipment sat out all night. Someone's dog? One of the cats that lived in the alley? *Oh, please, not the little rainbow mama.* A raccoon or possum or ... *Vet,* I thought. *Marietta's going to phone the vet on call for the trial.*

I climbed over the rope and joined the little group at the mouth of the tunnel. "Here!" I said, offering the phone. "What is it?" From the edge of my vision I saw Tom crawl into the other end of the tunnel and then back out.

Marietta pushed the phone back at me and said, "Call an ambulance."

My breakfast turned over and I felt my knees start to fold. *Not again,* I thought. I sank to the ground. I managed to hit 9-1-1, but when I tried to speak, nothing came out. Marietta took the phone from me and gave the operator the information, then tossed it back at me. The morning air was comfortable, but the night's frost hadn't completely left the grass and the cold seeped through my jeans and into my legs. But that wasn't what made me shiver.

"I can't believe this," I said, mostly to myself. I'd been down this road twice in the past half year and as much I wanted—needed—to know who was in the tunnel and how badly hurt she or he was, I couldn't ask. I looked the questions at Tom.

His mouth was tight, lips narrow, and when he spoke it was not to answer my question. "Call the police."

"Tom?"

"It's Rasmussen," he said, his tone flat. "He's dead."

# TWENTY

"WHAT DO YOU MEAN *dead*?" I heard a sudden ringing in my ears and felt as if my head might explode. *It can't be happening again, can it?* I closed my eyes and tried to shake some clarity into my brain. My first half-century was completely murder free, at least among people I knew, but in the previous six months I had been close to several violent deaths. *It can stop now.*

"Janet, are you okay?" Tom put his hand on my shoulder. "I think you need to sit down."

"No, no, I'm fine." I opened my eyes and looked at him, and my recent first-aid training kicked in. I stepped around Tom and crawled into the tunnel to see for myself.

Rasmussen was in there, all right. One arm stretched toward me, as if he had collapsed mid-crawl. Dark brown paw prints trailed along the vinyl floor from his head toward me, and a voice in my head whispered *blood*. The dogs who had made it through the tunnel had stepped in the man's blood. My stomach heaved. I had learned a bit about crime scenes over the previous few months, and I tried not to touch the paw prints as I crept closer to Rasmussen. *Maybe he had an accident,* murmured a hopeful voice in my head, but as I closed in on the body, I knew that this was no accident. Besides, how the heck did he end up dead in the middle of a twenty-foot agility tunnel?

My instinct was to back out of that tunnel as quickly as possible, but another voice said *you have to make sure he's dead.* As soon as I thought it, the macabre double meaning of the words hit me. I hadn't wished violence on him, but I still didn't like the man, and Janet demon urged, *yeah, Janet, make sure he's dead.* I couldn't keep myself from laughing even as I fought down nausea at the horror of it all. *Reflex,* I thought, trying to assure myself that I retained a morsel of compassion even for Rasmussen. Just a self-protective reflex.

My hand shook and my gag reflex continued to operate as I reached out to check for a pulse. Rasmussen's head was covered in blood that appeared to have sprung from several gashes in the back of his head and his temple. Something about the shape of his skull looked odd, like the side of his face wasn't right. It was hard to tell in the light of the tunnel, filtered as it was through red vinyl. I withdrew my hand and slid my sleeves as far up my forearm as I could, then reached again and pressed my fingers up under his jaw. His skin was cool, and no life beat beneath the surface.

I backed out, stood up, and said, "Dead." I took four steps backward and sank to the ground.

Tom knelt and laid a hand on my shoulder. "Janet?"

"How can this be?"

"Do you want some water?"

"No, I'm fine." *I'm not fine at all.* "Tom, how … Again?"

Marietta Santini stepped in close to us. "Are you sure he's dead?" she asked, and I nodded. "Oh my God." She pulled her cell phone out of her pocket, and as she punched in a number, she windmilled her other arm at the judge.

He slapped his thigh with his clipboard and glanced at his watch. "We're already twenty minutes behind schedule," he shouted. "Come on, let's get rolling." Marietta just kept gesturing for him to come on over as she spoke into her phone. He looked again at his watch, shoved his pencil behind his ear, and stalked across the course to join us beside the tunnel. Once he was informed, he wanted to tell the exhibitors, who were now clustered here and there around the ring trying to figure out what was going on.

"I don't think we should say anything except that there will be a delay," I said. "Not until the police get here."

The judge glared at me. He had gone from annoyed to supremely annoyed, as if we had planned a death on course to insult him personally. "Why is that?"

"Because they won't want people to leave until they say so." At least I didn't think they would, based on my limited but still too vast experience with murder investigations. If it was murder.

"I'm going to close the gate to be sure," said Marietta, already headed toward the entrance. She signaled Jorge to help her.

The judge was still staring at me. He seemed to have one standard question. "Why is that?"

"Because, if this is a homicide, they will want to interview people."

He rolled his eyes and said, "Oh, so you're a cop now."

Tom started to say something, but I cut him off. "They'll want to talk to everyone. Including you." I turned to Tom and said, "I need to see the boys." A laying on of paws would, I knew, make me feel enormously better. Tom took my hand as we walked away from the tunnel.

Exhibitors and spectators were gathered around the ring, and there were questions from all sides as we left the fenced area.

"Is someone hurt?"

"What's in there?"

"What's the holdup? I have a three-hour drive..."

Tom finally said, "Please, just relax and play with your dogs. There's going to be a bit of a delay. I'm sure someone will make an announcement soon."

We cleared the ring-side crowd and were half way to my van when Alberta spotted us and scurried over. She had a plastic bag filled with packages of cat treats in her hand. "What's happening?" she asked between wheezes. "I can't stay, have to replenish the cat-treat bowl, we've handed out a hundred and fifty of these already, can you believe it?" She swung the bag toward us with one hand and adjusted her glasses with the other. "So what's wrong with the tunnel?"

"Rasmussen. He's dead."

Alberta's face went blank and her mouth opened and closed several times, but no sound came out. Finally she said, "Charles Rasmussen?"

Tom and I nodded.

"Couldn't happen to anyone more deserving." Alberta sounded as if she were approving the High in Trial winner. I couldn't think of an appropriate response. I didn't like the guy, and I wouldn't miss interacting with him, but I couldn't rejoice in a violent death, either. Trite as they were, the words *it's complicated* were the only ones I could home in on.

A truck appeared from behind the training building and rattled over the sparse grass. His trajectory took him right by us, and I called to the driver's open window, "You're not taking them away already, are you?" In the bed, four plastic outhouses stood as if in casual conversation. Each of them, plus the door of the truck, sported the image of a dapper little man doffing his bowler under an arc of letters that spelled out "Johnny-Come-Early." The tea and water I'd been drinking were starting to pressure me, and I was hoping the rest of the slogan wasn't "Johnny-Leave-Early."

The driver stopped the truck and said, "No, ma'am. Just switched these out for nice fresh ones. Do that every Sunday for Ms. Santini." He grinned at us and drove on.

"Too bad Charles didn't fall down in one of those instead of in the tunnel."

"Alberta!" Okay, I admit that although most of me was horrified at her comment—a man was dead, after all—part of me loved the idea.

Alberta just shrugged and said, "Well, back to my display."

Tom nudged me and pointed my attention back to the driveway. A police cruiser and a black sedan had pulled in. A third cruiser stopped beside the departing truck, then parked across the end of the driveway. The officer, lanky and well over six feet tall, walked to the truck's driver, then waved him away. I turned to watch the other cars disgorge four more figures, three of them in uniform. The fourth, dressed in tan chinos, a plaid shirt, and a navy jacket, was Hutchinson.

"Oh, thank God," I said.

"I thought you thought he was kind of a bumbler?" said Tom.

"But he's our bumbler," I said, then thought better of it. "Besides, I don't think that anymore. He just works his own ..."

A voice that needed no bullhorn said, "Excuse me!" We both jumped and turned. The officer who had spoken to the truck driver was coming up behind us. She gave each of us the once over and, without breaking stride, said, "Don't leave the premises," and followed her colleagues to the competition ring.

# TWENTY-ONE

"I THINK I NEED to sit down for a minute," I said. My legs felt rubbery, and my brain fluctuated between spilling over and completely empty.

When we reached the van, Tom and I checked the big boys first, and I felt 200 percent better as soon as the two doggy tongues touched my fingers.

"You relax for a bit. I'll take these guys for a little walk." Tom kissed my forehead, then picked up Drake's leash and went to the back of the van.

Leo had come along again. He wouldn't be running agility, but I had offered to have him man, or cat, Alberta's information table for a while. I figured it would be good practice for his competition debut the following weekend. I got him out of his double-wide carrier and settled the two of us into the front seat. Whoever says cats don't care about people just never gave them a chance. Leo laid himself lengthwise along my torso and let his tail drape across my thigh. I looked into his eyes, all squinty with feline "I love yous." He mewed so low I almost didn't hear, then pressed a paw against my cheek. We stayed like that, Leo purring and me, eyes closed, counting my breaths. Inhale one-two-three, exhale one-two-three.

When the sound of a dog jumping into the back of the van opened my eyes, the dashboard clock said eleven minutes had slipped by. Tom loaded Jay and Drake into their crates and got into the seat beside me.

"Better?" He said.

"Much."

Leo meowed at Tom, and Tom ran the backs of his fingers down the soft orange body and let his hand come to rest on Leo's tail and my leg. We just sat like that for a few minutes, until I broke the silence.

"Everybody hated that guy, you know."

"He was easy to dislike, that's for sure," said Tom.

"What do you think?"

"About what?"

"Who killed him?"

"I'm sort of hoping he had some kind of bizarre accident." Tom craned his neck for a look at the ring. "We should go find out what's happening."

As soon as I stood up and the sharpening wind sliced into me, I realized I needed to make use of one of those newly refreshed portable facilities. "Getting colder," I said, more or less to myself. I put Leo back into his carrier, excused myself, and walked across the parking lot toward the front of the training building. The "Johnny" set up in the L-corner of the building there was probably the closest one. A woman I didn't know was scurrying in a different angle and got there three steps ahead of me. She had an unfair advantage—two malamutes were pulling her along. I wondered how she planned to manage. There was no way she and those big dogs would fit into the telephone booth sized bathroom.

"You go ahead," the woman said.

Normally I would have thought that unfair, but my bladder felt ready to explode, so I accepted. When I came out, I asked, "Would you like some help with those guys?"

She stepped into the plastic tube and fiddled with her retractable leashes, letting the cords play out to full length and laying the plastic handles against the inside of the door frame. "No, we're fine. We've done this before. But thanks." She pulled the door closed over the leashes, anchoring the dogs to the johnny.

*Bad idea*, whispered the voices in my head. They were right. I wouldn't have tried that stunt with my fifty-pound herding dog, let alone two hundred-plus-pound animals designed to pull heavy sledges across long miles of snow. I started to ask if she was sure, but the "Occupied/Occupado" indicator snapped into place, so I shivered, zipped my jacket to the top, and walked away.

The uniformed police officers were standing near the tunnel and a man with a bag was preparing to crawl into the tunnel.

"Who's that?" I asked.

"Coroner, probably. Or forensics?"

The police had removed everyone else from the area, and I scanned the observers standing around the ring. Marietta was talking to Jorge near the opening that served as a gate, and the stewards were gathered a few feet away. To my surprise, Hutchinson was outside the ring, leaning against the stewards' table.

I pointed toward Hutchinson and said, "What's he doing?"

"Or not doing," said Tom.

We approached from the side and Hutchinson turned.

"What's up?" asked Tom.

"You know who that is?" Hutchinson gestured toward the tunnel.

"You mean the dead guy?"

"Yes."

"Yes," Tom and I answered together.

"I took myself out of the investigation," said Hutchinson.

"Because of what happened yesterday?" I asked.

Hutchinson snorted. "That, and the complaint he filed against me."

"Really?" It made sense, I supposed, for Hutchinson to bow out, but I thought back to my first uncomfortable encounters with Hutchinson and his former partner, Jo Stevens. Suddenly I felt a little less secure about what might be coming. Okay, a lot less secure. I pressed on. "But that isn't *that* big a deal, is it?"

Hutchinson pulled a ballpoint pen from his pocket and began clicking it with his thumb. "Could be a conflict of interest," he said. "Jerk took it to the next level. Plays—played—golf with the mayor." He stabbed the tip of his pen into the picnic table top and turned to look first at me, then at Tom. "I might have been heard to react with a comment about 'dead meat.' So, yeah, conflict of interest."

"Probably a wise move," said Tom.

"Something weird, though. I know the guy didn't like animals, especially cats, but there's fur all over the front of his slacks." Hutchinson looked at me. "Like when Leo or Gypsy rub against my legs."

I started to answer, but a movement over Hutchinson's shoulder caught my eye, and I shifted my gaze. Jorge was standing near some shrubs near the front of the training building not far from where I had left the malamute owner. He bent over and reached toward the shrubs, and a small cat emerged from the evergreens and rubbed her head against his hand. I couldn't see well at that distance, but

115

assumed it was his little rainbow cat-mama. Jorge stood up, and I could see that he held something in his hand. He seemed to be talking to the cat, who was watching him closely, tail flicking. He started to walk toward the tree line where he had told me he thought the cat had hidden her brood of *gatitos*, and I smiled to see that the thing in his hand was a bowl. He was feeding the little family.

I turned back to Hutchinson and asked, "So what happens now?"

"They'll want to talk to people, so don't leave yet."

I sighed and muttered something even I couldn't make out. Tom started to say something, but a crazy loud banging and muffled yells and a duet of loud "awwooos!" snapped our attention toward the front of the training building.

Hutchinson jumped up, turned, and said "What the heck is that?"

For a long few seconds there was nothing to see other than the training building's calm facade, but the racket was getting louder. Then the malamutes appeared, their gazes fixed on the two figures I had been watching. Both dogs were woowooing and, judging by their postures, pulling hard into their collars. The cords of their retractable leashes stretched taut behind them, and everything about them screamed "get the cat!"

# TWENTY-TWO

THE TWO MALAMUTES WERE breathtaking, but my aesthetic appreciation quickly gave way to a more primitive primate response to the sight of predators in motion. I started to say, "This can't be good," but the scenario picked up speed as I watched and I never got the words out. Tom and Hutchinson turned to see what I was looking at and I felt all three of our bodies go rigid as the malamutes gained traction and speed and Johnny-Come-Early bounced into view behind them like an elongated ice cube skidding across a kitchen floor.

"What the ...," said Hutchinson.

*Gives a whole new meaning to portapotty*, giggled bad Janet. Good Janet warned that *Someone's going to get hurt,* and urged me to act.

The white cube swayed a different direction with each bounce across the dormant lawn, and every sway knocked a screech out of the vents at the top of the thing. "Ohmygod," I said, more or less to myself. "She's still in there." Then, raising the volume, I yelled, "There's someone in there!"

I felt more than saw Tom start to run, and turned just as he veered toward a potential interception point. Beyond him, Jorge and the little cat had both turned toward the noise. For a couple of heartbeats they stood there, eyes wide. Then the cat doubled in size as her fur stood straight up. She leaped into the air and spun around and ran for the brush along the fence line. The dogs were still at least thirty yards from him, but Jorge flung his arms wide. The bowl was still clutched in his left hand, and whatever he had planned to feed the cat fanned out in front of him and fell to the ground.

I turned back toward the escalating racket. The malamutes appeared to be hitting their stride, and the leading edge of the johnny caught on something, bounced and teetered, and then keeled over onto its side. The leashes slipped along the door frame and realigned the cube so that it was sliding and bouncing more-or-less floor first along the ground.

Hutchinson started to run toward the cube, and without deciding to, I felt myself moving toward the dogs' projected path. *If they dodge around Tom, maybe I can stop them*, I thought. They had closed the distance by half, but Tom was in place now next to Jorge, and if the dogs kept running in the same direction, they should run right into the men's arms. I glanced at the johnny as I ran and saw it wobble wildly and then turn ninety degrees so that it bounced along with the door on top. One of the leashes snapped free of its handle under the pressure.

The bigger malamute was now free and gaining speed, the thin cord of the once-retractable leash dragging behind. The smaller dog was left with the full weight of the johnny, and the bizarre cargo slowed perceptibly. If he stayed on this path, the dog would pass between a big pin oak and a limestone bench, and I hoped faintly that the johnny would catch between them.

Still, I ran as fast as I could, hoping to intercept the second dog just beyond the tree and bench. Hutchinson, on my right, had almost reached the bouncing toilet, although I couldn't imagine what he planned to do if he did catch it. I glanced to my left and saw that the first dog had stopped a few feet in front of Jorge to eat the cat's dinner from the ground and Tom was slowly approaching, clearly intent on a catch. *Thank heaven for smelly cat food*, I thought.

*Clunk!* One end of the white cube hit the tree and, half a second later, the other whammed into the bench and yanked the second dog up short. His rear end swung around from the impact and he yipped, but if he was stunned by the sudden stop, it wasn't for long. He turned back toward where his prey had disappeared and leaped forward. The johnny shifted and, just as Hutchinson reached for the door, it pulled loose, rolled a quarter turn, and began to trail behind the dog again, leaving a wake of fluorescent blue liquid.

I was in place, and the still-hitched dog had virtually no momentum. I called up my most commanding voice and yelled, "Down!" I'd like to say the command worked magic, but in fact the mal did not lie down. He did hesitate, though, and that was all I needed. I pulled a handful of treats out of my pocket and tossed them on the ground. The dog snarfed them up and looked at me with an expression that seemed to say, "If that's it, lady, I'm outta here." I reached into my pocket again and came out with the nearly empty tube of fish paste. Hoping it would be enough to hold the dog's attention long enough for Hutchinson to open the johnny door, I squeezed a fishy inch of glop onto the only thing I could find—a dry leaf. I held it toward the dog and down it went, leaf and all. The dog was still eyeing his buddy, who was now fastened to Tom's sturdy leather leash and walking toward us.

I heard the johnny door swing wide and bang against the side of the structure, then a thin, scratchy, "Oh my God! Oh my God!"

Hutchinson gave me the handle of the formerly retractable leash that still had a dog on the other end. He turned to help what appeared to be a seriously angry Smurf climb out of Johnny-Come-Early. The chemical stink coming from the johnny and the woman nearly knocked me down. *Just be glad it was a fresh, clean one,* I thought.

"Wow," said Tom, gaping at the sputtering blue woman. He offered me a folded handkerchief in exchange for the leash handle in my hand and said, "I'll manage the dogs. Why don't you help her."

The hankie removed the worst of the blue disinfectant water from the woman's face, but did nothing for the rest of her body or her rapidly declining emotional state. Hutchinson had run off but reappeared with a bottle of water, which he held toward her.

"Oh oh oh! Get it off me!" she said, her voice somewhere between rage and despair. She held her hands in front of her and Hutchinson opened the bottle and poured water over her hands.

"What happened?" Marietta Santini took in the scene and quickly figured it out for herself. "Oh, honey, come on. Let's clean you up."

"My dogs." The words came out like a whimper.

"They're safe," I said, gesturing toward Tom and the malamutes. The man must have been saying something fascinating, because the two dogs were sitting in front of him, apparently listening. Their owner told us where her crates were, and let Marietta lead her toward the training building.

I started to tag along to see if I could help, but Marietta looked at me over her shoulder and said, "Oh, I came over here to get you. The cops want to talk to you."

# TWENTY-THREE

JAY AND LEO AND I were home by five. They had plenty of pizzazz left, but I was completely wrung out, so I grabbed the essentials and decided that everything else could stay in the car until the next day. I dropped my tote bag on the kitchen table, exchanged my jacket for a warmer one, and went out the back door with Jay. The temperature had been slipping all afternoon, and the forecast was for a hard freeze during the night. Out of habit I checked that both gates were latched. Goldie wiped some fog off her kitchen window and we waved at each other. The air was rich with the fragrance of wood smoke and something delicious. Soup, maybe. And bread.

Jay tossed a tennis ball at my feet and bowed in front of me, tail wriggling. Who can resist an invitation like that? We played until I thought the edge was off his energy, and then I headed for the back door and heard the phone start to ring just as I pushed the door open.

"Wanted to catch you before you take your coat off."

"Hi, Goldie."

"And I didn't want to bother with mine." She asked how my day had been, and without waiting for an answer, said, "I have a nice big pot of soup and some homemade bread, just out of the oven. Is that handsome fella coming over?"

"Well, Jay and Leo are already here. Which handsome fellow do you mean?"

Goldie's laugh wrapped me up like a hug, and I smiled. "*Touché*, my dear. Let me rephrase. Are Tom and Drake expected? Because they are welcome, too. There's plenty."

"Nope, not tonight."

She sounded a tad disappointed when she said, "Then you come, with or without your boys."

I glanced into the living room. Leo was curled into a ball on the recliner, and Jay was stretched out on his back on the couch. "They're both sacked out. I'll just leave them here."

Goldie's kitchen wrapped me up in the same rich fragrances that had been mingled with wood smoke outside, plus the mellow warmth of soup steam and candlelight. I handed her the bottle of Chardonnay I had brought and pulled off my coat.

"Oh, perfect!" said Goldie.

"Wow, smells great in here." I closed my eyes and inhaled. "What's the soup? There's something…" I sniffed again, trying to place the scent. "It smells like… licorice?"

"Fennel."

"Fennel soup?"

"Fennel and potato and white beans and leeks." She poured the wine and raised her glass. "To friends!"

"To friends who are geniuses in the kitchen!" I said.

I hadn't realized how hungry I was until I tucked into Goldie's bread and soup. I didn't want to ruin the flavors with news of the day, so I held back and mostly listened to her report from the Fort Wayne Community Schools Clothing Bank, where she volunteers once or twice a month. "We've gotten good, warm coats and other clothes to nearly eight hundred young people already this year. I think that's fantastic. Not charity to my mind, just community as it should be." She cut another thick slice of bread and set it on my plate.

"I couldn't," I said, then picked it up and took a bite. "What do you do to this bread, Goldie? It doesn't even need butter." I took another bite. "I may explode."

Goldie giggled. "So, now that your appetite has been dealt with, tell me about your weekend."

I poured us each another glass of wine while Goldie cleared away the dishes, and when she sat back down, I told her about Rasmussen.

"Rasmussen?" she said when I had finished. "What's his first name?"

"Charles."

"Oh, him!" She made a rude noise. "I'm surprised it took this long for someone to knock him off." Another rude noise. "Especially his wife." Then her eyes went wide and she stared at me. "Louise didn't kill him, did she?"

I shouldn't be surprised at who and what Goldie knows anymore, but I was. "How do you ... ?"

She cut me off. "I've known Louise since we were girls. We went to school together. And I've seen her a few times since I moved back. Not often, and it's been, gee, maybe a year?"

"Did you know him, too?"

"No, not really. He's not from here."

"Hunh. I thought he was somehow." I tried to remember why I thought that, but all I had to hang onto was a foggy memory. "I thought he had family money, you know, from a local business here."

"Heavens no. Louise is the one with the money."

"But her father …," I started to say, remembering that my mom mentioned that Anthony had been an electrician at the GM plant. "Never mind, Mom gets things messed up."

"No, dear, Louise made the money. Not her dad."

Now that piqued my interest.

Goldie went on. "She invented some gizmo that helps slippery fabrics feed through sewing machines more easily. And some other thing, you know, I don't sew, so I don't recall the details. She had her own altering and tailoring business back in the sixties and seventies, and was clever at finding better ways to do things. She came up with the ideas and her husband made them work. Then they sold them for a bundle."

"So he did make the money? Or they did together?" I was confused.

"No, no. Not *him*. Not Rasmussen." Goldie snorted. "No, her first husband. Nice guy, now what was his name?" She paused, then waved a hand in the air and said, "Well, anyway, he was a lovely man. Killed in that crash in Tenerife."

I remembered that all too clearly. It was 1977 and I was scheduled to fly home from Paris the next day. I almost didn't get on the plane.

"Phil."

"What?" My brain had left the room briefly, and I had no idea what she was talking about.

"Louise's first husband. Phil. Phil Smithson."

"When did Rasmussen come along?" *And how does a self-made woman get stuck with a bully like him?*

Goldie studied something on the ceiling, then said, "I'm not sure exactly. She was dating him when I came back to Fort Wayne, and I think they got married a few years ago."

"I wonder what she ever saw in him," I said.

Goldie swirled her soup around, then said, "It's a mystery, that's for sure. He seems to have leverage in some quarters, but I don't know anyone who likes the guy."

"Yeah, Hutchinson mentioned that the guy has friends in high places," I said, and told her about the complaints Rasmussen had filed. "Hutchinson says he isn't worried, but I think he is."

"No one who cares anything about environment or wildlife will miss him, that's for sure." Goldie ripped a hunk of bread from the loaf, but she put it down and spoke again. "I asked someone from my birding group, and I was right. He's the one bent on developing a wetlands out east of town, and a couple of years ago he bought up some land that the Nature Conservancy was trying to acquire. A farm, I guess, and he made such an outrageous offer that the owner couldn't turn it down. My friend said it was a lovely fifty acres, half of it wooded, and Rasmussen's people cut down the trees, bulldozed, and put up a shopping center."

"I bet that was the place off Lima Road, just past DuPont." I had photographed a family of barred owls there over the course of several weeks and remembered the place well. "Big controversy about that at the time."

She shifted the topic then. "So, what happens now? Did the police seem interested in anyone in particular?"

"Hard to say. They seemed to be sorting out which of us might be worth a second look. They took names and contact information from a lot of us, but that's all. Tom and me. Giselle, too. Hutchinson said we'll hear from them within a day or two if they want to talk to us."

"And who do you think did it?"

"No idea."

"Oh, come on," she said, reaching across the table to squeeze my arm. "You're good at this amateur detecting. You must have your suspicions."

I'd had more than enough of amateur detecting, and I didn't feel particularly clever about it. "No, I'm not and I don't. Not really. I mean, it seems like everybody I know had some reason to want the guy out of their lives. But murder? I hate to think that anyone I know would go that far." But, of course, someone had.

# TWENTY-FOUR

FELICITY FELINE RESCUE, INC., looks more like a fairytale cottage than a shelter for cats. The outside of the house is painted a warm periwinkle blue, and, in summer, pink climbing roses flank the front door. Now, in chilly mid-November, the stoop was decorated with pumpkins and bittersweet, and a parade of wooden cat silhouettes in all colors of the feline rainbow marched along the sidewalk to the front door. Front doors, really. The entrance was designed to prevent escapes by landing you in a foyer that leads to a second door into the former living room, now lobby.

Felicity, the permanent greeter cat who inspired Angela Fong to start the shelter, yowled hello when I walked in. At least I hoped it was hello. Felicity is not particularly well-named, and she may well have been yelling "Get out!" She has good reasons not to like people, other than her own rescuer. Angela had found Felicity a dozen years earlier scrounging from garbage cans behind the Fong family's Asian grocery. The little cat had been starving and sick, the whole left side of her face ballooned from an infected wound and her tail rubbed raw by a string knotted around its base. The vet who treated her figured someone had tied something to her to frighten or hurt her. Angela said that finding Felicity was an epiphany, as she suddenly saw how many cats were scrounging for a living in that alley and beyond. She decided to do something about it.

Felicity hopped onto the desk and craned her neck at me, yowling every few seconds. Her face had once been round, but the infection had left one side of her jaw a little off kilter, and the outer corner of the accompanying eye drooped. Her body was stocky and her legs relatively short. Her coat was an odd mix, with tortoiseshell coloring in patches on her body and gray tabby stripes on her face. She had lost her left eye to the infection, but the remaining one was still bright, glimmering green. I was scratching her chin when I heard a door open and close and footsteps on the wooden floor.

"Janet! So good to see you!" Angela Fong wore a soft pink tailored jacket, black wool slacks, and a huge smile.

"Angela! I didn't expect to see you. Kim said..."

"Oh, I'm not staying. Meeting a client this morning," she glanced at her watch. "Wish I could stay for the shoot, but no can do. Actually, I'm running late. So..." She leaned in and kissed my cheek, ran a hand down Felicity's back, and turned to go. As she stepped through the inner door, she called, "Thanks so much, Janet! See you this weekend at the cat show!"

I found Kim Bryant, the shelter's day-to-day manager, in one of the group cat rooms. Two of the three bedrooms and the dining room housed cats who had been deemed healthy and social. The rooms were impeccably clean, and were furnished with shelves and cat trees for climbing, several types of scratching posts, and several self-scooping litter boxes. The other bedroom was set up with large enclosures arranged to give the residents maximum privacy, and this is where they housed queens with kittens and other cats who had passed the health clearances but were not so keen on feline companionship. The original garage had been converted into Angela's law office. The house was on a corner, and the garage faced the side street, so the shelter and her office had separate addresses, which I'm sure prevented a lot of confusion.

Kim chattered to me and to the cats as he waved feather teaser wands to help set up photos. "Angela wanted to be here for this," he said, setting a big tuxedo cat on a chair in front of me.

I kept shooting, but answered, "Right, I know she enjoys these photo shoots." I lay down on my belly to get a good angle on a pair of wrestling kittens. "It's okay, things come up." I resisted my nosy impulse to ask what had come up, figuring that if anyone wanted me to know, they'd tell me. Angela did a lot of *pro bono* work for low-income victims of domestic abuse, and more than once I had seen her leave an event early because someone needed legal help *now*.

Kim seemed to be bursting to tell someone what was going on, and said, "Yeah, some bigwig in town apparently pushed his long-suffering wife over the edge by threatening to move her father from a nursing home he likes." He paused, then said, "More to the point, apparently, he likes someone at the nursing home, if you get my drift. The old guy's daughter called..."

"What?" I lowered my camera and sat up to look at Kim.

"Yeah, right? What a jerk. Who cares if a couple of old people are gettin' it on?"

My cheeks flashed hot. *What are the chances?* I thought, and asked, "You happen to hear a name? Was it Marconi? Or Rasmussen?"

Kim shook his head. "Doesn't ring a bell. Not sure I ever heard a name, actually. Why?"

"No, nothing." But it had to be. I sat up and the big black-and-white cat oozed off the chair where Kim had put him and walked straight to me, sat down, looked into my eyes, and opened his mouth. "*Meeeeyowwwww!*"

Angela walked back in. She was very pale and she didn't smile or speak until she had a hot cup of tea in her hands. I kept taking photos, but glanced at Angela every couple of minutes until finally I couldn't stand it. "You okay?"

She seemed to come out of a trance. "What? Oh, yeah, fine. It's just… My client called. Her husband… We were about to file against him, but he was murdered Saturday night."

Kim said, "Whoa!" and I said, "Wow." I decided to keep my mouth shut for once and leave it at that for now. Ten minutes later I left with several hundred images to sort through, at least half of them in my mind.

# TWENTY-FIVE

By the time I got to the Firefly Coffee House, Giselle was ensconced at a table in the back corner, sipping green tea, nibbling an almond biscotti, and reading an e-book. I grabbed a cup of coffee and joined her.

"Oh, I didn't see you come in," she said, pressing a hand to her chest.

"Whatcha reading? Something fun?"

"Not really." She shut down her e-reader and tucked it into a big orange tote bag. "Elder abuse. Sociology."

Neither of us mentioned Rasmussen's murder. I had already decided to let Giselle be the one to bring it up. She had been badly traumatized twice in the past year, and I thought she should handle this new shock at her own speed. Besides, I'm no therapist, and I was never sure what to say that would help and not hurt Giselle. After we laughed a bit about the Johnny-Come-Early incident, Giselle said, "Janet, is your mom okay?"

That stopped me mid-sip. "What do you mean?" *And how the heck do you know anything is up with my mother?*

"Oh, yeah, you didn't know?" Back to Giselle's habitual interrogative inflection. She does that when she's nervous. "I've been working, you know, volunteering, I don't get paid, at Shadetree?"

"Ah." I had heard that Giselle was making regular visits with Precious, who was certified as a therapy dog.

"Your mom talks about you all the time."

"She does?" *What, she remembers me better when I'm not there?*

"Yes." Giselle smiled sadly. "I've heard about the wildflower hike with your Brownie troop, your piano recital when you wore a taffeta dress and slid off the piano bench, your..."

I couldn't help smiling at the memories, but I made a stop sign of my hand and said, "She has good days and bad. A lot of good ones lately, it seems. I think she's really happy again..."

"That man is just awful." Giselle was practically snarling. For a second I thought she meant Marconi, but the next sentence set me straight. "He brings his wife there and he pushes her around and he's rude to her father, Mr. Marconi, and *he's* such a nice old man, and now Rasmussen wants to make him move..."

I thought about what Kim had said, that Louise planned to take legal action to stop her husband, but it was all moot now and I kept it to myself. "Well, it was certainly mean-spirited to interfere with two people who have found a little happiness late in life."

"He's...he was wicked. He said such mean things, dirty things... He called them 'sinners,' for goodness sake!"

"You were there when he found out about their, uh..." I couldn't find a word that worked. *How about "love,"* whispered the little voices. Yes, love.

"They love each other, Janet," said Giselle. "You can see it, you can feel it." She paused for a moment, then said, "They're like you and Tom. Everybody can see it."

It had never occurred to me that anyone was talking about me and Tom. My cheeks went hot, and I shifted in my seat.

Giselle's face warmed into a grin. "It's good, Janet. You and Tom are perfect." The mood didn't last, though, and she went quiet.

"He—Marconi—was back at Shadetree last night," I said, "so all is well on that front, I think." At least I hoped so for both their sakes.

"I try not to wish bad things, especially after, well, you know," said Giselle, breaking off little bits of biscotti and dropping them into her plate. I did know what she meant. Giselle had found a murder victim six months earlier, someone she cared for, and she was still recovering from the shock. She put the biscotti down and wiped her hands, then looked me in the eye and said, "I shouldn't wish bad things, but I do sometimes. I wished that evil man all kinds of bad things."

"We all do that, Giselle."

"He called your mother some vile names, and he yelled at Ms. Templeton and the other staff, called them," she lowered her voice to a whisper, "whoremongers." Giselle rolled her eyes. "He even yelled at me and said Precious was a filthy cur!" Giselle's hand crushed her napkin in a white-knuckle fist. "That made me so mad!"

*Filthy*, I thought, remembering how Rasmussen had ranted about Gypsy and her newborn kittens as filthy carriers of disease and parasites. *The man has a filthy mind*, whispered a voice in my head.

"You know Candace? Candace Sweetwater?" Giselle sniffed. "He's the reason she lost her store."

"What store?"

"She had a little gift shop. It was all, you know, hand-crafted things by local artists?" Giselle was slipping back into her habit of turning every sentence into a question. "In that little shopping center where the Doggie Dog grooming shop used to be?"

"I remember that place. The front, anyway. It looked like a gingerbread house," I said. "I was never in it. Wasn't it called 'The Hand-made's Tale'?"

Giselle nodded.

"So what did Rasmussen have to do with that?"

"He wanted them to get out," she said. "I think he, his group, I think they built that office building that's there now. But Tory from Doggie Dog told me Candace didn't want to move and her lease had another year to go, so Rasmussen paid the owner of the shopping center to dig up the parking lot, and that was that."

"And that meant no customers," I said.

"When I heard him yelling at the trial on Saturday, I just snapped. I wished he would just fall down dead." Giselle's face was pale but for a couple of bright pink points on her cheeks. "I was cleaning up after Precious and watching Rasmussen yell. He grabbed Mrs. Rasmussen and I got madder and madder. Then later I saw him throw a rock at that kitty that Jorge feeds, and Jorge yelled at him, and he called Jorge all kinds of names, you know, bad hateful names."

Giselle was on a tear, speaking faster and faster, and I tuned her out for a moment, my thoughts bouncing through an array of faces in my mind. So many faces, all attached to people who hated Rasmussen, people he had assaulted one way or another. Giselle. Jorge. Alberta. Hutchinson. His wife, Louise, had plenty of reason to clobber him. I remembered him yelling at Marietta. My mom and Anthony Marconi, although Mom had neither the opportunity nor, probably, the strength to kill him. I didn't think Marconi did either. I could certainly picture Tom hitting the man again in self-defense, but he would never leave someone to die like that. I was beginning to wonder whether anyone who had ever met Rasmussen had *not* wanted to kill him. Surely he was a different man when Louise married him. What happened to make him so angry, so belligerent? And then Giselle's voice recaptured my attention.

"... and it was like a red veil fell over me and ..." Something in her tone seized me by the throat and I didn't think I wanted to hear the rest of this, but Giselle kept going. "I sort of blanked. I had the pooper scooper in both hands, and I was just swinging and pounding, you know?" Giselle's face was very pale and glistened with perspiration. "It was weird, Janet, because even when I realized what I was doing, hitting and hitting and hitting, I couldn't stop."

# TWENTY-SIX

ALBERTA LAID HER FINGER against her lips and moved in exaggerated tippy-toe posture. Goldie and I followed her down the hall, both careful to be quiet. That was no problem for Goldie in her soft-soled ankle-mocs, but I had to work to keep my boot heels from clacking on the hardwood floor. Alberta stopped and gestured into a bedroom, and we both peeked around the door frame.

Hutchinson sat on the floor beside a medium-sized plastic pet carrier. We must not have pulled off the stealth approach, because he turned and looked at us. When I saw the expression on his face, the word that came to mind was *ecstatic*. He looked as if he'd had an epiphany.

We all murmured our hellos, and I knelt on the carpet beside him. Goldie joined us and whispered, "Oh, aren't they beautiful."

The tiny calico who had so enchanted Hutchinson the night of the kittens' birth was snuggled against the man's chest. One hand cradled the kitten's body, and the other rested with fingertips under her chin. Hutchinson smiled at me.

"Looks like someone is content."

I meant the kitten, but Alberta grinned as she settled into a chair across from us and said, "That kitten is pretty happy, too."

Goldie leaned toward the carrier and asked, "Is it okay to hold them?"

"Best thing in the world for them," said Alberta. She reached both hands into the carrier and lifted the sleeping kittens, then handed the black one to Goldie and the gray tabby to me.

Goldie held the kitten against her lips and whispered, "Lovely, lovely, lovely." The little tabby nestled into the crook of my arm and went back to sleep, and all the craziness of the past few days faded, if only for the moment. "Boy or girl?"

"Yours," said Alberta, pointing at Goldie, "is male, and yours," she pointed at the tabby in my arms, "is female." Her use of the possessive pronouns was not lost on me. *Sneaky*, I thought. She finished up with, "And of course Homer's calico is female." I didn't think I'd ever heard anyone call Hutchinson by his first name.

"Ah, lovely," said Goldie, looking around the room. "And where's… what's her name? The mother?"

"Gypsy," said Alberta. "She's taking a little breather. I cooked her some chicken and veggies and gave it to her just before you got here."

"So, Hutchinson, any news from your world?" I meant the police investigation, and assumed that even if he wasn't on Rasmussen's case, he would hear things. I was a bit confused when he responded by grinning at Alberta. I said, "What's going on? You look like the cat who ate the canary," I said, and then added for Alberta, "pardon the expression." Alberta had a big flight cage full of finches in her family room.

"Yeah," Hutchinson said, looking from me to the kitten on his chest. "This is my new roommate. You know, when she's big enough."

I laughed, a warm tickle running through me. "That's great, Hutch." I had resisted calling the man by his chosen nickname since I met him, but the better I liked him, the more inclined I was to use the name he liked. He grinned and nodded, and I said, "In fact, that's perfect."

Goldie, who now had the black kitten snugged up under her jaw, murmured, "Mmm hmmm." I wasn't sure whether she was agreeing with Hutchinson, me, or the little creature in her hands.

"But you meant the murder," said Hutchinson.

And *voila!* The world was back. The tabby kitten pushed her head deeper into my elbow as if trying not to hear what Hutchinson had to say. I laid my free hand over her back and her breathing steadied.

"Too soon, of course, to have much. But I heard from ..." He stopped himself, and I assumed that he wasn't really supposed to know what was happening since he was potentially a suspect. But the guy had friends, at least on the force. "Well, I heard that someone clocked him pretty good."

"Right. I knew that." The memory of Rasmussen's bloodied and misshapen head sent a shudder through my shoulders.

Hutchinson gave me a blank look, and the shudder repeated itself.

"I saw him in the tunnel, remember?" No response. "On Sunday morning. I crawled in to see, you know, to check for a pulse." Hutchinson nodded. "His head was, I don't know, misshapen?"

"How awful," said Goldie, but her tone didn't fit her content. She sort of crooned the words to "her" kitten.

"It *was* awful," I said.

Alberta snorted.

"I know he was an ass, but still," I said. "I mean, I'd have been happy never to see him again, but I didn't wish him dead."

"Well, I suspect a lot of people did," said Alberta.

"From what I saw, he gave lots of people lots of reasons. I…" I glanced at Goldie and she stared into my eyes, flicked her gaze toward Hutchinson and back to me, and gave an almost imperceptible shake of her head. *She's right*, whispered my inner guardian angel. *He may be a friend of sorts, but he's still a cop.* Logic argued that it made no difference since I had done nothing wrong, but I decided that Goldie was right, I should for once try not to blurt out too much. "Never mind."

Hutchinson's lip twisted and he said, "So here's the odd thing. This came from the EMT at the scene." He paused to reposition his kitten. "He told me, you know, before I knew who the victim was, he said there was something mixed in with the blood on the guy's head. You know, on the wound, where he got whacked." Hutchinson repositioned his kitten. "So the guy, I mean the EMT, not Rasmussen, wondered what it was, so he touched it and smelled it, and he was pretty sure it was feces."

No one said anything for a moment, and then Alberta spoke.

"Always said he had shit for brains." Alberta looked at each of us in turn. "What?" No one said anything, and I confess that, although I felt guilty since a man was dead, I did have to agree with her. I didn't dare look at Goldie. I could *feel* her trying not to laugh.

When Hutchinson finally broke the silence, he just made it worse. "Isn't that bizarre? How in the heck would he get poop in his hair?"

I bit my lip and managed not to say what I was thinking about where Rasmussen seemed to have his head when I met him. I was

140

afraid to look at any of the others, and then a strangled squeal snuck out of Goldie's mouth, and Alberta started to titter, and Hutchinson laughed, and then we were all laughing. Finally Goldie said, "Oh, my. I am *not* laughing because a man is dead, but..."

I laid a hand on her knee and said, "We all know that. We all know."

When we were calm again, Hutchinson spoke. "I didn't see any dog poop, er, feces in there, you know, around the jumps and the tunnel and stuff, so I don't think he could have fallen in it."

"No, I've almost never seen a dog poop in an agility ring, and if they did, the ring crew would clean it right up," I said.

Alberta added, "Marietta keeps that whole place very clean. Well, Jorge does."

"Yeah, they do." I had been training at Dog Dayz for years, and she was right, the place was kept immaculate, other than the occasional gift from an antisocial dog owner. Even those got picked up quickly.

"So any ideas?" asked Hutchinson.

At first my mind was devoid of non-snarky ideas. Then, with the bite of ice water, a memory. Giselle. I had just left her a couple of hours earlier, and although I couldn't recall exactly what she had said, the fragments that came to mind scared the bejeepers out of me. *Pooper scooper... swinging and pounding... hitting and hitting... couldn't stop.*

She couldn't stop, but I had to. I pushed the half-formed accusation away and forced myself into the present. "I thought you were off this case?" I said.

Before Hutchinson could answer, Alberta said, "Hello, sweetheart," and I followed her gaze. Gypsy stood in the doorway, eyes wide and tail straight up and fluffed in alarm. Within seconds, though, she relaxed and strolled into the room, glancing from one kitten to another. I was closest to the door, so first on her list. She stepped delicately onto my thigh and leaned up and in toward her tabby daughter, saw that she was safe, and moved on to Goldie and then Hutchinson. When she was satisfied, she got into the carrier and began to wash her paws.

"Ooh wook jus wike your mama, don't ooh," Hutchinson said. Then he seemed to remember that he wasn't alone with his kitten. He pulled his shoulders back, cleared his throat, and said, "Yeah, the case."

"You're off it?"

"Yeah, for now. But my buddies tell me a little." He looked me in the eye. "You have any ideas?"

"How would I know?" It came out a little more high-pitched and whiney than I would have liked, but I wrestled my voice into submission and pressed on. "Everybody seemed to hate the guy. But not enough to kill him." I hoped I sounded more convinced than I felt.

"I did," said Alberta. "I mean, I hated him enough to kill him." She stared at Hutchinson over the top of her glasses. "But I didn't."

"Be careful who you say that to," said Hutchinson, and Alberta snorted.

"Maybe it was an accident," said Goldie. "I mean, what was he doing out there in the dark anyway? Maybe he tripped and fell."

"So what happens now?" I asked. "I mean, do they have a list of suspects or something?"

"They're waiting for forensics, I think, although I guess the lab guys are having a little trouble, considering how many dogs ran through that tunnel."

Goldie's black kitten began to mewl and wriggle, and as if that flipped a switch, the other two did the same. Gypsy meowed back, and Hutchinson said, "Okay, wittle girl, time for your snack." He placed her gently against her mother and stroked the older cat's cheek with one finger. Goldie and I put our kittens beside the calico. All four humans in the room watched in contented silence. We may even have been purring.

# TWENTY-SEVEN

GOLDIE TALKED THROUGH MOST of the drive home, beginning with variations on a theme of "aren't they amazing little creatures and isn't that black kitten the most perfect baby cat ever created?" I listened with half my mind while the other half teased apart a tangle of thoughts about motives, passions, and the potential for pretty much anyone to do things you don't expect. I knew all the potential suspects, some of them quite well. Did someone I knew and liked and basically trusted bash a man's head in?

*No, of course not*, whispered one inner voice. *It was someone else. A stranger. Maybe an accident.*

Then the other voice piped up. *It could happen.*

And based on the past year of my life, I knew that was true. Someone I knew and liked and trusted may have killed Rasmussen.

Goldie seemed to pick up on my thoughts, and her shift in topic penetrated the partition in my mind. "So who *do* you think did it?"

"No idea."

"Pfffttt. Come on, Janet. It's me you're talking to."

My fingers began to cramp and I realized that I had the steering wheel in a death grip. I forced my hands to relax a notch, and said, "No, really, I don't know that I seriously suspect anyone. But…" I took a deep breath. "But the guy was so nasty, so threatening, that I could see someone striking out in fear or self-defense or…"

"Rage."

"Yes, rage." We were on State, approaching Anthony. "Do you mind if I swing by Shadetree for a few minutes?"

"No."

"I'd like to check on Mom."

"No problem."

"It won't take long."

Goldie gave my shoulder a little push. "Janet, why don't we swing by Shadetree? I'd love to see your mom."

I turned south on Anthony and asked Goldie, "Have you ever been that angry? I mean, enraged to the point that you thought you could kill someone?"

"Yes," she said. "Once. I saw a man spit on a child in Birmingham." A strange hot thread wound through Goldie's voice, the anger still present all these years later. "The little boy was four or five years old. I thought he would be frightened, and I'm sure he was, but he just wiped his cheek and looked at the man and smiled. And the guy called him a string of filthy names, and the boy's mother started to pull the kid out of the way, and she screamed names of her own at the guy."

I pulled into the Shadetree parking lot, turned off the ignition, and looked at Goldie, waiting for her to finish. When she didn't speak, I said, "Black kid?"

"No. White. He was with his mother, and she was there like I was, supporting the cause."

"Pretty low, treating a child that way," I said.

"That made me angry, of course, but it was nothing out of the ordinary, considering the setting. But then he pushed them. He rushed them and shoved his hand against the little boy and practically lifted him into his mother, and they fell back and I could see that she was hurt, you know, actually injured. And I wanted to kill him."

"But you didn't."

"I didn't. But I might have tried if the little boy hadn't spoken right then." Goldie closed her eyes and took a long breath that I recognized as her centering technique.

"What did he say?" I asked.

"He picked himself up and looked at the man and said, 'I hope you find some happy peace, Mister.' I'll never forget those words. That was the last I saw of him. People sort of closed around him and his mother, and got her up and out of the way." Goldie turned and seemed to look right into me. "So I understand that kind of rage. And I know you don't buy some of the things I believe, but I think that boy was sent to teach me, and I think he saved me from doing something evil, then and later."

We sat in silence for a moment, then stepped out of the warm van into a stiff, cold wind. "Wow, it must be twenty degrees colder than when I walked Jay this morning," I said. I had to hang on tight to keep the door into Shadetree from flying wide when I opened it.

The lobby was warm and bright and welcoming. Jade Templeton, the manager, was speaking to someone near her office door, but she waved and smiled at us.

"Let's check the lounge and garden first," I said. "Mom is usually in one or the other this time of day."

"I'd forgotten how cheery this place is," said Goldie. "Oh, there's cute little Percy."

She was right. The little gray Poodle jauntied his way to us, tail wagging. He wriggled and whined and rubbed my leg, and I squatted to return his greeting. "You look like you own the place, little man," I said.

Goldie petted him as well, and said, "I'm so glad Ms. Templeton adopted him. A match made in heaven." Percy had moved in with Jade when his owners were killed, and now he came to work with her, serving as one of the resident pets to the many residents who missed their own animals. The other was a pretty little gray-and-white cat who went by whatever names the residents called her. The little dog took his duties seriously, and soon trotted off to greet a little group of residents who were sitting in a nearby alcove.

My mother was nowhere in sight, but Anthony Marconi waved from a bench in the indoor garden room and we made our way to him.

"Good morning, Janet," he said, then bowed slightly to Goldie. "And Goldie, I presume. Anthony Marconi."

Goldie held out her hand and said, "It's so nice to meet you finally. How did you know?"

"I've heard so much about you," Marconi smiled, but the look faded. "Your mother is, umm, not feeling well today. She just fell asleep a few minutes ago."

*Ah, shit,* I thought. I had hoped the Marconi spell would last.

"It's okay, Janet," he continued. "I sit with her and, really, it's okay when she thinks I'm someone else, you know, your dad or your brother mostly. I mean, what difference does it make, really, if she still loves me?" He smiled again, but it was different. Bittersweet.

"Mr. Marconi, I'm sorry for your family's loss," said Goldie.

For a moment, Marconi looked like he had no idea what Goldie was talking about, and when he recovered, he looked anything but grieved. "No great loss," he said, and followed with, "Sorry. That's rude of me, and I appreciate your concern. It's just that Charles, well … hard to explain …"

"No explanation necessary," I said. "I met him, and Goldie's heard about him."

"Yes, well, I'd as soon have been shed of him years ago," he said.

My judgmental left eyebrow wanted to grab my hairline, but I caught it in time. I couldn't resist a glance at Goldie, though, and she reciprocated, and I'm sure that the message going both ways was *Marconi could have done it.*

By the time we walked back to the car, the wind had strengthened and the temperature had dropped enough to make us pull our coats tight to the throats. It was still sunny where we were, but the sky to the northwest was a wall of cold gray and it seemed to be coming our way. As soon as we were in the car, we both started to talk.

"You first," I said, fiddling with the temperature and fan settings.

"What do you think?" asked Goldie, patting her own cheeks. "He was there, right? And he had plenty of motive."

"Oh, I don't know. I mean, come on, the guy is what? Eighty-three? Eighty-four? Besides, he wouldn't have been there that late."

"Have you felt his grip?" She asked. "And did you look at his cane? It's not plastic, you know. It's brier. I have a walking stick made of the same stuff. It's hard and it's heavy." She held her hands in batting position and swung. "Bam!"

I looked at her, then back at the road. She was right. Marconi was there on Saturday, and I couldn't forget the look on his face when Charles Rasmussen manhandled Louise.

Goldie declined my invitation to come in. She gave me a hug and left me feeling pretty glum as I pushed the button to close the garage door. As always, though, stepping into the furry arms waiting inside the door made the world a brighter place. Jay bounced and wriggled in front of me, and Leo rubbed against the backs of my legs and chirped. I let Jay out the back door and ran to the bathroom with Leo right behind me. He hopped onto the side of the tub and I stroked him and said, "Hang on, Catman. I'll feed you in a minute."

When I saw my hair in the mirror, I amended that. "Okay, Leo *mio*, hang on. Gotta tame this mess." The wind had tied my curly hair into knots, and I think I left half of it in my brush, but I got it smoothed down enough to twist it around and jaw-clip it into submission. I was back in the kitchen warming Leo's home-cooked turkey dinner when the doorbell rang. Jay barked and banged into the back door, and Leo yowled impatiently.

"Okay, okay." The doorbell rang again, and someone knocked. Loudly. "Hang on, will ya?" I shouted, setting Leo's food on his little table in the laundry room. I had created a cat station there and another in the garage to keep his food and litter box out of canine reach. I reset the baby gate to keep Jay out of there, and went to the front door. The knocking resumed as I unlocked the doorknob, and I had a mouthful of unfriendly things ready to explode from my lips. I did, that is, until I saw the two uniformed police officers on my porch.

# TWENTY-EIGHT

By the time I got to Dog Dayz for obedience practice, my stomach had let loose some of the knots the police had inspired, but my head was starting to pound. I wasn't sure which was worse. Either way, I figured I'd work Jay a little since he had been locked up most of the day, and then go home early and abandon reality for a good book.

"Helloo, Miss Janet." The voice was behind me, but I would know Jorge's breathy "j" anywhere.

"Hola, Jorge." The man was grinning like the Cheshire cat, and I couldn't help smiling back. "What are you so happy about?"

"You haff a minute? You come see?" He gestured a "follow me," so I made sure Jay's crate latch was secure and said, "Okay, if it won't take too long."

He was already walking toward the door to the office at the front of the building. There were two front doors, and the one he opened was not only locked, but had a sign that said "NO DOGS!" in big orange letters. Marietta often left her own dog loose in the office, so it was off limits, absent an invitation. Jorge had a key, and free run of the place, so I considered myself invited. I stepped into the warm room and wrinkled my nose at a distinctly fishy smell.

"Come, you see," he said, waving me forward with one hand and indicating a cardboard box with the other. "I find little Rainboo and her *gatita*."

I squeezed between the big desk and an enormous battered green filing cabinet and looked into the box. The little tortoiseshell cat I had seen at the tree line on Saturday was stretched full length, licking a carbon copy of herself. This kitten was older than Gypsy's brood.

Jorge reached into the box, picked up the kitten, and held her close. "Is beautiful *gatita*, no, Miss Janet?"

"She is beautiful, Jorge. They both are." The kitten had her blue-green eyes fixed on my face. They were fully open, as were her ears, and she was probably half as big as her mother, so I figured she was five or six weeks old. "Just one kitten?"

Jorge frowned. "There were more, but they disappear. Maybe *el gato*, you know, the male, maybe he kill the others." He shook his head sadly, then brightened. "But *la linda* is safe now."

"Her name is Linda?"

"No, no," he laughed. "She is *linda*, you know, pretty. *Muy linda*."

I reached out and stroked the side of the kitten's face and she pushed her cheek into my hand. "She's very comfortable with people for a feral kitten."

"I been seeing them, holding like this, since she very small. Eyes still closed when I meet her." I followed his gaze to Rainbow. She was still relaxed in the box and squinting cat love at Jorge. "Mamá Rainboo trust me."

"I see that," I said. "Jorge, are you okay? Yesterday was pretty tough."

He looked at me, and I tried to read the look in his eyes, but he had put them behind a curtain. "I ask Miss Marietta for bring Rainboo and *la linda* in here on Saturday. That man, he throw rocks at Rainboo and say he kill her she jump on car again." The kitten was wriggling to get down, so Jorge set her back in the box and placed a little stuffed bear in front of her. "I tell him he sorry he do that again."

"You might not want to tell the police that," I said, thinking *I wish you hadn't told me.*

Jorge laughed. "My English no *perfecto*, but I no stupid, Miss Janet. Police here today. They see my green card, ask questions. All okay."

"That's good, Jorge." To tell the truth, I was relieved to hear that he was a permanent resident. I knew he was from southern Mexico, from Oaxaca, but it had never occurred to me to ask about his legal status.

"My wife, she want *la gatita*, and we going to try Rainboo if she live inside happy." He brushed some fur off his sleeve. "I like you come for dinner my house sometime, Miss Janet. Mr. Tom, too. Maybe after the Thanksgiving, yes?" He smiled. "I make special food for you, Oaxaca food."

"You cook, Jorge?"

"I want Oaxaca food, I cook." He laughed. "I want American food, my wife cook."

The pounding in my head was worse when I got back to my van and I thought about just getting in and driving home. I scanned the parking lot, saw Tom's "LABMOBIL" plate, and changed my mind. I dug some change out of the stash I keep in the ashtray, got Jay out of his crate, walked him to the tree line and back, and went inside.

Tom was standing behind a free-standing barrier on wheels that Marietta moved around the obedience area, giving trainers a mobile hideaway for training their dogs for the out-of-sight stays. As I walked toward him, I could see the dogs lined up along the far side of the ring at the other end of the building. Drake was two dogs from the end.

"Hey you," said Tom.

"Hey yourself." Jay wriggled up to him and got a chin scratch, and I kissed him, then said, "Your dog is up."

One of Tom's endearing qualities is a mind as dirty as my own, and I had to laugh when he raised his eyebrows and said, "That's just my leash in my pocket."

"No, I mean your Labrador Retriever. He's supposed to be in a down, right?" All the other dogs were lying down, but Drake was sitting.

Tom stepped to the end of the barrier and took a look. "Oh, man."

"Want me to correct him?"

Tom held out his hand for Jay's leash and my training bag. The out-of-sight stays are very stressful for dogs and handlers alike, and sometimes a dog learns that if she breaks the stay, her person will come back. Having someone else put the dog back in place can break that pattern. I wasn't the best choice to correct Drake since I was his second-best person, but no one else was available, so off I went. When he saw me coming, Drake sank to the ground, put his chin on his paws, and conjured up his best Labrador sad eyes. I bent in front of him, put my hand around his muzzle, and, in my calm-and-in-charge voice, said "Down." He was still in that position when I got back to Tom.

"He hasn't done that in a long time," said Tom.

"Stress," I said, taking back Jay's leash and my training bag.

"What's he have to be stressed about?"

"Not him. You. Me."

"Right." Tom asked Clay Philips how much longer they had, then asked me, "You still on for Thursday?"

*Thursday?* "Yeah, sure."

"You forgot."

"No, I didn't forget." *I did, but now I remember.* "Just a little pre-occupied. So what time do you want to leave?"

Tom had been looking for a puppy for months. You would think it would be a snap to find one, since Labrador Retrievers have been the most popular breed in the U.S. for more than a decade. But Tom was determined to find a dog of type he loved—moderate size and build, strong work ethic, steady temperament—from a breeder who screened for inherited issues, socialized the puppies, treated the adults well, and didn't breed excessively. He had almost given up after several disappointments, but someone told him about a breeder they thought might fit the bill, so we were off to see her and her dogs.

"She has a litter on the ground, right?" I asked, meaning already born. I wondered whether we'd be bringing a puppy home with us.

"Yes, but they're only five weeks old. Anyway, this is just a look-see. I don't want a puppy until spring, and besides, this is a yellow litter. I'm thinking I should stick to black so all the dog hair on my clothes is the same color."

I brushed some long white hairs from his pants and said, "Too late."

When I looked back at his face, the muscles around Tom's eyes had tightened and he wasn't smiling. He said, "What?"

"What what?"

His right eyebrow rose, as if I should know what he was asking, but he didn't say anything.

Everyone else behind the barrier was so intent on their dogs' stays that they probably weren't listening, but I still wasn't comfortable talking openly about being a possible murder suspect. I edged Tom a few feet away from the others before I whispered, "The police came to talk to me this afternoon."

"Me, too."

"Really?"

"They didn't actually come. They offered to come to my office, or I could go to the station. So I went there after my last class." My heart went into sprint mode, but Tom looked like he'd just told me he went for bread and milk. He grinned and added, "I didn't want them hauling me out of the university in handcuffs."

"That's not funny."

"Oh, come on," said Tom. "More to the point, I didn't want the dean making a fuss about how bad it looks to have police questioning faculty." He laughed. "Although on second thought, that might be kind of fun." Tom and one of the deans had been sparring over whether or not Tom could bring Drake with him to his office, something he'd been doing for years.

I thought back to my own afternoon chat with the officers and felt a little sick. They must have called Tom right after they left my house. A scratch surrounded by fading blue bore witness to Rasmussen's backhand to Tom's cheek on Saturday, and I was sure the police would see physical assault as provocation. And Rasmussen's insinuations about making trouble for Tom with the university could be construed as motive. What was it the cop shows say a suspect needs? Motive, opportunity, and means. Tom had all three, at least from where the investigators stood.

# TWENTY-NINE

CLAY CALLED TIME, so Tom and the others returned to where they had left their dogs in out-of-sight stays. Jay and I found a chair by the adjacent ring where heeling practice was already underway. My conversation with Tom had left dancers clogging on my skull, so I got a cola from the machine, took two aspirins, and sat down for a moment. Marietta was in the center of the ring calling commands. She waved at me, then asked someone to take over for a few minutes. She stepped over the accordion fencing that defined the ring and sat down beside me. Jay leaned into her leg and she scratched the sweet spot over his hips, freezing him in place.

"What a screwed up weekend."

I nodded. "What happened with the johnny business?" I'd gotten so wound up in Rasmussen's demise that I had almost forgotten about the crazy portable-potty chase.

Marietta rolled her eyes. "Was that the stupidest thing you ever heard of? I mean, sled dogs? I wouldn't hitch a Pomeranian to a portable toilet, let alone two malamutes." She let out something between a laugh and a snort. "Served her right. And John is threatening to sue her for damages. He says the unit is ruined."

"John?"

"John Johnson owns Johnny-Come-Early, if you can believe that."

"What's in a name?" I asked. We both chuckled, and I went on. "At least no one was really hurt," I said. "It's a good thing he had just switched out the johnnies."

"Took an hour to wash that crap out of her hair and off her skin." Marietta said and wrinkled her nose. "Well, not actual crap. But that blue disinfectant stuff is clingy. Yuch. Had to use dog shampoo and stick her in the grooming tub. I hope I get my clothes back. I loaned her my favorite sweat pants. Gad, people."

"Speaking of people ... How long were the police here?"

"Hours. They finally let Clyde Williamson off the hook." She was referring to the agility judge. "He flew in Saturday night and didn't have a car, plus no motive. He was pretty cranky about the whole thing."

"I noticed that."

"Yeah, we won't be hiring *him* again." She stopped scratching Jay and told him to lie down. He looked at me for confirmation, then lay down across my feet. "The cops talked to me and to Jorge. He was pretty shook up," said Marietta, "but I think that was more about those cats he's been feeding than about what's-his-name. What *was* his name? Rapscallion?"

"Rasmussen." I wanted to ask her what else the police wanted to know, but my phone started to ring. "Shoot. I thought I turned that off," I said. I checked my pants and jacket, then remembered that I had dropped the silly thing into my training bag. By the time I fished it out from under my spare leash, spilled liver treats, a dumbbell, a tennis ball, and a couple of toys I use in training, it was quiet. I looked at the missed-call number and said, "Hutchinson. Maybe I should call him back."

Marietta didn't seem to hear me. "Jorge was pretty mad at that guy, though. He saw him throw something at that little mama cat in the afternoon, and later in the evening, after you left, he said he saw the guy chasing the cat out near the agility ring."

"No! He came back onto your property?" The image of Rasmussen sitting in his car across the street came back to me. At the time, I thought he was watching for Louise to leave. She was having pizza with Alberta and some other folks, and I had no idea how long that little *soirée* lasted. Maybe he got tired of waiting for her. "And chasing a cat? Why would he do that?"

"That's what Jorge said, but it was dark out there, so maybe it wasn't the guy, Ratsass or whatever. Maybe someone was out there running the course without a dog. Practicing their handling moves. Who knows?" Marietta stood and stepped back into the ring. "Jorge yelled at whoever it was, but he was bringing a forty-pound bag of dog food in from his truck so he didn't go out there right then."

"That's so weird," I said. "Who runs around an agility course in the dark?"

Marietta shrugged. "The main lights were off, but there was some light from the back of the building and the parking lot."

"But Jorge wasn't sure it was Rasmussen?"

"Oh, he seemed pretty sure. He sputtered and swore while he dumped the dog food into the bin. Then he went back out to police the yard and said he'd take care of it."

"Did he see anyone out there?"

"He said he saw someone walking along the edge of the parking lot, but not on the agility course. It was odd, since almost all of the competitors had left long before that," she said. "He did say it wasn't Rasmussen though."

"How did he know?"

"Too small."

Marietta resumed control of the practice ring and I just sat there for a few moments. I should have called Hutchinson right then, but I didn't think I could stand to hear about any more friends being murder suspects and I couldn't think of any other reason he would be calling. I closed my eyes and pressed the cold pop can against one temple, then the other, then my forehead. The icy pressure loosened the pain a notch, but the harder I tried to disentangle my thoughts, the tighter they wound themselves.

Jay whined softly and shifted off my feet.

"Okay, you're right, Bubby," I said, looking into his hopeful eyes. I strapped on my treat bag, and picked up my leash. "Come on, let's work a little." I'd say I did all this training and competing for Jay, to channel his high-energy mind and body into acceptable activities, but the truth is that I do it for myself. Working with my animals never fails to center me. Besides, they're both so gorgeous, they take my breath away.

There were only a dozen human-canine pairs working in the main ring. Rhonda Lake and Eleanor were there, and several people I didn't remember seeing before. Probably recent graduates of the basic obedience course, I thought. Collin Lahmeyer waved at me, his Chesapeake Bay Retriever, Molly, at his side. I stepped into a gap in the line circling the ring and glanced down. Jay looked up at me, already aligned in perfect heel position, a jaunty little bounce in his step.

"Fast!" said Marietta.

The people in the ring shifted to jog speed. The more experienced dogs sped up and stayed in position, adjusting their strides as needed. One of the new dogs, a big brindle boy who appeared to be some sort of hound cross, bounced up and down, started to bay, and took off at a run. His owner, a thirty-something blonde in desperate need of more secure footwear for dog training, pleaded, "Stop, Billy Bob! Billy Bob, stop! Oh!" Her cute little ballet flats pitter-pattered on the ring mats but gave her no traction at all. Billy Bob let out a long "Awooo!"

"Halt!" said Marietta.

Everyone pulled to a stop. Except Billy Bob. He was in full cry now, although I had no idea what he was chasing. Pure joy, probably.

"Billy Bob! Oh, oh, oh …" Billy Bob's owner sounded like she might start a full cry of her own, but I had to give her credit for hanging onto that leash. Her dog probably weighed nearly as much as she did, and he had the advantage of two additional legs and a low center of gravity.

Marietta tried to intercept Billy Bob, but she was too far away and he seemed to be focused on something near the pop machine by the far wall of the room. A voice in my head wondered *What is this, runaway dog week?* I shifted my focus from the hound and spotted a display of collars and leashes and, just beyond, something new. A rack of stuffed dog toys. I turned my gaze back to Billy Bob just as he leaped, trying to clear the folding gates that defined the ring's perimeter. It wasn't much of a hurdle for a big, leggy dog.

Billy Bob rose a few inches off the ground, but he was handicapped by the woman who still clung to his leash. "Awooo!" he cried, and crashed head-first through the gate. The diamond-shaped opening slid over his head and neck and caught against his shoulders. Billy Bob's momentum slowed, but he kept running, bowing the center of the gate like an arrow, his own body the point he aimed at his target. The ends lifted off the stanchions as they stretched and flapped behind him like wings. His owner took several tripping steps, stumbled to her knees, and let go of the leash.

Giselle had appeared from the back of the building. For an instant she stood slack-jawed between Billy Bob and the toy display. Then she let out a scream, scooped Precious up from the floor, and scampered back the way she'd come in. Tom and the rest of the group in the other ring were turning toward the ruckus with various levels of comprehension.

Billy Bob folded his front quarters in an obvious attempt to stop, but he was off the mats and his elbows skidded across the smooth concrete. He crashed into the toys, knocking the rack up against the wall, and his wooden wings flapped and stretched open around him, wobbled, and finally stopped. Billy Bob pulled his head out of the gate and loped back to where his person crouched weeping on the floor. He sat in front of her, his body cocked sideways onto one hip and one long ear flipped rakishly back across his neck. He put a big paw on the woman's shoulder, an oversized pink-and-purple octopus dangling from his mouth.

# THIRTY

By ten o'clock I was snuggled into Tom's big cushy armchair, a fleece throw tucked around me and an "Archeologists do it in the dirt" mug of Irish coffee warming my hands. Tom sat facing me on the couch, feet stretched onto a hassock and a dog cuddled up to him on each side. Drake had rolled part-way over for a chest-and-belly rub. Jay was snuggled up close with his nose nearly touching Tom's and a love-gaze locking them together. The rest of the world receded and I knew somewhere deeper than words could reach that this was everything I had always wanted—love, loyalty, and my freedom to boot.

Jay lay down and heaved an enormous sigh, and Drake rolled fully onto his back. The spell was broken, but the afterglow lingered, even when Tom said, "You goofy dogs."

I swallowed some more coffee and licked the whipped cream from my lips. "Why do you have an archeologist mug?" I asked, enjoying the low buzz as the whiskey spread itself out from my center.

"Gift from a cousin who calls me Indiana Saunders. He thinks all anthropologists are treasure hunters."

I cocked my head at him.

"It's true, we are. But not all treasures are buried under the ground."

"I wish I'd had my camera tonight." Billy Bob's great escape kept rerunning in my mind.

Tom laughed. "That was a pretty spectacular crash into the display. I felt sorry for Billy Bob's owner, but it was funny."

"But did you see him when he went back to her?" I asked. "Those beautiful eyes, and the paw on her shoulder." My voice broke on the final word and I almost burst into tears.

"Hey, you okay?" Tom started to get up, but I waved him off. "Is this the 'I love dogs so much I get all choked up' thing or something else?"

He knows me too well. *He knows you just right*, whispered my snarky little inner demon. *Besides, your dog and cat love him and trust him. What more do you need?* It was true. They would have brought him home and kept him months ago.

I smiled at Tom, squirmed deeper into the chair, sipped my Irish coffee, and screwed up my courage. "Tom, I've been thinking..."

Drake snapped his head up and knocked into the mug in Tom's hand, sending an arc of coffee into the air. "Hey!" yelled Tom, pulling his other arm free of Jay and trying to get up from under the dogs. Drake froze, his lip caught on his canine and one ear folded back, and rolled his eyes toward the front of the house. Jay bellowed, "*Boof!*" The two dogs launched themselves from the couch, their back feet shoving with a combined force of a hundred and fifty pounds. The couch, and Tom, slid a couple of inches, and another slosh of coffee rocketed out of the mug.

Tom was on his feet, swearing, holding the mug at arm's length. I was up and untangling myself from the fleece wrap. I took the mug from Tom's hand and stifled myself long enough to ask, "Are you okay? You didn't get burned, did you?" When Tom said he was wet but not scalded, I started to laugh. And laugh.

"What the hell was that?" said Tom, pulling his wet shirt away from his chest with fingertips. He started to laugh, too.

I was still laughing when I followed the dogs and opened the front door just as the man outside reached for the bell.

"Oh!" said Hutchinson. At first I thought he was just surprised that I had opened the door, but when I saw that he was rigid and the dogs were jostling and sniffing all around him, I realized he wasn't completely cured of his fears.

"Come on, guys, let him in," I said, tapping each dog on the fanny and signaling them into the house. "You, too," I told Hutchinson, and he relaxed a tad and followed me in. Tom told the dogs to lie down, and then he disappeared into his bedroom. Hutchinson started to sit on the couch, but I aimed him at my chair and said "Hang on." I got a towel and, as I blotted the coffee from the couch, said, "Little mishap when the dogs heard you coming." I spread a second towel over the wet spot and sat down. "Thank goodness for microfibers."

Tom reappeared in a dry sweatshirt. They shook hands, but Hutchinson declined refreshments. "I can't stay, I just ..." He sat forward in the chair, elbows on his knees. "Alberta was picked up for questioning this afternoon. I tried to call you ..."

*The phone call.* I had meant to call him back, but between Billy Bob's escapade, my headache, and the rainy drive, I had forgotten about his message. "Sorry, I would have called …"

Hutchinson nodded. "No problem."

"Wait. What do you mean 'picked up'? They interviewed *me* at home."

"No, it's fine," he said, not really answering the question. "She asked me to see if you could go feed her dogs."

"Oh!" I glanced at my wrist, but didn't have my watch. "Are they … I can go now …"

"I took care of it," said Hutchinson. "Twinkle needed her medicine, and Alberta was worried."

That took me up short. Alberta had four Welsh terriers, and their barking could be intimidating if you didn't know them. Maybe Hutchinson was more cured of his cynophobia than I thought. "You went and fed her dogs?"

"Yeah," said Hutchinson. "They know me, you know, from my visits to see the kitties."

"Where is she now? Is she okay?" asked Tom.

"Yeah, she's back home now." His forehead was wrinkled up, but he said, "She's mostly ticked off. But a little scared, I think."

I thought back to my own adventures in police interrogation and said, "You guys are terrifying."

Hutchinson's eyebrows shot up, and he stared at me and finally said, "I guess. Anyway, she's not off the hook yet. They—we, I guess—just don't have enough to arrest her."

"Oh, come on." I said. "Alberta? She's five feet tall and can't walk three feet without wheezing. Rasmussen was a big guy. She couldn't have killed him."

"You'd be surprised what people can do given the right weapon," said Hutchinson.

"Do they have a weapon?" asked Tom.

"They might," said Hutchinson.

"What does that mean?" I asked.

"What do you mean?"

"Do they have an actual weapon, or do they think they know what kind of weapon it was?" I asked.

"They found something," said Hutchinson. "On Sunday. They just aren't sure yet that it was used to kill him."

Tom and I asked simultaneously, "What is it?" and "Where was it?"

"They sort of have two things," said Hutchinson.

"What do you mean, sort of?" I asked.

"Look, I'm not on the case, so I'm getting bits and pieces as I can. I'm still on the potential suspect list myself, so some of the guys are careful what they tell me." He stopped talking and signaled Jay to come to him, then continued to talk while he scratched behind Jay's ears. "Remember I told you the E.M.T. found shi..., er, feces in the guy, Rasmussen's, wound and hair?"

I nodded.

"They found one of those whaddyacallums, you know, for picking up dog, umm, droppings..."

"Pooper-scooper?" I asked.

"Yeah."

Tom and I exchanged a glance. "There were pooper-scoopers all over at the trial," I said, mentally taking stock. "At least five of them. Probably more." But even as I said the words, I heard Giselle telling me how she had swung and hit with a pooper-scooper, over and over and over. At the time I had assumed she had been hitting the ground. Now part of me wished I had asked her, and part of me didn't want to know. The old Lizzy Borden jump-rope rhyme surfaced from deep memory, but in a new version. *Giselle Swann had a scoop, Hit Rasmussen with the poop, When she saw* … Hutchinson's voice broke in and drew me back to the moment.

"No, yeah, I know. No, this one was in the garbage. They're pulling prints and checking for trace, you know, blood or whatever. The handle was broken. Snapped through."

"That would take a pretty good force," said Tom. "Skulls just aren't that hard. I don't think the handle would snap from hitting the guy."

The voice of reason. I thought I might be able to breathe again.

"I don't know," said Hutchinson. "Just telling you what they found."

"But prints? They're going to find just about everyone's prints, you know." I tried to remember whether I had used any of the scoopers over the weekend. I didn't think so. I rarely do unless my pockets are out of plastic bags.

"I suppose," said Hutchinson. "But placement of the prints will say a lot. You know, how the person gripped the handle."

Then I remembered something. "You said they had two things, possible weapons. What's the other one?"

"Yeah, they found blood on that table thing."

*Table thing?* I stared at him.

"You know, that thing the dogs sit on." Hutchinson used his hands to shape a square.

"The pause table?" said Tom. "Where the dogs sit or lie down during their runs?"

"Yeah. The pause table," said Hutchinson. "But they don't know that it's his blood. Could be from a dog, right?"

"Could be," I said, although it seemed extremely unlikely to me. I tried to remember where the pause table was in relation to the tunnel where Rasmussen's body was found. As I recalled, it was about twenty feet out and just off a beeline to the tunnel's mouth. I'd have to check my photos, although I had only taken a few that morning. I wasn't the official photographer, but I had gotten a few shots of my friends' runs.

Tom said, "Nobody hit him with a pause table, that's for sure. So it if *is* Rasmussen's blood, he must have fallen." He looked at me, then at Hutchinson. "And that would make it an accident."

*Unless someone shoved him,* I thought. *Or tripped him, as I had done during the kerfuffle earlier on Saturday. Or whacked him with the pooper-scooper so that he fell and hit the table.* My imagination went wild and a series of candidates lined up in my mind—Alberta, Jorge, Giselle, Anthony Marconi, Rasmussen's not-so-grieving widow, Louise. Even the police officer sitting here petting my dog.

"Here's something funny, though," said Hutchinson, although he wasn't laughing. "There were odd footprints on the table."

That didn't seem all that odd. The ground had been soft and damp in spots, and probably a hundred dogs had landed on that table on Saturday. But then a horrifying thought hit me and I asked, "Bloody footprints?"

"No," said Hutchinson, and I let out my breath. "Just a little mud. But Gerald, you know, one of the other cops? He's taken a lot of tracking courses and he hunts, too. He's the one that noticed them among the others."

"And?" asked Tom.

"Cat. He said they were from a cat."

Marietta had said that someone had been chasing a cat across the agility course. Or at least that was what Jorge told her.

Hutchinson gave Jay a last chin scratch, stood to go, and said, "I hope she didn't do it. But Alberta really hated that guy."

*Who didn't?* I thought.

# THIRTY-ONE

THE FRAGRANCE OF WARM yeast enveloped me when Goldie opened her door, and I thought I might swoon. Goldie had taken Leo to her house the night before, as she often did if I stayed at Tom's after doggy school, and I was there to pick him up. I had thought I'd just pop in, grab my cat, and go right home, but who can resist fresh, homemade sweet rolls? So at nine thirty Tuesday morning, I was sitting in my best friend's kitchen sipping a breakfast blend from Charleston Tea Plantation and nibbling my second sweet roll. Leo purred like thunder on the chair beside me, and Goldie told me about her newest project.

"I think I'll give it a try," she said. "I need a new project for the winter, and I do have a lot of odd recipes."

"Creative, not odd," I said, although she was right, some of her concoctions were nothing short of odd. White chocolate and lavender cookies. Chicken licorice soup. Pasta with pine nuts and violas. "If you need photos, let me know. I've always wanted to take photos for a cookbook."

"So did you ask him?" Goldie has been my biggest cheerleader in the game of love ever since I met Tom, even when I'm not sure what a "win" might look like.

I shook my head, and Goldie's shoulders sagged. I said, "I was just about to, but Hutchinson showed up, and then I called Alberta to see if she was okay. Tom made me a second Irish coffee, and by the time I finished that, I couldn't keep my eyes open."

Goldie rolled her eyes and got up from the table, our mugs in her hands.

"I'm going to talk to him today. It's better, really, in the cold light of day." I wasn't sure whether I was talking to Goldie or myself. "Not so hormonal, you know?"

Goldie peered out the window as she poured more tea. "Looks cold out there."

"Miserable. The radio said it's thirty-eight degrees, and it's trying to rain. But it *is* November." I closed my eyes as another bite of sweet roll worked its magic on my taste buds, then said, "We lucked out for the agility trial."

"Not everyone," said Goldie.

"No, not everyone," I said. "I meant the weather. And I'm not sure luck had anything to do with Rasmussen's demise."

"And the police questioned you?"

I thought about the two humorless cops who had come to my house the previous day. "I spent about ninety minutes with them. I'd forgotten how terrifying that is," I said. "I guess Jo Stevens and Hutchinson scared me like that at first." Stevens had been Hutchinson's partner when a series of murders rocked the obedience community earlier in the year. We had ended up becoming friends, but I had definitely been on her person-of-interest radar at first.

"Oh, yes, my dear. You were a mess," said Goldie, stirring a spoonful of honey into her tea. "So what did they ask?"

"A lot of questions about where I was all day, and what I was doing. They knew that Rasmussen's father-in-law was my mother's, umm, friend. They knew Rasmussen had threatened to have me arrested for trespassing last week." I felt a little woozy and stopped to take a couple of deep breaths. "I think I'm basically off the hook. I mean, Tom vouched for my whereabouts," I giggled at the sound of that, "and I vouched for his. I'm quite sure our stories matched up, since we both told the truth."

"Almost always a good idea," said Goldie.

"So then they asked what I knew about other people's feelings about Rasmussen. I hated that," I said. "And besides, I have no idea where anyone else was when Rasmussen was killed. Tom and I left long before that."

"But you have your suspicions. Who do you think it was?" Goldie's eyes sparkled.

"You have a very nosy streak, you know that?" I said.

"Like you don't."

"No idea. Alberta hated his guts, of course." Goldie already knew about Rasmussen's attempts to develop the wetlands and woods next to Alberta's house, but she didn't know about their conflict over the cats. I told her about his campaign against Alberta's trap-neuter-release efforts in their neighborhood. "He wasn't alone, of course, but I guess he was the most vocal and the most threatening." I pictured him bullying his wife in her studio and at the agility trial. "And he had a violent streak."

"But why did he care if she fed a bunch of poor, homeless cats?" asked Goldie. "Why would anyone object to kindness?"

"Some people say that feral cats kill too many birds and other animals," I said. "And that is a problem in some places. It has been in some environments, like islands, where any kind of predator can be a problem for ground-nesting birds, or any endangered species."

Goldie snorted. "I think there are a lot of bigger dangers to creatures of all kinds in that neighborhood. Like the chemicals they use on the golf course and on their perfect lawns and manicured gardens." Goldie has a stunning organic backyard filled with flowers, herbs, vegetables, and fruit three seasons of the year. Four, really, since she plants shrubs that have winter berries for the birds.

I put down the sweet roll I was nibbling. Talk about ecological violence always hits me with a cocktail of fury, sorrow, and despair. "I know. Every time I see ducks and geese on the pond by the entrance, I think about the chemicals swimming there with them."

"So Alberta has been angry at Rasmussen for a long time, right? Why would she kill him now, and why do it at the trial?"

"Well, she was pretty angry about what how he treated his wife, and she probably knew that he tried to move his father-in-law out of Shadetree because his so-called morals were offended," I said, thinking I'd better go check on my mother when I finished with Goldie.

"Did something push her over the edge, you think?"

Rasmussen's face as he spewed venom at Alberta came back to me. "He said he had 'taken care of' the cats and rats. We all assumed he had set poison out. Alberta was in a complete panic, of course."

"That's terrible!" Goldie chopped her sweet roll in half with the butter knife. "He killed the cats?"

"No, Louise made a call and people went out looking for any sign of poison, and they picked up the food that was out, but there was no sign that he had actually done anything."

Goldie clucked and shook her head. "Emotional violence."

"And of course his wife … widow … Louise. Her anger had been building for years, but apparently the way Rasmussen treated he father put her over the edge." I knew that Goldie's next question would be 'why Saturday, why there,' so I said, "He yelled at her father, Anthony Marconi, in front of everyone, and shoved him."

"So Marconi had motive, too, then."

"Yes. But I just don't think he could have done it."

"Maybe Rasmussen didn't see it coming," said Goldie. "Marconi could have clocked him from behind, right?"

I nodded, and went on with my list. "Remember Giselle Swann? She hated Rasmussen, too. And she told me she had sort of blown a gasket at the trial, she was so angry."

"What did she do?"

I didn't feel comfortable repeating Giselle's story about swinging the pooper-scooper, so I ignored the question. "And Jorge, the handyman at Dog Dayz, hated Rasmussen, too. But I don't know, Jorge is small, shorter than I am and skinny. And that kid, Rudy Sweetwater. But I saw him leave with his mother and he's only fifteen, so he couldn't have driven back."

"Maybe it's like *Murder on the Orient Express*," said Goldie.

"What do you mean?"

"Maybe they all did it."

# THIRTY-TWO

As USUAL, THE PARKING lot at the university was packed. Waves of rain and dry leaves whirled in short, raw blasts of wind. As I drove around looking for a space, I spotted Giselle getting out of her car in the far end of the lot. Her wool poncho billowed around her as she hugged a backpack to her body and wrestled with the wind for possession of her umbrella. A sudden gust spun rain and leaves in the air and shook my van. I pulled up beside Giselle just as her umbrella flipped inside out and half the fabric tore loose.

"Get in," I shouted.

Giselle didn't need a second invitation. "Oh man," she said. "You're like an angel. Thank you."

"Ha! I haven't been called that in a while," I said. "Where are you headed?"

"I have biology class?" Giselle often spoke in the interrogatory when she was stressed.

"No, I mean where? Which building?"

"Oh." She pulled a tissue from her backpack and blew her nose. "Right here?"

We were approaching the row of visitors' spaces right in front of the doors when a pair of tail lights flashed and a car started to back out. "Looks like you're my good luck for the day," I said. "I drove by here about five times before I picked you up."

"Yay," said Giselle, although her tone belied the usual excitement of the word.

"Are you okay, Giselle?"

"Oh, sure? You know, just busy and everything?" She started to open the door, then sat back and stared at my glove compartment door. "I'm tired of talking to the police, that's all." Sniff. "And I kind of hope they don't even catch whoever killed that horrible man." There was no question at all in her tone.

We parted in the lobby. I started down the hall to Tom's office but caught a glimpse of my hair in a glass trophy case and back-tracked across the lounge to the restroom for some repair work. I couldn't do much about my fiery cheeks, gift of the sharp November wind, but if I could find a comb, I could at least make it look less like I was wearing a fright wig. I fished around in my tote bag. "Oh, that's where you are," I said, pulling my missing dog-nail clippers out from under my wallet and a small sample of cat treats I'd forgotten about. I had a nail file and a jaw clip, but no brush or comb, not even Jay's.

"Must be windy out there." It was Tracy, the secretary from Tom's department. As always, she appeared to have just come from a fashion shoot, which she may have, since she does some part-time modeling.

"Cold, windy, and wet," I said. I bent over and used my fingers to comb my hair, then stood up, gathered the curly mess, and closed the clip over it. I looked in the mirror and then at Tracy. She shook her head slightly.

"Right," I said, removing the clip and shaking out the curls.

Tracy smiled and left me searching for my lip balm. I was smearing it on when two young women came in. They both wore jeans, hiking boots, and loose ponytails, and they both seemed to be speaking at once while they scrubbed their hands.

"Couldn't happen to a more odious man," said the tall one in the cable-knit sweater.

"I know," said the short one in the turtleneck and sweatshirt. "I hope they never catch the guy who did it."

"How do you know it was a guy?"

Sweatshirt pivoted toward her friend and, by default, me, her eyes wide. "You're right. It could have been a woman." She lowered her voice and said, "I heard he beat his wife." She glanced at me, and as I returned the look, I read the writing on her sweatshirt. *See the Future with ESP*, it said, and below that, *IPFW Environmental Studies Program*.

The two women exchanged a look and stopped talking while they dried their hands. They resumed as they went out the door, and the last thing I head was, "Do you think this will stop the development?"

They must have been talking about Rasmussen. Hadn't Tom mentioned a protest from some of the environmental studies students who didn't want the university to accept scholarship funding from him? I couldn't remember the details, but Tom would know.

I shifted my thoughts to the reason for my current visit to the university. I gazed into the reflection of my own eyes for a moment and took three deep breaths. In one-two-three, out one-two-three-four. Then I marched myself out the door and across the lobby, rehearsing what I planned to say. We could combine households, maybe rent the house we aren't living in for a while until we decide, or ... *Really?* asked my companion voices. *You're going with the oh-so-practical appeal for cohabitation?* I decided to stop rehearsing. My guardian angel whispered, *Just say what you feel.*

As I approached Tom's office, I heard his voice. He sounded like he was on the phone. "Okay ... Yes ... Any other titers besides rabies? ... How long in advance?"

I stopped outside his door.

"Yes, just a year." Silence. "And no quarantine, correct?"

My knees went wobbly and my mind raced. Although I had always known that Tom had a sabbatical coming, it had never occurred to me that he might be planning to go abroad. But if he was checking on quarantines and any other antibody titers besides rabies, he had to be thinking of taking Drake out of the country. My mind raced to remember the possible research projects he had told me about. Something in Mexico? I thought so. And some tiny island in the Caribbean, if memory served. Something caught in my chest and I leaned into the wall.

Tom was still speaking, but all I really heard was "... list of local veterinarians" and his email address, all wrapped up with, "Okay, thank you very much ... Goodbye."

I pulled myself upright and debated what to do. I didn't want him to know I'd been listening in. On the other hand, his door *was* wide open. I decided to leave. I didn't get far.

"Janet?"

I turned and tried to smile, but my mouth didn't want to cooperate and I was afraid I might start to cry. *Stupid hormones.*

Tom said, "I'll be back," and pulled the door shut. "Where are you going?" Tom caught up to me and kissed my cheek. "I just finished my mountain of papers. Why didn't you come in?"

"Oh, I, uh, was just going to the restroom."

"I was just going to grab a cup of coffee. Come on." He wrapped his arms around my shoulders and I let myself be steered toward the cafeteria. Tom stopped outside the women's restroom and said, "I'll wait here."

For a moment I had no idea what he meant, then remembered what I had said. I went into a stall and leaned against the wall, and told myself it wasn't the end of the world, or even our relationship. *Then why do I feel like I might barf?* I splashed cold water on my face and patted it dry.

"Are you okay?" Tom asked when I returned.

"Sure. Why?"

"You were in there a long time." He studied my face, started to speak, and then stopped. "Let's get that coffee."

We found a table near a window that looked out across an expanse of grass along the Saint Joseph River. Rain slanted into the glass and a bank of indigo clouds hung low over the trees to the northwest.

"What's up?" asked Tom.

"No, nothing," I said. I tried to smile at him, but my mouth felt lopsided.

"What are you doing here on such a rotten day?" He grinned at me.

"Just, you know, running some errands and thought I'd stop and say hi," I said, marveling at the dopiness of it all. I wanted to ask about what I had heard from outside his office, but I was afraid I'd embarrass myself if he said he was leaving for a year.

Tom gave me the look that said he knew there was more, but he let it go for the time being. "The forecast is a bit better for Thursday. That's good, because I'm not driving to Indianapolis in freezing rain."

"So you're still planning to go?" *How could he get a puppy if he was also planning to go abroad for a year?* I wondered.

"Of course," said Tom. "Why wouldn't I?"

I started to feel angry, although I wasn't sure whether it was for my own inability to ask straight out what was happening, or at Tom for not telling me. But I didn't want to get into it in a public place, especially not where Tom worked, so I changed the subject. Again.

"I saw Giselle on my way in," I said. "She ..."

Tom was staring over my head and pointing at something. I was about to turn around when an image on the television across the room caught my eye. A "Breaking News" banner in the upper corner of the screen where a reporter spoke in front of a bevy of emergency vehicles with their lights flashing. A news crawler moved across the bottom, and I caught "... bomb squad called to home in southeast Fort Wayne." Two men were visible behind the reporter. One was Homer Hutchinson. I whipped my head around and saw that the same scenario was playing on another TV behind me. The whole thing was unfolding in front of a house I knew.

# THIRTY-THREE

"THAT'S ALBERTA'S HOUSE." THAT'S what I meant to say, but when I opened my mouth, nothing came out.

"Isn't that Alberta's house?" asked Tom. He stood and pressed the volume button so that we could hear.

"…the bomb. One person was slightly injured and there is major damage to the home. This is Ro…"

"Oh my God," I said, and realized that my hands had clasped themselves over my mouth of their own volition.

The image shifted to a traffic accident on Interstate 69.

"Try another channel," I said, forcing my hands down to the table.

Tom tried two more news stations before we hit one that showed the same chaotic scene in front of Alberta's house. The camera angle was different, and the open garage door showed no vehicle inside. The camera panned past the emergency vehicles in the driveway and on the street and stopped in another driveway. I recognized the Rasmussen home, and Alberta's SUV in the Rasmussens' driveway. *Just one Rasmussen*, a voice in my head reminded me. A police officer appeared at the back of Alberta's vehicle, popped the hatch, and picked up a pet carrier. It looked like the one Gypsy and her kittens had been in when I visited. Another man appeared with four Welsh Terriers on leashes. Hutchinson. He followed the officer with the cats in through the garage.

Tom sat down beside me as the image shifted to a distant view of the back of Alberta's house, where a half dozen police officers and a couple of fire fighters were doing what they do. "… through a large window. Police have not yet determined whether the incidents are connected." The reporter pressed her ear and held her hand up in a "wait a minute" gesture, then spoke to the camera again. "We take you live now to police spokesperson Captain Vicky Miller."

A crisp woman in a jacket with police insignia on it was now addressing a dozen reporters. "… short statement. The bomb squad responded this afternoon to a report of a suspicious package delivered to a home in Fort Wayne. It was determined that the contents of the package were designed to look like a bomb, but no explosives were present. The back window of the same home was broken at about the same time. We have not yet determined whether the events are related. We will keep you informed as we learn more." The Channel 15 reporter started to ask a question, but Captain Miller signaled "stop" with her hand and said, "We have work to do" and the image shifted again.

The camera panned across the front of Alberta's yard to the pond and woods, and the reporter spoke again. "We have learned that the owner of the home, Mrs. Alberta Shofelter, has been embroiled in a number of neighborhood disputes over the past few months."

"'A number of disputes?" I said.

"Two is a number," said Tom, holding up his hand to stop me talking.

"... feral cat colony, and an unrelated dispute over potential development of this empty lot."

My shoulder muscles spasmed at that. "Empty lot? It's woods and wetlands and meadow, you moron."

Several people turned to look at me, including the two young women I had seen earlier in the restroom. Sweatshirt smiled at me and said, "You're right. It's a beautiful place, and not empty at all."

The television shifted again to a view of Louise Rasmussen's house across the street, and then a photo of Charles appeared on the screen. "... developer and philanthropist Charles Rasmussen, who died Sunday under suspicious circumstances."

"Good riddance," said a young man sitting with the ESP women. The three of them stood up, dropped their refuse into the recycle bins by the wall, and left.

The TV news shifted to another story, and Tom turned the volume off.

"I need to check on Alberta," I said. "She may need some help." I pulled my phone from my pocket, but Tom stopped me. "Let's go to my office. It's quieter."

It was no surprise that Alberta didn't answer her phone. Even if she had it with her, she had to be shook up. I left a message and tried Hutchinson. No luck there, either. I didn't have Louise's number, but I knew someone who did. Jade Templeton answered on the first ring, and I told her what was going on.

"I can't give out residents' numbers except to family," she said. "But hang on ..." I heard a door close, and Jade said, "Mr. Marconi is in the garden with your mom. Hold on. I'm on my way ..."

Drake's head rested on my thigh, and I fondled his silky ear while I waited.

Then another voice. "Janet?"

"Mr. Marconi. Something has happened to my friend, well, her house, across from Louise's place. I really need Louise's phone number." I wrote it on a pad on Tom's desk and said, "How's my mom today?"

"Better, much better," he said. "She's been telling me about your upcoming exhibit of photos from North Africa."

I closed my eyes and took a deep breath.

"Something wrong?" he asked.

"That was in 1990."

"I know," he said, the kindness in his voice tangible over the airways. "She's really looking forward to the opening, and she's very proud of you."

"Wow. Just wow," I said after I closed my phone. I told Tom what Marconi had said, then punched in Louise's number. She didn't answer, either, but I left a message.

"I'm going," I said.

Tom grabbed his jacket from the back of the door and snapped Drake's leash to his collar. "Who's driving?"

I stepped out the door and nearly walked into the young woman in the Environmental Studies sweatshirt. She said, "Oh!" and took a step back. "Sorry. I just, uh, I thought you might be here at Professor Saunders' office so …" She thrust a flyer into my hand and said, "Here. I wanted you to have this. If you're interested."

The flyer's headline was "DON'T LET THEM PAVE PARADISE." Below it was a call to a teach-in, a term I hadn't heard since the sixties and seventies. My mother was fond of teach-ins in those days.

The theme was "Wetlands and Woods in Winter," and it was scheduled for the first weekend in December.

"Okay, I'll look at the website," I said, and started to walk past her, but the woman's face lit up and she said, "You will? Oh, that's great. We could use a photographer."

"How do you know I'm a photographer?"

Tom closed his door and said, "Guilty."

The woman gave Drake a good back-scratch, then held her hand toward me and said, "Sorry. I should introduce myself. I'm Robin." She glanced at Tom. "I took Professor Saunders' class on ethnobotany. He showed us an article about that award you won last year for your environmental photography."

*He did?*

Tom shrugged at me.

"Robin, look, we really have to go, but I will look at the website."

"Can I call you? Or, you know, text you?" The fire of youthful passion lit her face.

"Sure, call or email. Email is better. No texts. You can get my email from To…, er, Professor Saunders." I started to go, but turned back and asked, "What's your last name?"

"Byrde. With a 'y' and an 'e.'"

When we were out of earshot, I said, "Seriously? Her parents named her Robin Byrde?"

"Beats 'Princess.' I had one of those once."

The subject of goofy names was therapeutic, if bewildering. Coming up with more of them cracked the glacier of stress that had been smothering me since I arrived on campus, if not before. "What do you suppose Robin's relatives are named?" I asked.

"There's her brother Hawk."

"And the twins, Wren and Sparrow."

"Don't forget Uncle Booby," offered Tom. "He wears blue suede shoes."

"And Auntie Ostrich, with the long neck."

"We're awful. She seems like a nice person," I said, wiping my eyes.

"Auntie Ostrich?"

"Robin."

"She is. At least she was a good student." He slowed down for the turn into Alberta's subdivision, and gestured for me to look down the street. The fire truck we had seen on television was gone, but two police cars, one of them unmarked, still had their lights going, and a K9 handler was standing on the sidewalk in front of the house, a black German Shepherd dog by his side.

# THIRTY-FOUR

"I'm going to park down here," said Tom, pulling to the curb several houses down from Alberta's place and clear of the police cruisers' flashing lights of a fire truck, a panel truck with "Fort Wayne Police Department Technical Response" on the side, and an unmarked vehicle like the one Hutchinson drove. "There's an umbrella in the back if you want it."

The mist was turning into a more serious drizzle, but I declined the umbrella and pulled my hood up, trading peripheral vision for hands free to tuck into my pockets. Tom put on a cowboy hat he had brought back from New Mexico. I didn't say a word, but he still offered, "Keeps the rain off, ma'am." By the time we had walked the half block to Alberta's house, I wished I had my rain pants. My jeans were soaked through and the wind was cold. I shoved my hands into my pockets and found a happy surprise. Gloves.

Hutchinson saw us coming and left an older man in a FWPD parka to intercept us. "Alberta is with Louise. Nobody's hurt."

Hutchinson sported a butterfly bandage over a long gash under his right eye.

"The TV news says one person was hurt," I said, gesturing toward his face. "You?"

He touched the bandage with one finger and winced. "Yeah. It's nothing."

"Looks like it needs stitches," said Tom. "What happened?"

"I stopped by on my way to the station." He glanced at the other cops and lowered his voice. "I come to see the kittens almost very day."

"I don't blame you," I said, and Hutchinson nodded at me.

"Alberta's dogs started raising hell, and wouldn't be quiet when she told them, like they usually are." I remembered well the power of Alberta's *quiet!* command. Hutchinson continued, "So she went to see what was wrong. I looked out the window and saw a mail truck back out of the driveway, and I heard Alberta open the door, but didn't think anything about it until she said 'Oh my God.'"

"A package?" said Tom.

"She came back to the kitty's room and said I'd better come see. Said it was a bomb." Hutchinson fidgeted slightly. "Honestly, I thought she was imagining things. She's been, you know, kind of on edge."

*Who hasn't?* I thought.

"Can't blame her there," said Tom.

"Yeah. Well, anyway, the box was on the coffee table, and just as I walked into the living room, there was a loud *crack* and the window exploded. Glass flying all over the room," he said.

"It went off?" I asked. "I thought they said..."

"No, not the package. Something hit the window." He shook his head. "What a mess. I turned around and pushed Alberta back into the hallway and, you know, made sure she was okay. "I didn't know I'd been hit until Alberta looked at me and screamed. I wanted to scream, too, when I looked in the mirror." He started to smile but winced and raised a hand to his cheek. "Long sliver of glass was still stuck in my face."

"Oww!" I wanted to scream just thinking about it.

"I told Alberta to get the dogs and get out of the house. Then I looked in the box and, well, it looked like a bomb, all right. Luckily Gypsy was in her carrier nursing the babies, so I just grabbed them, got out of the house, and called it in."

"So it was the big window?" I asked, picturing the expanse of floor-to-ceiling glass at the back of Alberta's house. Hutchinson nodded, and I said, "You were lucky you weren't hurt more seriously."

"But what was it?" asked Tom. "What broke the window?"

"They're working on that," said Hutchinson. "And yeah, real lucky. We were just coming into the room, and Alberta was behind me, so she didn't get hit."

"The dogs? They weren't hurt?" I asked. Alberta's dogs spent a lot of time in the living room, sprawled all over her couch.

"She put them out in the side yard before she came to get me. So they're okay."

"Why did she do that?" asked Tom.

Hutchinson shrugged. "Said she had a bad feeling. Lucky."

"If you can call a bomb scare and shattered window 'lucky,'" I said.

"I really thought it was a bomb," said Hutchinson. "Scared the stuffing out of me. It had wires all hooked up to a battery pack, and a cell phone taped to it." He leaned forward, rested his hands just above his knees, and shook his head. I laid a hand on his shoulder. "I admit it, I was scared. Now I'm just pissed off."

A panel truck crept down the street, Handy Andy painted on its side. The driver stopped and spoke to one of the police officers. "I called them," said Hutchinson, pointing at the truck. "Let me go talk to the lieutenant in charge, see if we can at least get some plastic sheeting up over the window while they're processing the room."

"Wait, Hutch," I said. "Was there anything else? I mean, why send a message without a message?" I remembered Alberta telling me about having *Crazy Cat Lady* sprayed across her garage door. If this assault on Alberta's house was meant to scare her off, it seemed to me that whoever was behind it would want to be explicit.

"Oh, there was a message. A card taped to the battery pack. I think it's from a book or something."

"What did it say?"

"The fire next time."

# THIRTY-FIVE

LOUISE USHERED TOM AND me into a kitchen that was half as big as my house. Alberta's dogs rushed us when we stepped over the baby gate that kept them corralled, but yapping turned to squealing and wriggling as soon as they heard my voice. I'd spent a fair amount of time photographing them, and that always involved food and toys, so they liked me well enough.

Tom took a seat at the table across from Alberta. He reached down to pet Indy, Alberta's multi-titled champion Welsh Terrier, and as soon as the dog felt the hand on his head, he popped onto Tom's lap and settled in. Tom grinned at me, then turned his attention to Alberta, "Are you okay?"

"No, I am not. I'm mad as hell," said Alberta. The expression on her face backed her up. "If they think this will stop me, they'd better think again. I'll *buy* that piece of land if I have to, and I'll put up a cat shelter right there by the pond."

"Do you think it's the people who oppose the TNR program or Rasmussen's partners in the development?" I asked.

Alberta shrugged and said, "Yes."

"No, I meant ..."

"I know what you meant."

Louise set a carafe of coffee and a plate of pound cake on the table and made a second trip for plates and two more mugs. In the wake of the day's events, I'd kind of forgotten that Louise was so newly widowed. I looked at her and said, "I'm sorry. We ... I was so worried about Alberta, I wasn't thinking."

She patted my shoulder and said, "Not at all, dear. I'm worried about Alberta, too."

I looked around the kitchen and breakfast area. "Louise, is that one of yours?" I asked, indicating a luscious oil landscape over a buffet.

She followed my gaze and said, "The painting? Heavens, no. I don't paint."

"But the studio?"

"Oh, that," she snorted. "Charles thought it impressed people if he said his wife was an artist." She touched the faint remains of bruising under her eye and said, "He made me take a couple of classes, but I was no good. He never forgave me for that."

Louise might have said more, but the doorbell rang. She came back with Hutchinson in tow and set one more place.

"I don't think you should stay here tonight," said Tom. "Either one of you."

"Oh, come on," said Alberta. "It was just a stupid bluff. As long as the window gets covered ..." She looked the question at Hutchinson.

"Actually, I agree with Tom," said Hutchinson. "If you have somewhere else you could stay tonight, away from here, I think it would be a good idea."

"I'll tell you what would be a good idea, young man," said Alberta, pointing her fork at Hutchinson's cheek. "Stitches would be a good idea. That's bleeding again."

She was right, the cut below his eye was seeping blood. Hutchinson touched it gingerly and looked at his fingers. "Damn."

"Let me drive you to the emergency room," said Louise. "It's just down the road."

"And I'm picking up the bill," said Alberta.

That made Hutchinson laugh. "I have pretty good coverage."

"You promise to stay somewhere away from here tonight, both of you, and I'll promise to go have this looked at."

"Well, forget that," Alberta said. "I can't go to a hotel with four dogs and four cats. You did call Handy Andy for me, didn't you?"

Hutchinson nodded.

"I have a place," said Louise. "I mean, a place we can go."

"What about the animals?"

I started to offer to take the dogs or Gypsy and her brood for a night or two. I knew that Goldie or Tom would take Jay and Leo for a while, and I could keep the terriers or the cats but not both in my small place. It would be chaotic, but I could manage. "I . . ."

Louise said, "Yes, the animals too. My dad's house. He still owns it and I have a key. It's not huge, but it's comfy and no one around here knows anything about it."

That was a relief.

We left Hutchinson to help them pack a few things and a bunch of critters, and we headed back to campus for my van. The dark cloud that I had watched earlier on the horizon had found us, and although it was no longer raining, the low black canopy of sky made it seem much later than it was. My mind wandered and I wasn't really listening to what Tom was saying until I thought I heard, "I could list my house as a rental with the faculty housing service."

"What?"

He proceeded as if I knew what he was talking about, which I would have if I'd been paying attention. Part of me wanted to ask him to start over, but my thoughts flew to the questions I had overheard about quarantines and titers, and I was afraid I didn't really want to know what was up. Not right then. My mood went darker than the sky as I tried to sort out what he was talking about without asking directly.

"The personnel office maintains a list, you know, to match up incoming or visiting faculty who need housing and faculty on sabbatical with property to rent or sell."

"Ah." I was no closer to comprehension and we had arrived at my van. I should have asked for clarification, and I started to do just that. Better to know what was going on, even if the news was bad. The parking lot was nearly empty, and I thought about asking him to back up and repeat whatever I hadn't heard, but the rain had started again and the way it pinged against the glass told me it was turning icy. I wanted to get home. *You want to curl up in a fetal lump,* said my Janet demon. Really, though, I wanted to curl up with Jay and Leo. And I knew with a certainty that brought tears to my eyes that I wanted Tom and Drake there, too.

"Why don't I pick up some Chinese and we'll talk about it in the comfort of home?" He put his van in neutral and took my hand in his. "Your home, since it's closest and your kids are there."

"Pizza," I said. "And cheese cake."

Tom had a few things to do at the office before he called it a day, so we agreed that he'd see me in a couple of hours. "But if this really turns to sleet, just come, okay?" I said. I transferred Drake to my van and Tom drove off to the faculty lot. I started the car and just sat there for a moment. I turned on the radio and landed in an NPR program on the blues. Robert Johnson wrapped up "Crossroads," and the reporter began to speak about the story linked to the song. "Some people say that Robert Johnson really did sell his soul," he said, and I pushed the button for an oldies station in search of lighter fare. Although I didn't expect to meet the Devil there, I felt we were barreling toward a crossroads of our own, Tom and I. Or maybe I was alone in this maelstrom of indecision. Maybe Tom saw the road ahead as straight and smooth. He always seemed to know what he wanted, but I couldn't decide which I wanted more, *me* or *us*. Since I had met Tom, I had managed mostly to have both. *Why does anything have to change?*

Drake whined and whacked his tail twice against the side of the crate, and when I glanced in the rearview mirror to see if I could see him, I noticed a white SUV idling in the drive. There were two people in the front seat and I thought someone was moving in the back seat as well. That seemed odd, since there were plenty of open spaces. Maybe the driver was just giving me a chance to back out. "Okay, you're right, Drake," I said. "Time to go." The white vehicle didn't take my space, and when I stopped to turn onto the road out of the campus, it was right behind me.

Normally I would have turned left onto Coliseum, but the SUV made me nervous, and although it seemed silly to change my route, I drove straight onto Anthony instead. The other car was still with me, but I reminded myself that that didn't mean anything. A lot of people used North Anthony to get in and out of campus. I pulled into the Firefly Coffee House parking lot and slid into a space. The other car also turned into the lot, but parked on the other side, in front of the health food store. No one got out.

My heart started to beat a little too fast, and I whispered, *I don't need this crap.* I went into the Firefly and ordered a mocha. I was fourth in line, so it took a few minutes to get my drink. When I came out, the other car was gone, or at least I couldn't see it. I set my mocha in the cup holder and got Drake out of his crate and had him lie down on the floor in front of the back seats. I kissed him between his eyes and said, "I know you're basically a big friendly lug, but I feel better with you not locked up." Besides, I knew from experience that he would try to protect me and Tom if necessary. Drake slapped my mouth and nose with his sloppy warm tongue, and I felt safe, body and soul.

I drove south out of the parking lot and made a left onto East State. The freezing rain was coming harder now and starting to stick, and the back window wore a curtain of icy water drops, fog, and lights from the next car back. I pushed the anti-fog button and turned on the rear wipers long enough to clear the glass. The road ahead had the dull sheen of a well-used nickel and all I could see of the cars coming toward me was their headlights. Drake sat up and lay his head on my arm rest, his muzzle touching my coat sleeve just hard enough so say, "I'm right here." The light changed, and as we accelerated away from the car behind us, I got a look in the mirror. It was the white SUV.

# THIRTY-SIX

THE WHITE SUV WAS still behind me when I reached Georgetown Square. Part of me, egged on by my Janet demon, wanted to hit the brakes and have it out with the driver right in the middle of East State. Another voice whispered, *Janet, Janet, tut tut. There's more than one white SUV in Fort Wayne.* Which was confirmed when I checked my driver's side mirror. It showed another one coming up on my left. Still, my inner wimp said, *Pull into the shopping center. Don't lead a stalker into your badly lit neighborhood.*

I signaled for the right lane and checked my rearview mirror again. The road behind me was empty for a block or more. The car on my left had stopped in the turn lane, and there was no one on my right. I let out a long breath and Drake nudged my arm lightly as if to assure me that all was well. *Except my mind, which I seem to have left somewhere,* I thought.

Full dark had all but settled in for the night by the time I pulled into my driveway. I had knocked the garage door opener off the visor earlier, so I put the car in park and fished around on the floor.

When I finally pushed the button, nothing happened. I held the gadget at arm's length and pushed the button again. Nothing. A few choice words that I've been trying not to use shot out of my mouth as I shook the remote and tried again. Drake's tail banged against the back of my seat when the overhead door finally opened.

I took the dogs out back and they raced off in a joyful chase, Jay in the lead, as always. Goldie's house was dark but for the front and back porch lights and I smiled. After successful cancer treatment, which she had hidden from me for months, she was healthy again and taking full advantage. Bird walks two or three mornings a week, a new book club, a writing class to help her work on her cookbook. Tuesday, if I remembered correctly, was figure drawing class, which she claimed was about much more than the naked young man who modeled for them.

A thin film of ice glittered on the patio, so I stepped carefully back to the door. The doggy boys were playing keep-away with a long rope toy, so I left them outside. I put a kettle on for tea, changed into my only not-too-ratty gray sweat pants and a deep-raspberry fleece top that always made me feel warm and secure. I started back to the kitchen, but caught a reflection in a picture-frame glass and backtracked to the bathroom. I brushed my hair into a semblance of control, and put on some eyeliner and light shadow per an article I'd read in a waiting room a while back. I think the title was "Make Up Tricks for Mature Eyes." I stepped back and assessed the results. *Better*, I thought, despite the blue puffiness that proclaimed my exhaustion from the past few days. I smeared some tinted balm onto my lips just as the kettle began to whistle.

The dogs were on the patio, but I figured they could wait while I put my tea to steeping. Jay thought otherwise, and just as I put the lid on the teapot, the back door banged open and the two galoots slid into the kitchen, their wet paws like skates on the vinyl floor. Jay stopped mid-kitchen. Drake banged into a table leg, pushing the table sideways, knocking over the salt and pepper grinders and launching the tabasco bottle into a fatal roll. I almost managed to snatch it from the brink.

"Okay, you guys, in here." Jay and Drake had both sobered up at the sound of glass breaking, and they obeyed my directive with ears back and heads low. "Down." They lay down. I tried to give Drake a stern look, but it's very hard to be upset about a little spilled hot sauce caused by pure doggy joy. "It's okay, guys. I just don't want you to cut yourselves." Their eyes brightened and they both smiled and wagged at me.

I was pulling the dust pan from under the sink when "From Me to You" announced a call from Tom. I dampened a sponge, opened the phone, tucked it between my chin and shoulder, and got down on my knees by the table.

I meant to say "hello," but it came out as more of a grunt.

"What's wrong?" asked Tom.

"Cleaning up a mess your dog made."

"My dog? My dog wouldn't make a mess. What kind of mess?"

"A small mess."

"Best kind," he said, and I could hear the soft sparkle I knew would be in his eye. "So, I'm going to call in the pizza order in a few minutes. What do you want on it?"

We sorted that out, and I told him to be careful of the ice that was starting. I figured I had three-quarters of an hour, so once I got the table back in place, I freed the dogs, poured my tea, and sat down to check my email and Facebook page.

Most of my emails were various newsletters and other missives that I had signed up for but never had time to read. I scanned topics, saved a handful to read later, and moved the rest to trash. There was one from Robin Byrde, whose email moniker was "rockin-robin," inviting me to the "Wetlands and Woods in Winter" teach-in on Sunday morning. I wrote her back and told her that I would regretfully have to pass because my cat and I were competing in feline agility this weekend. Just writing that made me smile. I invited her to my Facebook page, Animals in Focus, signed off, and sent it.

I was about to shut down my computer when I saw that I had a new email from Norm, which made my heart go pitty pat because Norm never emails me and I figured it was trouble. Besides, the subject line was "Lawsuit." *Don't open it,* I thought. *It can wait until morning. Things look better in the sunshine.* But I knew I wouldn't be able to get it out of my head, and certainly wouldn't sleep if I didn't know what it said, however bad.

Then another new email popped onto the list, this one from Jade Templeton at Shadetree Retirement Home. That didn't worry me. Jade emailed me pretty frequently with updates about events at Shadetree or to arrange photo shoots, which we had been doing every couple of months lately for the residents who wanted better-than-cell-phone photos with their kids and grandkids. Then I saw the subject line, and let my body slide low in my chair to match the sinking I felt inside.

# THIRTY-SEVEN

I PUNCHED IN THE speed dial number for Shadetree Retirement Home. Jade was not available, and the receptionist couldn't—or wouldn't—tell me anything, so I left my number and typed a return email as well. The parts of Jade's email to me that ran over and over in my mind were "respiratory distress" and "nonresponsive." I checked for signs of life at Goldie's again, and looked out the front window, knowing Tom wouldn't be there yet but vaguely hoping to see his van. The dogs, sacked out in the hallway, roused themselves enough to watch me, but went back to sleep when I returned to the kitchen. I pushed Tom's speed dial number, but closed my phone before the call want through. Bill, my brother, was away on business, so I called Norm's number to see whether Shadetree had tried to reach them. My call went to his voice mail. He would be at the gym, I knew.

I got my coat from the closet, bringing the dogs to their hopeful feet, but threw it onto a chair. For all I knew, my mother was on her way to a hospital, and I wasn't sure which one. I stared at my phone,

203

willing it to ring. Two warm chins found my lap, and I leaned into the tops of the dogs' heads and breathed in their warm presences. "Everything will be okay, right, guys?" I said. They both pressed into me a bit more firmly.

A car door closed out front, and I heard the double honk of Tom's van locking. Then my phone rang. I answered as I unlocked and opened the front door.

"Getting nasty out there," said Tom, pushing the pizza through the door ahead of him. A grocery bag hung from his wrist.

I nodded at him, listening to the voice through the phone. When she finished, I asked, "Are you sure?"

"Yes. There's nothing you can do here, she's fine now, and the roads are getting really nasty. Stay home."

"But…"

"Come tomorrow," said Jade. "I'm staying here, and she's sleeping now. I'll check in with you around ten if you like."

"If anything changes, you'll let me know?" I asked.

"Of course." Jade's voice is so soothing, I almost relaxed. "Try not to worry."

Tom stood watching me, his coat still on. "What's happened?" he asked when I set my phone down. "Your mom?"

"Jade called it a 'respiratory event.' She collapsed and couldn't breathe. Mom, I mean."

Tom pushed a chair up behind me and guided me into it. "Sit down," he said, and poured more tea into my mug.

He was right. I felt a respiratory event of my own coming on. I stared into the dark, fragrant tea and worked at that steady breathing thing. *In one-two-three, out one-two-three-four.*

"If you want to head over there, say the word," said Tom.

"Everything's apparently under control and Mom is sleeping. I guess … Jade will be there all night and promised to check in at ten." To be honest, I wasn't sure what to do. If she was well and truly out of immediate danger, there was no point sitting there at Shadetree all night. "Damn, I don't know what to do." Then I had another thought, but decided to wait and discuss it with Norm, not Tom. Norm was Mom's attorney, after all. He had drawn up and I had witnessed her directive.

The phone rang. I expected it to be Jade or Norm, but it was Alberta. "Janet, are you okay?" She didn't wait for an answer. "Louise told me about your mom."

That made no sense at all for a moment, and then it did. Anthony Marconi would have called Louise, and Louise must have told Alberta.

Alberta was still talking. "Tell me what you need. Anything. You have someone there with you? We can come if you need us. You shouldn't be alone. We're over here at Louise's, well, her father's place. It's not far, you know."

I didn't know. I had no idea where Marconi's house was. "Alberta, I'm fine, really, and I just talked to Shadetree. I appreciate it, but I need to keep this line open. I'm expecting a call from my brother, and Shadetree will call me if anything … So, thanks again. Goodnight."

"Oh, right, okay, I ju …" I flipped my phone closed.

Tom hung his jacket on the back of the chair and got a couple of plates and a cake server. He opened the pizza box and pushed it toward me, then checked the fridge. "No pop?"

"There's beer in the back if you want it."

"No, not tonight." I knew he meant "in case we have to go back out for your mother," but was glad he didn't say it.

"Laundry room," I said. I realized that I wasn't speaking in full sentences, but couldn't seem to do any better than that. "Root beer."

Tom set two glasses with ice on the table, poured root beer over the ice, and sat down. He watched me for a moment while I stared at an olive on the pizza, then lifted a slice with the spatula, slid it onto my plate, and said, "Come on, eat. You have to eat something."

I picked the olive off my slice and dropped it onto my tongue. The briny bite reminded me that I was thirsty, and I drank down my whole glass of root beer. I took a bite, forced myself to chew and swallow, and set the slice back on the plate.

"She didn't tell you anything specific?" asked Tom. "She isn't asthmatic, is she?"

"No, never has been." The sugar seemed to hit my brain all in a rush, and I woke up a bit. "They sent a report to Mom's regular doctor. I'll check with her in the morning."

The dogs both leaped to their feet and ran to the front of the house, and a few seconds later the doorbell rang. Tom gestured for me to eat, and followed the dogs. The next voice I heard was Goldie's.

"Whew, boy, it's slicker than snot on a doorknob out there."

Leo bounded into the kitchen, still in his harness and dragging his leash. He hopped onto the chair next to me and leaned in for a nose bump. I heard some near-whispers in the other room, and then Goldie was beside me, unwinding a long orange scarf from her neck with one hand and gripping my shoulder with the other.

"Tom told me," she said. "What do you need?"

"I'm fine," I said. I smiled at her, and at Tom. He unbuckled Leo's harness and started to refill my root beer but I waved him off, rinsed the glass, and filled it with tap water. I nibbled at my pizza slice and listened as Goldie turned the conversation to her evening.

"There's going to be a teach-in on wild areas in urban and suburban settings. Several groups are involved. I'm sort of helping the organizers, you know, organize." Goldie's face was glowing.

"This is out at Alberta's place, right?"

"Is it?" She frowned as if she needed to think about it, then smiled. "I hadn't put it together. You're right."

"What's happening with that now that Rasmussen is out of the picture?" asked Tom.

Goldie said, "He wasn't alone. There were five partners, so four now, and they're going to try to go forward, and we're going to stop them." Goldie leaned toward me and said, "Janet, guess who I saw at the meeting tonight?"

"Who?"

"Our old partner in crime."

Tom laughed and asked, "Which one?"

"Peg. You know, Peg from your vet clinic." I had to smile at the idea of Goldie and Peg together again. The consortium may just have met its match in those two. "I just love her!"

I started to ask whether she knew Robin Byrde, the environmental studies student who was also involved in the teach in, but the phone rang and I excused myself as I answered.

"Hi, Norm."

"Janet. Did Shadetree reach you?"

"Yes. I spoke to Jade."

"Okay. And how much did they tell you?" There was a sharp edge not usually present in my brother-in-law's voice.

Suddenly I needed to sit down. I backed up and sank onto the bed and said, "What do you mean? What did they tell you?" Leo reached out from the pillow where he had been sleeping and tapped my leg.

His tone softened slightly, and he said, "No, nothing. Sorry, I didn't meant to upset you. I'm just concerned about ..."

I knew there was more. I knew what he wanted to say and why he was having trouble saying it, so I helped him. "The directive, right?"

Norm let out a long breath and said, "Yes. I'm concerned about your mother's wishes being followed, or not. I'm making some calls right now. I just wanted you to know that."

Goldie was telling Tom about her painting class when I rejoined them. They both watched me settle into my chair. Neither of them asked what Norm's call was about, but I had the sense that they both knew. We had all discussed the ins and outs of do-not-resuscitate directives, and we had all agreed that it was Mom's choice to make.

I felt a warm muzzle in my hand and looked into Jay's soft brown eyes. Drake stepped up and laid his chin on my arm, and Leo strolled into the kitchen and rubbed against my leg. Something alarmingly tear-like filled my eyes, and I knew it was all true. I was fine, or would be, because I was not alone.

# THIRTY-EIGHT

Goldie decided to high-tail it back home before the sidewalks got any more treacherous, and I thought a long, hot shower would do me some good, so I left Tom watching a NOVA show about melting glaciers and ducked into the bathroom. I set my phone to maximum volume and laid it on a towel beside the bathtub. I turned the shower on as hot as I could stand it, sprinkled a few drops of peppermint essential oil under the spray, and stepped in. I'm worlds away from New Age-y, but I have to say there really is something to the revivifying effects of peppermint essence and steam.

When I stepped out of the shower I checked my phone for missed calls, and again after I dried my hair, but no one had called. My face was red from the hot water, so I patted on some moisturizer and stared into the mirror. The woman staring back at me looked older than the one who lived inside me, and she still looked tired. I fished around in a drawer and found some eyeliner and beige shadow. They helped a lot, even without the mascara I couldn't locate. I re-secured my towel and scurried into the bedroom, where I stepped into clean, comfy yoga pants and pulled a soft gray cardigan over my black t-shirt. The mirror over my dresser revealed a much more human-looking being than I had felt like half an hour earlier.

The ten-o'clock news was on when I rejoined Tom. Robbery at a fast-food place. Some political idiocy. Several accidents attributed to the icy roads. Better weather on its way. Tom clicked the TV off and said, "Feeling better?"

"Much," I said. "Think we could rearrange the seating assignments?"

Jay was stretched out beside Tom, his hind feet pushed up against the cat in Tom's lap and his head on my embroidered Australian Shepherd pillow at the other end of the couch. Drake was on the floor, belly up, a round chewy hanging from his forearm like an enormous bracelet.

Tom set a protesting Leo on the floor and said, "Jay. Off."

Jay opened one eye and looked at me as if to say *Really?* I felt like a heel since he looked so comfy, but I signaled him to get off, and he rolled his feet to the floor, toddled a few steps, and crashed. I'm not sure he ever woke up completely.

Tom wrapped his arm around me and we sat in silence for a few minutes. "Jade hasn't called."

"She will."

"She said she'd call at ten."

Tom hugged me. "She'll call. She has a lot on her plate there."

I knew it was true, but couldn't help feeling that my plate—Mom's plate—should have priority tonight. "I'll give her ten more minutes. Then I'm calling her."

"I think this is a time when no news is probably good news, Janet," said Tom, and I knew he was right. Someone would call if my mother had another "event." I decided to change the subject.

"Goldie's trying to recruit you for the teach in, right?" I asked.

"Sort of. Mostly she wants me to take a look at the flora out there. See if there's anything of note."

"Of note? Like endangered or something?" I knew there were quite a few endangered species in Allen County and other parts of Indiana, so it wasn't a crazy idea. "Could they stop the development if there's an endangered species out there?"

"It's possible," said Tom. "It's not that simple, but it could be an argument in their favor. But here's the thing," he said, and paused. "I didn't want to get into it with Goldie tonight, but I think they need to think this through. At least Alberta needs to if she wants to keep the cat colony out there, too."

"What do you mean?"

"Well, endangered plants are one thing," said Tom. "Endangered mammals, birds, or amphibians are another."

The light went on. "Oh, crap. So the opponents of Alberta's TNR program could use an endangered animal as an argument to remove the cats."

"Exactly."

"But the cats have been there for years, according to Alberta," I said. "So if they've been living alongside the endangered animals..."

"There's no way to know whether the cats are a problem for other species without a field study, and we don't have any such thing for this piece of land," said Tom. "I looked at some of the studies but they're scattered, and they don't necessarily apply here."

"So Alberta is going to have a moral dilemma on her hands," I said.

"Maybe, " said Tom. "But I …"

My phone cut him off.

"So sorry, dear," said Jade. "The time got away from me." She assured me that all was well, and that she would be there all night. "I'm not officially on duty, but I'm going to sleep here just in case."

I said I'd be over first thing in the morning.

Tom got up and looked out the window. "Looks like the rain has stopped, at least for now. Drake! Jay! Let's go out before it starts again."

I pulled my old blue afghan from the back of the couch and wrapped it around me. My mother had knit it for me the summer before my freshman year in college. Thirty-some years of spin cycles and tumble dries had softened the yarn, and a spot near one edge sported a slightly different blue yarn where Mom had repaired it after a puppy got hold of it, but it was big and warm and felt like love.

Love. Tom's voice floated to me from the kitchen, where he was toweling eight wet feet and talking some sort of silliness to the dogs. I heard the refrigerator open and something about a treat. Leo heard, too. He focused all his senses on the sounds, then leaped off the chair and hurried to join them. *I could live this way,* I thought. But as soon as I thought it, the voice of doubt piped up. *You like your freedom,* it said. I closed my eyes and listened to the sounds in the kitchen. A knife hitting the cutting board, *sit* and *down* and *spin* commands. I could almost hear Janis Joplin singing about freedom and loss.

Exhaustion was taking me again when the phone in my kitchen startled me back to the moment. "You want me to get that?" asked Tom.

"Please."

The usual greetings followed, and then Tom said, "Hutchinson."

I abandoned my warm afghan nest and went to the kitchen. "Wonder why he's using the land line," I muttered, wishing I had put socks on. The vinyl floor was cold. Tom smiled at me, and he and the critters went back to the living room. I sat down, pulled my feet up onto the chair, and wondered why I had never trained my dog to fetch my slippers.

"Sorry to call so late," said Hutchinson. "I heard about your mom. I just wanted to see, well, you know, to check on you?"

I filled him in, and thanked him for his concern. I thought he was about to hang up, but then he said, "My buddy who's on the Rasmussen case called me. He wanted me to know that I'm in the clear."

"That's good," I said.

"Yeah. I guess sometimes it pays to be on the Internet at odd times." He lost me there, and I didn't say anything. I was starting to shiver, and wanted to cozy up between Tom and my afghan again. I stood up and paced the floor.

"You know, the timeline on Facebook vouched for my being online."

"Ah. Well, that's good, Hutch." I gazed at the knife and cutting board. Tom had washed them and put them in the rack to dry.

"Yeah. I mean, I wasn't really worried, but it's better for the investigation if they narrow the suspect list," said Hutchinson.

What had Tom cut up for the dogs?

"He had something else, too. Nothing official yet, I mean, you know, a report, but the coroner says..."

I opened the refrigerator and looked in, half listening to Hutchinson. I stared at the shelf for a minute, trying to figure out what was missing.

"...that Rasmussen was hit..."

I knew what they had eaten. The leftover eggplant parmesan I'd been saving for lunch.

"...by at least two different weapons."

"Dammit," I said.

"What?"

"Sorry," I said, shutting the fridge. "Two weapons? So that means, what, two killers?"

"It's possible," said Hutchinson.

It was hard enough to believe that any of the people I knew to be on the potential-suspect list could have killed a man. But two of them? Conspiring to commit murder took Rasmussen's death to a whole new level.

"So, I wanted to let you know," said Hutchinson, "because they may be talking to people they know might, you know, work together."

I held my breath and waited for the other shoe to drop.

"People who had problems with Rasmussen," said Hutchinson. He sounded a bit apologetic. "Like Louise and her father, or Marietta and Jorge,..."

I closed my eyes, knowing what was coming.

"...you and Tom."

# THIRTY-NINE

THE PHONE JOLTED TOM and me off the couch. As I shot straight up and climbed over Tom to answer, the previous evening played at warp speed in my mind, beginning with an achy awareness that we had never talked about whatever Tom had started to bring up the previous afternoon. I had been thinking about so many other things at the time that I had tuned him out until he said something about listing his house for rent.

And what about that conversation I had overheard about quarantines and rabies titers? The two things had to be connected. He must have been talking about Drake, about taking him to another country. Tom had a sabbatical coming up next year or the year after, and he had mentioned the possibility of doing research or teaching abroad, but he hadn't said anything specific. If he intended to begin something the following summer or fall, his plans must be well underway by now.

I felt wrung out from grappling with my mother's latest health problems and another murder up close and way too personal, even if I wasn't fond of the dead guy. Top all that off with what Tom's plans might mean for our relationship, especially in light of the obvious fact that he had kept me in the dark, and I wanted to run away to a wild place to be alone with Jay and Leo and my tangled thoughts. I should have asked him right then and saved myself a lot of heartache, but by the time I had the right words and thought I could keep my voice under control, Tom had fallen asleep. I had lain awake for what seemed like hours, listening to Tom's heart beat and feeling more alone than I had in years.

Clearly I had fallen asleep at some point, but I was wide awake now and fighting off the adrenaline rush that comes with being startled out of sleep. Jade's voice on the phone brought me fully into the moment, and I looked into Tom's eyes and mouthed "hospital" as I listened. I tapped my wrist where my watch would have been if I could find it, and Tom said, "Quarter to three." He got up, let the dogs out, and disappeared into the bathroom. By the time he came back, I had put on jeans, socks, and shoes. I took my turn in the bathroom and clamped a jaw clip around my hair while Tom got the dogs in. We were out the door in eleven minutes flat.

The sleet had stopped and the wipers handled the windshield ice easily, so it had softened in the past few hours. "Looks like the warm front has arrived," said Tom. He reached for my hand, but I left it where it was, tucked into my jacket pocket. He laid his hand where mine might be, but when I didn't react, he turned the radio on. "Maybe we can catch the forecast," he said.

The news had just started. Another downtown convenience store had been robbed, and a portion of West State Street would be closed while a culvert was replaced. It was all so much background noise until the voice said, "Fort Wayne police say they may be close to making an arrest in the murder of area entrepreneur and philanthropist Charles Rasmussen, who was found dead early Sunday morning under suspicious circumstances."

I blurted, "Philanthropist?" and turned the volume up.

"Police spokesperson Suzanna Idris said that the exact cause of death has not yet been determined, but that Rasmussen was struck several times, and foul play is suspected." They went on to the next story, and I turned the radio off.

"Nothing really new there," said Tom.

"No, but who are they going to arrest?" My stomach knotted up as I thought about my last conversation with Hutchinson. I should have felt some compassion for Rasmussen, but the man was making me angrier than ever. Irrational as I knew it to be, I couldn't help thinking, *It wasn't enough to cause my friends trouble when you were alive? You have to keep at it now that you're dead?*

"We'll get through this," said Tom. I was glad he hadn't tried to tell me everything would be okay, because I knew that an inane comment like that would set off the explosion building inside me.

I watched homes and businesses slide by, their darkened windows punctuated by the occasional garish glare from an all-night convenience store or fast-food joint or all-night drug store. We turned onto Jefferson, hit a red light at Clinton, and sat there idling. "Does this light seem long to you?" I asked after a few hours, or maybe just seconds.

"We're almost there," said Tom, and a minute later we pulled up in front of the emergency entrance and for the first time since we'd been jolted awake, I really looked at Tom. I wished I had let him take my hand in the car. "Seems like *déja vu* all over again, doesn't it?" I whispered, thinking of how Tom had helped me through Mom's first day at Shadetree Retirement. And I hardly knew him then.

He squeezed my arm and said, "Go on. I'll be right there."

I found my mother on the third floor. She was sitting up in bed, pale but perky, eating what appeared to be raspberry sherbet. Norm sat by the bed, and a big woman in a white jacket stood on the other side. She spoke in a low contralto that rolled up and down with the rhythms of South Asia.

"Mom?"

The big woman stopped speaking and turned toward me, smiling and stepping back to make room for me.

My mother tilted her head and waved her spoon at me. "Oh, hello, dear. So glad you could make it."

I felt my eyes widen and felt both guilty for not getting here sooner and a little ticked off and hurt. Then I realized that her tone was upbeat and almost giggly, and that she meant exactly what she had said. "Mom, how are you feeling?"

She tapped her lips with her spoon and gazed at me, then said, "I know we've met somewhere, but I just can't remember your name."

I glanced at Norm, but he was watching Mom. "Janet," I said, leaning lightly into the bed. "I'm Janet."

Mom turned her focus to her sherbet, which suddenly seemed to be all-consuming. I looked at the woman in the lab coat and said, "I'm Janet MacPhail. Daughter." I glanced at the name embroidered over her pocket. A capital K followed by a very long last name. Then I looked up into her face.

"Yes, I see," she said. She was very tall and neither slim nor fat. "I am Doctor," and the very long last name rolled off her tongue.

"Don't worry, I couldn't pronounce it myself until I was nearly out of medical school. Call me Krishna." Her features were coarse, almost mannish, but her smile lit the room, and I knew my mother was in good hands, at least for now. "May we step out to the hall for a moment, Janet?"

Norm smiled and waved me on, and I followed Krishna out of the room, past another room, and into a small lounge.

"So how is she, really? This isn't what I expected to find."

"No, she did not look like this when she arrived." She checked her watch. "Such fast responses always make me marvel." She rocked her head from side to side, and then said, "We still are waiting for some of the lab results. The short of it is that your mother's sodium levels plummeted and she became unresponsive."

"They told me she'd had a respiratory event."

"Yes, she was also in some respiratory distress. That is why we are checking her blood chemistry." She smiled. "It is really quite common in the elderly and may be also related to other issues."

"And what happened, I mean, what did they, you, do . . ." I couldn't find a way to ask whether she had actually stopped breathing and been resuscitated. Mom had made out a directive, legally executed, several years ago, long before her competence could be questioned. I knew how the idea of being kept alive by machines horrified her. But how do you ask a doctor you don't know why your mother wasn't allowed to die?

# FORTY

"Rest assured, she never stopped breathing, but her breathing was very labored," said Doctor Krishna. We were standing a few feet from the door to my mother's hospital room. The doctor's gaze slipped sideways. I heard footsteps behind me, and then Tom was at my side.

"This is my, uh …" *We really need to come up with something better than "my uh,"* I thought.

Tom spoke up before my hesitation became even more awkward. "Tom Saunders. Friend of the family."

"Ah." She looked from Tom to me the same way Goldie does when she knows more than I think she should, but she didn't comment. The good doctor returned to the subject at hand. "Janet, we are aware of your mother's wishes and I—we—will honor them if it comes to that. I do not think we are at that point. But we would like to keep her here and run some tests to determine the cause of this misadventure."

"How long will that be?"

"Depending on what we learn, we may release her this afternoon, or it may be a day or two," said Krishna. She gave me her card so I could reach her directly and walked away.

I went back to the room and found Norm and my mom in deep, apparently serious, conversation.

"Janet," said my mother, patting the bed beside her.

"Don't let me interrupt you," I said, relieved that she knew me again, at least for the moment.

"We're finished," she said, patting the bed once more. I perched there, and she took my hand, surprising me with her grip's boniness and strength. "I'm glad you're here, dear, but I don't want you worrying too much." Her eyes were clear, and my real mother seemed to be fully present, the shadow at bay for now. "I've given Norm my power of attorney regarding medical decisions. I won't want you to be hurt by that. I just don't want you or Bill having to make those decisions."

"Okay," I said. "Norm, are you okay with this?" My brother-in-law has a deceptively tough, rational shell over a very tender center, and I wondered whether he really wanted this job.

"Yes, it's fine. I'm fine." He and my mom exchanged a smile. "I think we're all fine." He stood and reached for his pocket and, although I hadn't heard it ring, pulled out his phone. "That was Bill. Let me go call him back. I left a message to call me, but he had early meetings. He doesn't know..."

"Where is he, anyway?" I asked.

"Amsterdam." He picked up his jacket and turned to my mother. "I'm going to go now. But I'll be back later to check on you." He kissed her cheek and then he was gone.

Tom teased Mom a bit about making him come out in the middle of the night. "I had more carousing to do," he said, and she giggled.

A nurse came in and said she had a few things to do if we could give her twenty minutes. I didn't want to know what kinds of things. Just the thought of jabbing sharp implements into flesh makes me want to scream and flail my arms. I picked up my tote bag and said, "Okay, Mom, we'll be back in a bit."

"Coffee?" asked Tom.

We took the stairs down two floors to the cafeteria. It was a stark place of plastic and chrome, and very quiet. A couple of nurses ate salads by the windows and a family huddled over coffees and soft drinks in the back corner, but that was it.

"Are you hungry?" asked Tom.

"Just tea," I said. I sat down at an out-of-the-way table and took stock. My mom was, apparently, going to be okay, at least physically. There's a big fat thumbs up. My brother-in-law is taking charge of the messy world of legal directives. Another thumbs up. Tom is planning to leave the country and hasn't told me. Big fat thumbs down. And I'd become embroiled in another murder investigation. Even worse, the suspects are all people I know and like. Including Tom. And me. Possibly in cahoots with one another, according to Hutchinson's source in the investigation.

Tom returned with a cardboard drink carrier loaded with a cup of coffee, another of steaming water, a tea bag, two creamers, and a flimsy paper plate struggling to accommodate a big fat Danish oozing golden goo from one end. He set a pile of napkins on the table, unloaded the carrier, took it to the recycle bin, and returned with a plastic knife, which he used to saw the Danish into quarters. I ripped open the packet and pushed the tea bag into the cup of water, then bit into the gooey end of a bit of pastry. It tasted like sweetened cardboard. I ate it anyway.

A blast furnace seemed to have opened around me. I leaned back with a thud against the chair and fanned my face with a napkin. *Great. That's all I need*, I thought. *Hot flashes.*

Tom was talking, but once again I managed to tune out the first part of what he said. I tuned back in just as he said, "... because life's too short not to do what we know we want to do, don't you think?" I looked at him, and he winked and said, "Besides, it will be fun."

*So he* was *planning to go somewhere.* My whole body felt hot and clammy, my temples throbbed, and I thought my brain might explode. I said, "I need some water," and started to get up.

"I'll get it," said Tom. He stood but hesitated as he studied my face. If it looked anything like I felt, it must have glowed like Rudolph's nose. He put his hand on my shoulder and leaned into me. "Are you faint?"

I shook my head. "Hot flash." *And, oh yeah, my mother and my relationship may both be dying and then there's that matter of the police* ... "And I feel a headache coming on. Water and drugs should do the trick."

The ice dispenser sounded as disturbed as I felt, and it may have been having a hot flash, too, because no matter how many times Tom shoved the cup into the release level, it didn't give up a single cube. He went to the counter and handed my cup to the woman behind the rgister and she disappeared into the kitchen.

I reached into my tote and rummaged around until my fingers found a bottle. I pulled it out. Anti-nausea meds for Jay, expired two years earlier. I shook the bottle, and heard the sound of one pill clapping around. I set it down and resumed my search, intoning, "Drugs, drugs ..." I didn't think I mumbled all that loudly, but two young men wearing lab coats with stethoscopes in the pockets both looked up from the files they had been poring over. I smiled and they looked away as my fingers closed over another plastic bottle.

Tom was still waiting for the glass of ice, and I felt a pang as I watched him. I couldn't tell who I was most upset with, him or myself. I pushed and twisted the top of the bottle but couldn't open it. I watched the woman hand Tom the glass of ice as I pushed and twisted again. Nothing. Tom turned away from me, headed back to the water dispenser on the pop machine. I muttered and set my teeth for one last attempt on the bottle before I resorted to violence, talking myself through the process. *Push down hard on cap. Twist firmly.*

I twisted a little too firmly. Despite pressure and stress, the cap remained attached to the bottle, and the two together leaped out of my hands. I tried to catch them, but as I lunged forward, my chair skidded on the waxed linoleum and I nearly fell out of it. The bottle hit the floor with a loud *clack!* and rolled. The acoustics in the cafeteria were terrific, and the pills on plastic sounded remarkably like popcorn popping. The young doctor who had his back to the ruckus whirled around and said, "What's that?" The other one started to laugh. The bottle passed under a table and finally rolled to a stop under the next one.

"Sorry," I said, walking to the second table. "It got away." I tried to reach the bottle, but it was too far under the table. I pulled a chair out, got down on my hands and knees, and grabbed it by both ends. The cap came off in my hand.

# FORTY-ONE

Tom and I talked about my mother's hospital adventure and the investigation. No, that's not quite right. Tom did most of the talking, and I vacillated between giving him my full attention and none at all. My eyelids felt like sandpaper as the dry heat of the hospital joined forces with fatigue and I wondered where I might find a secret sofa for a twenty-minute nap. I may even have been drifting into sitting-up sleep when Tom's voice broke in.

"How are you doing?" asked Tom.

*Swell.* "I'm okay."

I didn't look at him, but I could feel his eyes on my face.

"It doesn't look as dire as we thought at first," he said.

"Nope."

"Did I do something wrong?" He sounded confused with a hint of annoyed.

"Not that I know of," I said, and immediately wanted to kick my own butt. *Passive aggressive, anyone?* I looked at Tom. He was leaning forward, both forearms resting on the table. His face was relaxed, but there was something in his eye that said he didn't like this game. I didn't much like it either, even if I was the one making the moves. *You're out of control,* said a voice in my head. *My whole life is out of control,* said I. Aloud I said, "I'm tired and I'm worried and I'm the tiniest bit terrified."

"Of what?"

"Of what? Are you kidding?"

"No, but she's doing okay, unless I missed something. What did the doctor say?"

I filled him in on what Doctor Krishna had told me before he arrived. Three women sat two tables away, so I leaned across the table and lowered my voice. "And there's the little matter of our possible status as murder suspects."

He laughed at that. "Oh, come on. That's just the police brainstorming possibilities. Lots of people saw us leave the trial long before Rasmussen was killed."

"Did they?" I thought back to Saturday at the agility trial. I was pretty sure that no one stood in the parking lot at Dog Dayz and watched our departure. Why would they? "Even if someone did see us leave, who's to say we didn't go back? I mean, Rasmussen himself left and came back."

"What else?" asked Tom.

I took a long moment to answer, "I don't know." It seemed less confrontational than *you tell me.*

"So what do you think? Should I put my house up for rent?"

"Do whatever you want," I said. I tried to keep my voice noncommittal, but my tone came out sharper than I intended. *Then again, you're the one with the secret plans,* I thought.

Tom looked like I had dumped the missing ice in his lap, and I could heard the tight bands of control around his voice when he said, "What?"

I knew I should shut up, but my mouth took off on its own. "Apparently you've already decided what you're going to do, so why ask me?"

"What are you ta..."

"I think I'd like to be alone," I said. *I'm terrified of being alone again.* But that wasn't what frightened me, and I knew it. Being alone is not the same as being apart from someone you love. What I should have said was *I think you're leaving, so I'll just make sure of it.*

Tom picked up all the trash except my cup and the plate with the remaining half Danish, the cardboard pastry now trapped in congealed goo. The clock on the cafeteria wall hadn't moved since we came in, and it didn't move after Tom walked away, so I have no idea how long I sat there wanting to punch someone.

Mostly myself.

My hot flash had been replaced by a chill, and a shiver shook me out of my paralysis. I got up. I would find Tom and we would find a quiet spot and I would apologize and then I would shut up and hear what he had to say. I scurried down the hall.

A nurse had just left Mom's room, and she intercepted me. "She's finally fallen asleep."

"I won't wake her," I said. "Is anyone else in there?"

"No, just Mrs. Bruce," she said, and bustled off.

I wouldn't have answered my phone, but its ringing seemed obscene in the medicinal quiet of the early morning corridor. I thought I had turned it off, but lately nothing I thought seemed to be right.

I flipped it open and ducked into the stairwell, trying to keep my voice low.

It was Alberta. She wanted me to photograph the feral cats and the cat colony set up. I assumed this was a request for *pro bono* photography, since most rescue groups have no discretionary funds, but she said, "Okay if I give you the retainer when I see you? Or I can send it by, what's that computer thing?"

I told her not to worry, she could pay me when I finished. I was happy not to be paid at all this time, but I couldn't afford to turn down the money.

"Any chance you can come this afternoon or tomorrow? I mean, if your mother is okay?" It seemed like an afterthought. "It's so nice out, I thought you could get ..."

I filled her in. "But I don't need to be here at the hospital all afternoon," I said. "Tomorrow's out. I'm going with Tom to look at a litter of puppies. At least that's the plan, unless something happens." We set a time and I walked back to Mom's room, thinking Tom should be back by now.

He was not. I checked the waiting area where Doctor Krishna and I had spoken, but he wasn't there either. He wasn't in any of the other sitting areas on that floor. My pulse thundered in my ears. I went back to Mom's room, thinking he might have left me a note. Maybe he had gone to the lounge downstairs.

He hadn't, and his jacket was no longer draped over the chair where he had left it earlier. The tea and morsel of Danish I'd eaten turned to lead in my stomach, and then I saw something on the bureau. No note. Just my keys. What was it I had told him in the cafeteria? *I think I'd like to be alone.*

I had never felt so alone.

# FORTY-TWO

Doing something with my dog and cat usually dulls whatever pain bedevils me, so I headed straight out the back door when I got home. Jay brought me his tennis ball, I threw it, and he took off with Leo right behind him. I broke the film of ice that capped the birdbath and threw the ball again, but the boys ignored me and shot around the side of the house. They reappeared a few seconds later, dancing around Goldie's feet. She wore a bright-blue ski jacket and a Fair Isle cap in lollipop colors, and carried a covered baking pan.

"How's your mom?" She obviously saw the surprise on my face and said, "I saw Tom get out of the taxi this morning. He told me."

I filled her in, and said, "She was sleeping when I left. I'll call in an hour or so for an update."

"Tom must have had an early class," said Goldie, bending to pick up Leo. He settled into her arms and I could hear his motor running from three feet away. She smiled at him and I swear he smiled back.

"You need a cat, my friend," I said. I felt more comfortable talking about cats and dogs, or even my mother, than about Tom at the moment. Besides, Goldie had talked to Tom and probably already knew that all was not well.

Jay shoved his tennis ball into my knee. I started to tell him the game was over, but the anticipation blazed across his face stopped me. I took the sopping ball out of his mouth and told Goldie, "You might want to put Catman down before I throw this."

"Good idea," she said. Leo was finely focused on Jay, and he poured out of Goldie's arms and tucked himself into a crouch that said, "Ready!"

I got three more tosses in before we reached the back door. Each time, Leo chased Jay and Jay chased the ball. They followed us into the house, both of them panting, and lay down together on Jay's bed. Leo patted Jay's muzzle with his paw, and was rewarded with a slurp across his neck and cheek.

Goldie pulled her cap off, releasing a tumble of silver waves that stood out in an electric halo. "Oh," she said, shaking her head and crinkling her nose, "that static tickles my nose." She set the pan on the table and peered over her glasses at me where I had collapsed into a kitchen chair. "Shall I get you a plate and put the kettle on for tea?"

"No, thanks, but help yourself," I said, kicking my shoes off and crossing my feet on a chair. "I ate at the hospital."

Goldie's eyebrows rose.

"Cardboard pastry, but filling."

She sat down across the table from me and asked for more details about my mother. Then she switched topics, as I knew she would. "What's up with you and Tom?"

I didn't answer. Goldie fished some hair pins from her pocket and began twisting and looping and pinning her hair, and I marveled at her ability to create an intricate up sweep without benefit of brush or mirror. I can barely manage to catch a clump of my hair in a giant jaw clip. She finished her do and sat watching me, her fingertip tapping the table.

As much as I didn't want to talk about my so-called love life, the subject was gnawing at me. "What did Tom tell you?" I asked.

"That you needed to stay with your mom and he had places to go," said Goldie.

I wasn't surprised that Tom would keep our problems to himself, but I also wouldn't have been surprised if he had told Goldie every stupid little detail of our conversation, if you could call what we'd had that morning a conversation.

"But he looked like he'd been run over by a truck," said Goldie.

*Maybe the same truck that ran over me when I overheard him asking about quarantines and vaccine requirements for dogs?* "Probably tired."

"Uh huh. I'm sure that was it."

I really didn't want to get into the disturbing trajectory of my relationship, so I said, "If all is well with Mom, I'm going to photograph Alberta's feral cat colony in a bit. You want to come? We can visit the kittens, too."

She said yes, she'd love to go. "Do you have any of that blackberry sage? A cup of tea sounds good." I started to get up but she waved me to stay where I was and went about the tea making.

"Could you please grab me an egg from the bowl in the fridge?" I asked. "I think I need some protein." *I think I need a week in Tahiti.*

My cell phone rang and I answered, thinking it might be the hospital. Or Tom. *Let it be Tom.* Of course, I knew by the ring that it wasn't him.

"Janet, how are you doing?" It was Norm, and he didn't wait for an answer. "I'm back at the hospital and thought I'd fill you in."

Goldie set a mug in front of me and I inhaled the sweet fragrance. Blackberry sage tea never fails to calm and lift me all at once. I mouthed a thank you and she squeezed my shoulder and sat down.

"They wanted to run a bunch of tests but Mom is feisty this morning and she has declined," said Norm. He lowered his voice a notch and continued. "Her boyfriend, Anthony, is here with his daughter. They're so cute together I can't stand it. Him and Mom, I mean.

I had to smile at that. "I know."

Norm went back to his normal voice. "Anyway, she doesn't want more tests, so she's going back to Shadetree any time now. We're just waiting for the ambulance or transport vehicle or whatever they call it."

"Okay," I said, "I'll leave in a few minutes."

"No need. She's really tired and will probably fall asleep the minute she's in her own bed. I'll follow them and stay until she's settled. Then I'm off to pick Bill up. He caught an earlier flight and will be in at two-ten."

"But I should..."

"Let's do this in shifts, okay?" He chuckled. "Besides, Mom was pretty adamant that she wants some private time with Anthony, and doesn't want us hanging around her as if we're on a death watch. Her words."

Yes, they would be, I thought. Terrible words. I felt myself spinning off into a deep space of loneliness, all my tethers suddenly torn loose. Then Norm's chipper voice threw me a lifeline and I floated back into the moment.

"Be sure to keep your phone charged," he said. I'm notorious for letting the battery run down. "And go do something fun. Go take some photos or play with the fur boys, or," he filled his tone with innuendos, "that big handsome boy of yours."

Have I mentioned how much I love Norm? He gives me all the brotherly affections that my biological brother, Bill, finds so difficult. If Bill hadn't moved in with him, I'd have to adopt Norm myself.

I called Alberta to see if we could meet her in about ninety minutes. Fine with her. Goldie went home to change into suitable pants and boots, and I slipped into a quick shower. My peppermint essence steam trick worked its magic and I stepped out feeling slightly more able to function. On a scale of one to ten, with one being comatose and ten being gung ho, I moved up to about a three.

Leo was waiting for me on my bed, and he meowed and stretched when I entered the bedroom. "Hey, Catman." I sat down and ran my hand over his long, sleek felineness. "We'll practice this evening, okay, Leo *mio*?" He squinted at me and chirped. "I know, you don't really need the practice." Which was true. I was the most-likely-to-mess-up team member whenever I performed with my animals. I got up and pulled clean jeans and a sweatshirt out of the closet, and realized that Leo had bumped me up another notch on the functional scale.

And then I opened a drawer in my bureau. I was looking for socks, but I didn't expect the ones that I saw to be Tom's. It used to be my sock drawer, but I had cleared it to give Tom a place to park a few necessities. Apparently the stress of the past twenty-four hours had pitched me back into my old routine. Next to the brown fuzzy socks was an olive green T-shirt, the one that brought out the green flecks in the man's brown eyes whenever he wore it. I picked it up and held it to my face, but it smelled of nothing more personal than dryer sheets. I laid it back in the drawer, smoothed it out with my palm, and gently pushed the drawer shut.

By the time I had my jeans and sweatshirt on, I was angry at myself for being such a wimp about asking straight out what Tom was planning. I even thought about calling him to apologize and to plead insanity at the thought of his leaving, even if it wasn't forever. But that thought conjured the betrayal I had felt when I heard him on the phone. If he was planning to take Drake abroad with him, he had to be planning to be there a long time. From there my heart whirled back to old betrayals, years old but still thinly scabbed. I yanked the knot tight in my boot laces, feeling even angrier, but no longer at myself.

# FORTY-THREE

"ARE YOU SURE YOU heard what you think you heard?" Goldie and I were headed for the feral cat colony managed by Alberta and her friends, and now that she had me captive in the car, Goldie had steered the conversation back to me and Tom.

"I know what I heard," I said.

"Maybe," said Goldie I glanced at her, but she had her eyes averted, as if there were anything interesting to see on this familiar stretch of downtown road.

"Look, if you know something I don't but should, just cough it up, would you?"

Goldie shifted toward me as far as her seatbelt allowed and said, "You're under a lot of stress, and it's possible you're overreacting. Things aren't always what they seem."

"And besides, it's okay to keep big fat secrets from friends who love you, right?" *Put a sock in it, Janet,* whispered my guardian angel.

But Goldie *had* kept a big fat secret all summer, and although I understood, sort of, why she had chosen to do so, I wasn't entirely over it.

Goldie sighed a little too dramatically and said, "That's not fair. I really don't think this is the same." She paused before she said, "Besides, Tom isn't Chet." Meaning my jerk of an ex-husband. "I think you should tell Tom what you overheard and ask him outright what it's all about."

"He's planning to rent out his house, Goldie. He's obviously going somewhere."

"Maybe not as far as you think." I barely heard her.

"What do you mean?"

She didn't answer. I might have pursued it, but my phone rang, so instead I said, "Could you get that? Might be about Mom."

"Oh, hi," she said.

"Who is it?" I asked.

Her hand fluttered at me. "Yes, I understand." Pause. "We're on our way there now…Yes, to Alberta's place and then the cat colony… Okay, yes, I'll let her know." She flipped my phone closed.

"What? Who is that?"

"Your policeman friend. Hutcherson, is it?"

"Hutchinson."

"He said he'll talk to you when you get there."

"About what?"

"He didn't really say."

Which I didn't believe for a second. "My friends sure have a lot of secrets," I said.

I knew as we approached the entrance to Alberta's subdivision that whatever was going on, that was the place.

"Oh, no, this is *déjà vu* all over again." A police cruiser blocked the road between Alberta's driveway and the bulldozer that was still sitting on a flatbed trailer by the pond. I caught a glimpse of something big and orange in front of the trailer, but lost sight of it when I turned into the driveway.

Hutchinson left Alberta standing on her front porch and came out to meet me. "What now?" I asked.

"Vandalism. Someone spray-painted the rocks," said Hutchinson.

At first I thought he meant the boulders that Alberta had incorporated into her landscaping, but they looked normal. Then Goldie started to laugh. Her left hand pointed past the flatbed and her right fist was raised in the air. "Don't let them pave paradise!" she shouted.

The pile of bland white rocks that the community association planned to dump along the edge of the pond to "improve it" looked from that distance like coals ready for a giant's cookout. Then I realized what had happened, and smiled. Someone had spray painted the whole lot of them fluorescent orange.

"They have any clues?" I asked, hoping that whoever did it got away.

"Oh, yeah," said Hutchinson. "Two college kids. Apparently the one they caught has had a couple of run-ins with the police before."

I couldn't think of any eco-terrorists in my immediate circle of friends, although I was sure Goldie wouldn't mind wearing the label. The young women I had met on campus flashed into my mind. "You get a name?"

"I didn't. Why?" Hutchinson frowned at me. "What do you know about this?"

"No! Nothing. I mean, I met some kids on campus, that's all."

Hutchinson gave me an odd look but didn't say anything more. I heard voices and looked toward the far end of the pond, where a group of six or seven people were emerging from the woods. "What's that all about?"

Alberta spoke for the first time. "They're surveying the woods and wetlands."

"Who are they?" I asked.

"A group of university students, a couple of volunteers from my birding group."

I squinted at the group. "Is that Peg?" Peg was the office manager for my veterinarian.

"Oh, goodie," said Goldie, elbowing me. "The gang's all here!" Goldie and Peg had become friends after I got them together a few months earlier.

Alberta said Peg was a member of her birding group, and then said, "We also have a professor from Purdue." She laughed. "I believe you know that one, Janet."

As Alberta spoke, the group skirted the pond and emerged from the shadow of the woods, making my heart beat a little faster. I did indeed know the professor. I knew the light in his graying hair and beard, I knew his jacket, I knew the angle of his shoulders and the way he moved easily across open ground. I also knew the way he made me weak in the knees, and none of my feelings of the past twenty-four hours muffled that response.

Goldie gestured toward Tom with her head, as if I should go talk to him right then and there. I stepped away from her and turned toward Hutchinson.

"Were the women with that group? The one you've arrested and the other one ?"

"I didn't arrest anyone. I'm off-duty today," he said. " But no, from what I gather the girls…" He looked at me and said, "Women?"

I suppressed a smile and nodded. Apparently my efforts at consciousness raising were having an effect.

"The young women came later. The neighbor called it in." He looked away from the pond and pointed with his chin, and for the first time I noticed an elderly man standing on a porch, leaning into a walker. "He says he saw them pull up and start monkeying around near the trailer. He thought they were trying to sabotage the bulldozer. Says he had just come out for some air and didn't even know the other group was here, so they don't seem to be connected. At least not at first glance."

That was a relief. Tom was possibly a murder suspect as it was. He didn't need to be implicated in vandalism, too.

A uniformed officer appeared from the other side of Alberta's house, a handcuffed figure walking a few steps ahead of him. It was Robin Byrde's friend from the college cafeteria, and she and the officer were on a collision course with the group that Tom was with.

"What are you guys doing here ?" asked the woman. If her surprise was an act, she was very good.

"What are *you* doing?" asked a tall, intense young man with streaks of shocking blue in his spiked-up carrot-top hair. He looked at the flat bed and bulldozer, and his voice pitched an octave higher when he said, "What have you done?" Then the painted rocks seemed to register. He leaped into the air, let out a whoop, and yelled, "Totally!" I had no idea what it meant in that context, but the gist was clear.

Tom laid a hand on the young man's shoulder and looked at the handcuffed woman, who was grinning back at the group even as the police urged her toward the cruiser. Tom called after her, "Don't say anything until you have an attorney present. Do you need us to find you one?"

She shook her head and shouted from the cruiser, "Already called my dad. He's meeting me at the lock up." She was still grinning when the officer guided her into the back seat and shut the door.

Most of the group was now scattered across Alberta's driveway and yard, except for one of carrot top's friends, who was taking photos of the glowing rocks with his cell phone, and a straggler who was still back by the pond. Tom met my eyes but kept his distance. He said, "How's your mom?"

"She's doing okay. Going back to Shadetree."

He nodded at me, and for the first time since I'd known him I couldn't read his expression. It wasn't exactly blank, and it wasn't cold, but the heat and humor I had come to expect didn't dance in his eyes or the curve of his lips. I thought I saw something like pain, but then he looked away and I couldn't be sure that it wasn't my own.

Alberta's voice broke through the quiet that had descended on the group. "Did you find anything interesting out there?"

"Who else was in that car?" asked carrot top. He was looking at me.

"I don't know. Tinted window…" I was about to ask whether it might be my new friend Robin, but then I saw her waving at me as she ran up the slope from the pond.

"Hi! Did you guys see the nests hanging in the cattails down there?" She was grinning and bouncing. "Anybody know what kind of birds…?"

"Red-winged blackbirds," said Peg. "You need to come out in the spring and watch them, and hear them trill. It's magic." She pointed at the flatbed and bulldozer and added, "And those are the tools of the evil giant who would take the magic from us."

# FORTY-FOUR

ALL EYES IN THE group seemed focused on what Peg called "the tools of the evil giant."

Finally Alberta broke the silence. "Well, we're all giant killers." She put a hand on Tom's sleeve and asked. "So what about the woods and wetlands? What did you find?"

"Did they do any other damage?" Peg still had her binoculars aimed at the construction equipment. "I don't see anything from this side."

Tom looked at Alberta and said, "Hold that thought." Then he turned to Hutchinson. "That's a good question. Did they do anything to the equipment?"

Hutchinson nodded. "Just paint. No real damage."

Tom seemed to breathe a little easier. I didn't think he would encourage vandalism, but he obviously liked these kids and their cause. He glanced at me but didn't linger before turning to Alberta's question. "It's not the best time of year to assess the wetlands. A lot of plants have died back and aren't immediately apparent, and the amphibians and reptiles, and some of the mammals, are holed up. And of course a lot of the birds that are here in summer are migratory. But Jordan," he indicated the redhead, "is doing a count of migratory fowl."

Jordan's head bobbed wildly and he said, "I'll be back at dawn. Best time to spot them."

Tom went on. "We'll check the survey maps. If the wetlands are being used by rare migratory birds, we may have a case. So, we have more work to do, but this is a good start. Let's pull what we have together." He hesitated. "And although I don't encourage anyone to commit acts of vandalism, that," he pointed at the fluorescent rock pile, "at least delays the planned destruction of the pond's perimeter. We have an attorney working on a temporary restraining order against the so-called improvements."

"Speaking of vandalism," I said, "is there any news about the damage to Alberta's house?"

"It was a golf ball that broke the window," said Hutchinson. "They found it wedged into a bookcase. A Callaway. Top of their line."

"My dad used to use those," I said. I only knew that because I made doll furniture out of the empty boxes.

Several of the group members walked toward a beat-up car parked on the street. Tom and Jordan, the red-headed kid, were talking about whatever was in Jordan's notebook. I wanted to ask Tom if we could meet later to talk, but I didn't want to interrupt. Alberta tugged on my jacket and I turned toward her.

"Can we go take the cat photos now? I think it would be a good time to get pictures of most of them," she said. She went into a convoluted explanation of the kinds of photos she wanted, as if I wouldn't know how to get good pictures of felines, and finally wrapped up by saying, "Sally usually feeds them about now, so they come in for that."

"Sure. Let me grab my camera, and give me a second." I turned around, intending to ask Tom if we could grab a minute, but all I saw was the back end of his van as it accelerated away from me.

*Focus on your work*, whispered the voice that had helped me get past tough times before. I wasn't sure it would get me through this, but having a job to do did keep me from dropping into a whimpering mess on the cold, wet grass. I got my camera from my own van, returned to Alberta, and said, "Okay, let's do it."

I could have walked to the cat feeding station in five minutes, but Alberta slowed me down. She had moved a lot faster with the adrenaline pumping through her when we were searching for Gypsy, but now she went at something between a toddle and a stroll. She was telling me about the current feeding and shelter situation for the cats, and what her little group of volunteers had in mind for the future.

"Right now we just have a few medium-size crates out there with the doors off and some straw inside. We've wedged them between bales of straw for the winter, for insulation." She stopped and put her hand on her chest for a couple of breaths, then walked on. "If we get the permit, we're going to put up a more permanent, insulated facility with access points so they can come and go as they please."

"It sounds great," I said. We were walking along the back of the clubhouse, and if I remembered correctly, the cat station was just a few yards farther past the corner of the building. "How will you keep wildlife out? I mean, it sounds like the perfect place for raccoons and possums and things, and they could cause a lot of problems, I would think."

We rounded the corner and stopped short. Alberta let out a long moan, and I felt as if cold claws had sunk into my belly. Clearly wildlife were not the biggest danger for feral cats at The Rapids of Aspen Grove.

Alberta stopped moaning and began to swear. She was very good at it, and she had reason. The last time I had seen the shelter and feeding stations set up by Alberta and her network of volunteers, the place had been tidy and clean. It couldn't be called an eyesore because it lay in the right angle where a storage building met a row of juniper bushes and was invisible from the club house and road. For a stop-gap pending a better arrangement, it had looked pretty impressive.

Volunteers had built a frame of two-by-fours into which they had placed straw bales with plastic cat carriers tucked between them at staggered heights. At each end of the structure were feeding stations well-stocked with dry food and clean water, all checked and replenished at least twice a day. The top and three sides of the affair had been covered with heavy plastic sheeting, stretched and stapled, to fend off wind and rain.

Now it looked as if a tornado had hit the place. The wooden frame had been pulled over, and many of the boards broken. The binders had been ripped from the straw bales, and the November wind had scattered straw far out into the golf course. Someone had taken something heavy, perhaps a sledgehammer, to some of the plastic crates, smashing and cracking them to uselessness. Food and water bowls had been tossed here and there, and the padlock had been broken off the food-storage bin and cat food lay everywhere. There was no sign of a cat anywhere.

# FORTY-FIVE

Alberta stepped toward the mess that once was the clean and tidy feral cat shelter.

"Wait," I said. "Don't touch a thing. Call the police. I'll get some photos while you do that."

She looked at me and nodded, her face very pale. She held a hand to her chest and said, "The cats."

"I'll look around. Come here," I said, looping an arm around her shoulders and guiding her to a golf cart parked up against the club house wall. A piece of paper was taped to the seat. Rain and ice had obliterated most of the writing, but I made out enough to know the thing was out of commission. It still had seats, though, so I sat Alberta behind the wheel. "Call the police." I was worried about her, but short of taking her home, I couldn't think of anything to do better than keep her occupied. Besides, I knew she wouldn't leave until I checked on the cats. The question was, where should I look? They weren't likely to shout "here we are" after what must have been a traumatic experience.

I clicked off a series of shots, recording the damage from all sides. I had never used the video function on my camera, but this seemed like a good time to give it a trial run. I panned across the entire scene, slowly taking in the surrounding structures, the edge of the golf course, and houses in the distance. I walked slowly toward a clump of naked forsythia, thinking that if any cats were around, they would be hunkered down in whatever hidey holes they could find, watching.

It took me two trips around the sprawl of yellow-brown branches before I saw anything remotely feline, but finally I spotted a tuft of black fur fluttering from the sharp end of a broken twig. A minute movement caught my attention, and I stared into the tangled branches and debris toward the center of the shrubs. *There.* Once I saw the cat, I couldn't *not* see him, but I marveled at the camouflage that made that first awareness so elusive.

"Hi, kitty," I said very softly. "Are you okay?" The cat was a big gray tabby. One ear was missing its tip, marking it as a trapped, neutered, and released member of the colony. "Did you see who made that mess over there?" I knelt, sinking my knee into a mat of cold, wet leaves. "Where are all your friends?"

The cat didn't come to me, but seemed to relax. I raised my camera, took a couple of photos, and slowly panned the underbrush in hopes that my viewfinder would show me something I hadn't noticed. It did. Another cat, a black-and-gold tortoiseshell, was tucked into a nest of branches about five feet from the tabby. "Pretty girl," I said. "Everything will be okay." She looked like she had her doubts. I checked the whole sprawling mass of vegetation again, but those were apparently the only cats holed up there at the moment.

I walked all around the club house and peered under the shrubbery and planters, earning some semi-hostile stares from a group of well-coiffed older women on their way to the front door. No cats. I was almost back to where I had left Alberta when I noticed someone watching. The sweatshirt was different—mustard yellow instead of navy—but I was sure it was the same person who had been watching me at the pond. He, or she, was too far away for me to get a good view, so I raised my camera and *click click clicked*. I expected him to turn away, but for a long moment there was no reaction. Then the figure raised one languid arm, gave me the finger, and walked away. *That was interesting.* I'd be able to see who it was soon enough, I thought.

The weather hadn't been bad for November when I started out from home, but the wind was beginning to pick up and the temperature was dropping. Low, blue-gray clouds had arrived in the past half hour, casting a cold shadow, and I started to shiver. I would check in with Alberta and then run back to my van for my warmer coat, thankful that I had thought to grab it on my way out of the house. I capped my lens and hustled around to the back of the club house.

Alberta was right where I'd left her, talking on the phone. She hung up when I reached her and said, "I've called the press."

"What?"

"It's time to get the public on our side. People will be outraged about this," she swept an arm toward the vandalized cat colony and almost toppled out of the golf cart. "I know people. I called my contacts at the *News-Sentinel* and *Journal-Gazette*, two radio stations, and Channel 15 News. Someone will come, and these people," she tipped her head toward the club house, "won't like negative publicity." She wriggled forward on her seat and stepped out of the cart.

"Did you call the police?" I asked, hoping they would at least get there before a mob of reporters, if reporters actually found this newsworthy. I crossed my arms and tried to suppress the goose bumps and shakes the cold wind was giving me.

"They're on their way. And I called Homer, too."

Homer Hutchinson. It always took me a second thought to put the first name with the man. *Can't hurt*, I thought. Even if he wasn't on the vandalism case, he might nudge someone to give it careful attention. Then again, this wasn't like the attack on Alberta's house.

A knife of wind sliced through my sweatshirt and I felt as if my torso were turning to ice. I told Alberta that I really was chilled and had to go for my warmer coat. Cradling my lens to keep my camera from bouncing, I ran around the club house and all the way back to Alberta's driveway, where I jumped into my van and set my camera into the case on the passenger seat. I would warm up and go back, I thought. Alberta wore a ski jacket, mittens, a mad-bomber hat, and yellow rain boots, and she had been tucked into the lee of the building while I was out in the wind, poorly dressed. She'd be fine until I got back.

My fingers were so cold that I fumbled my keys and they disappeared under the seat. "D-d-dammit," I said through chattering teeth. I got out and bent down to look under the seat. It was dark under there, and at first I couldn't see much. Then an empty potato chip bag and a couple of gas receipts. Something shiny. I reached for it, thinking it was a key, and my fingers closed over my long-lost watch. I stared at it and said, "S-s-so there you are," and shoved it into my jeans pocket. My keys had somehow fallen out of reach under the back of my seat.

By the time I closed the back side door and climbed in again behind the wheel, I was shivering nonstop and had to try a couple of times before I hit the ignition slot with the key. I turned the heat up full blast but it came out cold, then lukewarm. I pulled my down jacket from the back seat and draped it over myself like a blanket. It was cold, but I hoped my now nonstop shivering would generate some heat that the down-filled nylon would trap for me. *I wish I had a nice warm cat in my lap and a dog stretched out beside me,* I thought. *Or a nice warm Tom.*

The heat finally kicked in, but my body still shook and my teeth clackety-clacked. Still, I thought I could manage a conversation. I punched Tom's speed dial number, almost hearing his voice through the ringing. Then I did hear his voice. Or, more accurately, his voice mail message. In spite of the heat now blasting out of all the vents, I felt a new chill well up from somewhere deep and lonely.

# FORTY-SIX

My van took about five minutes to crank up the heat, and I sat there for another five, letting the heat blast out of the vents until my feet and my cheeks were warm and I had mostly stopped shivering.

I shut off the engine and reluctantly stepped from the warm van into the cold, damp wind. I tried to pull my down jacket on over my hoody, but couldn't make it work. Maybe I was just tired, but the jacket sleeves didn't want to slide over the sweatshirt. "Dammit," I said. I really wanted the hood to keep my head warm. I fished around the back of the van on the off chance that I might have left a hat in there, but no luck. I tried once more to urge the sleeves to just get along, but no dice. I threw the jacket onto the front seat and pulled off my hoody. All that remained between me and the wind was my long-sleeved t-shirt and my undies. I may as well have been nekkid. By the time I got my down jacket zipped up to my chin, I was shivering again.

I jumped up and down and fished around in the pockets again. One thin knit glove. "Better than nothing," I mumbled, pulling it on.

At least my right hand would be moderately warm. *Good thing you aren't caught in a blizzard,* said a voice in my head. *Nag, nag, nag.*

I jogged back to where I had left Alberta, and by the time I got there my body was a little warmer. My face was another story. My cheeks felt as if someone were giving me a facial with one of those hand-held vegetable shredders, and I was afraid I had icicles hanging from my nose. I had no tissue, so I gave up, blew my nose into my glove, pulled it inside out, and shoved it deep into my pocket.

"Elegant," said Alberta. I looked at her to see if she was serious, and as soon as my eyes met hers we both started to laugh. It was one of those tension-breaking, ridiculous laugh fests that shift the universe a hair, and by the time we stopped, I felt that I—we—would get through this convergence of crises. Somehow.

"Oh, man," I said, wiping my eyes with my jacket sleeve. A question had occurred to me on my jog back from the car, and I asked, "Alberta, who actually owns this land?" I gestured toward the piece of ground where the bales and crates were scattered.

"Community association," she said.

"And you have permission for the cat colony to be here?"

"Sure," she said.

"Really?" I didn't entirely believe her. "I thought a lot of the homeowners opposed the TNR program, and cats?"

"Some do," she said. "My friend Sally is vice-president of the homeowners' association. And she's passionate about the cats. She drummed up a lot of support, and they took a vote about allowing this set-up through the winter. Then we'll reassess."

I had more questions, but Hutchinson and two uniformed officers appeared from around the corner of the building. Hutchinson waved but walked with the officers to the perimeter of the damage.

I heard one of them let out a long whistle. After they had taken a good look, Hutchinson and one of the others, a young woman with dark hair and ice-blue eyes, walked over to us.

"Ladies," said Hutchinson, nodding. "This is Officer Lindemann. She has a few questions."

"Are you on this case, Homer?" asked Alberta.

Hutchinson shook his head. "Not officially, but I asked my lieutenant to let me take a look because this might be linked to the other vandalism on your house." He looked me up and down and said, "You look cold."

"Freezing," I said, and realized my body was shaking again, although not so violently as before. "I can't seem to warm up."

"You can go in a minute," said Officer Lindeman. "I need you to answer a few questions first."

My teeth started to chatter, but I clamped them together and answered her questions—when had we found the damage, were any animals hurt, had we touched anything, and so on. I told her I had taken photos and she gave me her email address so I could send them, promising to print any she wanted once she had seen the digital versions.

When she was gone, I started again to excuse myself, but Hutchinson asked Alberta, "How are the kitties?"

"Doing great," she said. "You must come see them."

Hutchinson looked at me, his eyes sparkling. "Their eyes are open now, you know."

Who couldn't smile back at such news delivered with such wonder? I wondered whether my lips were blue. The police had just finished marking the area off limits when a small gaggle of people appeared. They were talking in friendly tones but walking toward us as if in a race. Reporters. I decided it really was time to make myself scarce before they trapped me there and I froze to death.

The wind was in my face all the way back to my van. I tried to run, but my eyes teared so much that I couldn't see, so I walked with my head down and shoulders hunched. My hair whipped around so wildly I thought it might just blow away. At least without my camera I could keep my hands stowed in my pockets. *Note to self: Winter is coming. Soon. Outfit your car.*

Something was flapping in the wind. I could hear it as I crossed Alberta's side yard and approached the driveway. Had I not noticed a flag out here? But when I was a few feet from my van and finally looked up, I saw it. A big sheet of poster board flapped crazily from its duct-tape anchor on my windshield. "What the … ?" I grabbed the near edge and pulled, but whoever taped the thing to my van meant it to stay there, at least for a while. I needed better leverage.

I opened the back of my van and looked for something I could stand on. My grooming box would have been perfect—big and sturdy—but I had taken it to the garage to tidy Jay's coat up before the agility trial. The only thing I could find was the small plastic tackle box I used to hold a few basic tools—hammer, pair of screwdrivers, pliers. It would have to do.

It didn't do at all. I could barely fit both feet on it, and as soon as I leaned over the windshield, the stupid box tipped out from under me. If I could get into Alberta's garage … I tried the front door, hoping it would be open. No luck. When I turned away from the front porch, the little creep who had been stalking me was standing between the two houses across the street, sporting the navy hoody this time. "I hope you freeze your noogies off," I muttered.

The poster board smacked flat against my windshield and I saw that there was writing on it, albeit faint and hard to see. Pencil, maybe. I grabbed the bottom corner and yanked. The tape held to the glass, but I managed to tear off about two-thirds of the sheet. I had to play with the angle to get the light just right on the graphite before I could read it. "Take you're camera and go." *You're a moron*, I thought, *and your spelling sucks*. Any inclination I may have had to laugh went up in smoke when I read the next line, written near the bottom of the sheet. It said, "Remember: the fire next time."

"What's that?"

I think I might have sailed right over my van if I'd had any forward momentum, I jumped so high. The voice was right behind me.

"Sorry," said Hutchinson. "Sorry." He reached for the poster board in my hand. "What is that?" I handed it to him and he said, "That's the same as the note to Alberta. 'The fire next time.' I don't like this at all."

"Hutch, don't make a big deal, but if you look across the street, the guy who's been watching me is over there, between the houses." Honestly, I wanted him to make a big deal. I wanted him to catch the guy and find out why he—or she—was following me around, and whether the stalking and this threat were connected.

"There's no one there now," he said. He was right. I wondered whether he thought I was making this up, but he said, "I'll take a look around."

The warming effects of the adrenaline had worn off, and my shivering came back at a whole new level. Hutchinson said, "Get in and start the van and warm up."

"But I can't drive…"

"Get in. I'll get that crap off your windshield."

He was back in five minutes with a step stool, a can of adhesive remover, and a putty knife. I stepped out of the van and asked where he got all that.

"I keep a lot of stuff in my trunk. You never know when you'll need it."

My motto exactly.

I watched him work from inside my warm vehicle and tried to think, but I was too tired and too cold. The same four thoughts played over and over.

*I want my normal, boring life back.*

*I want to talk to Tom.*

*I want to curl up on the couch with my dog, cat, and a hot toddy.*

*I don't ever want to talk to Tom again.* How could he ... ?

Hutchinson got the tape and most of the adhesive off and signaled me to open the window. "It's not perfect, but you can see to drive." He held the bottle of remover toward me. "You want this?"

"Thanks, I think I have some."

"Okay, then." He stepped back from the van. "See you."

Traffic was light and I made it home in record time. Leo was perched on his favorite length of windowsill, and when I pulled into the driveway, Jay popped up behind him on the couch. Home. All I wanted was a quiet evening at home.

# FORTY-SEVEN

My house was quiet. If I hadn't been nodding off on the couch with Leo purring on my chest and Jay mostly on my lap, all fifty-five pounds of him, I might have said it was too quiet for eight o'clock. As it was, though, I probably needed a little down time after the bone-and spirit-chilling events of the afternoon. The van had warmed me up on the drive home, but once I was there, it took only five minutes outside with Jay to set my teeth to clacking again, even bundled up with coat, hat, and mittens. I fed the critters and opened a can of chunky vegetable soup, but once I had it in a bowl in the micro-wave, I realized there was no way around it. I was still chilled.

Twenty minutes later I stepped out of a hot shower, dried off, pulled off the shower bonnet I had pilfered from a motel ages ago, and jumped into pink polar fleece pajamas with dancing penguins, two pairs of thick slipper socks, and my ancient thick-chenille bathrobe. Warm at last. My face felt chapped from the wind, so I captured my crazy hair in a headband and slathered on some moisturizer. I gazed at the frump looking back from my mirror and told her, "Just look what that silly man is missing." My phone was on the counter beside the sink, and for half a second I considered taking a selfie, but quickly came to my senses. What kind of advertisement would that be for my own photography?

The soup came out of the microwave way too hot to eat, so I treated it as a sort of inhalant while I munched crackers and sorted my mail from the past couple of days. I couldn't help noticing a pattern in the messages plastered across the junk-mail envelopes. *Don't Miss Out! Act Now! ... Before it's too late!* I gathered them up and chucked them into the recycle bin.

Leo strolled into the kitchen and lay down with Jay on the big red dog bed in the corner. They both watched me as if waiting for an explanation. "What?" I asked. Jay swiveled his head and Leo tucked his front feet under his chest. "Just lie down," I said, which was ridiculous since they already were.

I hunched over my soup and tested a spoonful. It was tomato-y and rich, and I closed my eyes and tracked the heat slipping through my throat and chest and into my stomach. I tried to shut everything else out and let eating become a mindful meditation. Lift the spoon, hold while the good, earthy fragrance of roots and leaves and the fruit of the tomato vine rises into your consciousness. Blow gently. Let the fire go but hold the warmth and take it in.

Jay sighed and I looked at the big red bed. He and Leo had apparently given up on me and were sleeping, my little orange cat snuggled tight against the side of my dog's head. Suddenly I realized that I missed the big black dog. It wasn't so much that Drake and Tom were absent tonight. That wasn't unusual, since we spent maybe half our nights together. But knowing they would soon both be gone for months, maybe a year, maybe even longer, created a gaping void in what had become, over the previous months since I'd met them, my life.

*If that's what he wants, fine,* I thought. I cleared the table and put the kettle on. Goldie's lights were on and there were two cars in her driveway and two more parked at the curb. Must be her book club night, or meditation, or … I was happy for her that she was back in the social swing that she had let go while she was ill, but a little disappointed that she wasn't available for a chat. I walked to the big red bed, squatted down, and stroked Jay and Leo. "At least we have each other, right boys?" Leo opened one eye, gave me the "I'm sleeping" look, and curled up. Jay stretched his back legs and relaxed back into his snooze.

I sat down at the table with a cup of Earl Grey and unwrapped a bar of dark chocolate, because if nearly freezing to death isn't a reason to eat chocolate, I don't know what is. As the bittersweetness spread across my tongue, my thoughts spread out as well, beginning with events of the afternoon. Who in the world had taped that odd threat to my windshield, and why? I had been threatened before for taking photos of things someone wanted to remain unseen, but images of dormant woods and wetlands in the bleakness of November didn't seem worth the trouble. Or was it because of my involvement, sparse as it was, with Alberta's cat colony? And who in the world was that creepy person who was, apparently, stalking me? There was something familiar in the posture, but I couldn't put the pieces together.

My thoughts traveled back, then, to earlier events. The thought of those ugly chunks of rock rendered even uglier by the orange spray paint made me smile. I couldn't understand why anyone would think those bland bits of limestone made for a better pond's edge than the natural grasses and reeds, and the thought of destroying habitat that nurtured the trilling blackbirds and myriad other creatures filled me with fury and hollowed me out all at once. Did the people who made these decisions simply not understand the environmental impact, or was there more to it? I thought about the little group who had been there to survey the area that was at risk, and that led my wandering mind back to Tom.

*Admit it*, said my Janet demon. *You think about Tom all the time, even when you're not thinking about him.*

I moved on to thoughts of the police car, and Robin's friend being guided into it, handcuffs on her wrists, the police officer's hand on her head, and defiance on her face. Who else was in that car? Someone had been arrested for vandalizing the rocks and the bulldozer. That would delay destruction of the pond's edge by a day or two at best, I knew, unless the activists were successful in their legal efforts. I decided to call a few people later and see whether my photos would be of any use to them. I wished I had gone out in summer as I'd talked about. The greens of summer are much more appealing than browns and grays.

Browns and grays. Tom flashed into my mind's eye again, the brown of his eyes, the gray edges of his hair.

*Go away.*

*Dammit, come back.*

*What time is it?* All my time-keeping devices were in the other part of the house, so I pulled my robe around me and padded off to the bathroom. In my half-frozen state when I got home, I had tossed my jeans into the hamper without emptying the pockets. I found them under several other articles of clothing and pulled out my cell phone and my watch. It was almost nine. I had two messages.

261

The first came in late afternoon, and I recognized the number. Giselle. I realized for the first time that I hadn't seen her with the environmental group at the pond. She had been pretty excited about the trip when I talked to her at Dog Dayz and I had expected her to be there. Something must have come up. I'd call in a few minutes.

The other message was from Tom. "Hi, you … Sorry we didn't get to talk today. It didn't seem like the right place … Anyway, I'm glad your mother is doing better." *Oh, crap, I need to call Norm and Bill*, I thought, still listening to Tom's message. "So, call me when you get this, okay? It's, uh, seven p.m. on Wednesday. I … Okay, call me." There was a long silence, as if he might have wanted to say something else, before the message cut off.

Something told me I wasn't going to enjoy either conversation, and I had an almost overwhelming urge to turn off both phones and crawl into bed with my dog and cat and a good book.

# FORTY-EIGHT

LEO GOT UP, STRETCHED, and strolled over to rub himself against my fleece jammies. One second he was on the floor, the next he was on the table, leaning toward me with his squinty "I love you" look. We bumped noses and I said, "So, Catman, we didn't get our practice session in today."

He yawned, which I took to mean he could run the agility course backward with his eyes closed. But his eyes were wide open and he was looking right into me. I stroked his head and he pushed the top of it into my palm. I glanced at Jay. He was on his back, hips rolled one way and front legs the other, like a loosely wrung towel. His head was tilted back and gravity had pulled his upper lips into a passive snarly face. I looked at Leo and said, "Your brother looks like a doofus."

He said, *mmmrrrwwwwllll*.

"So, what do you think?" I asked my cat. "Should I return those calls?"

"*Mmmrrrwwl.*"

"Should I call Giselle first, or Tom?"

He kept his opinion on that to himself and jumped down, so I pushed Tom's speed dial button and was about to push "call" when my land line rang. I picked it up.

"Janet, I'm so upset? I don't have a lawyer, should I talk to your, Bill's … you know, I don't know …"

When she stopped, I said, "Giselle? What's happened? Why do you need a lawyer?" And suddenly I knew who was behind the tinted window in the back of the police car. I started to laugh, not because I wished her trouble with the police, but because it made me happy to know that Giselle was progressing from passive-aggressive silliness to full-out civil disobedience.

"What's funny?" she asked, more than a hint of hurt in her voice.

"No, it's not funny," I said. "Giselle, did you spray paint those rocks?"

"Yes?"

"Well done!"

"Really?" her tone shifted to something like tentative satisfaction.

"Oh yeah. Brilliant, really," I said. "Although bummer getting caught."

"I'm out on bail?" Her voice lost its confidence. "They have evidence, they say …"

I cut her off. "Right, the nosy old neighbor saw you do it. Call my brother-in-law Norm in the morning. If he can't handle it, he'll refer you to another good attorney. But I bet they'll back off. They aren't going to want the publicity."

"No, Janet, I mean, yes, I need an attorney, but it's not the stupid rocks," she said. "It's murder. They think I killed that Rasmussen guy."

That shut me up for a few seconds. Finally, I said the only thing I could think of. "What?"

She described her arrest, and I asked, "Are you okay? I mean, if you want you can come over here, stay in my guest room. You and Precious are welcome." I thought about her little dog and added, "And Precious is welcome here if you need a place for him, you know, for a while." *Like twenty-five to life*, I thought with a jolt.

"No, I'm okay. My friend is here." There was a long pause, and then she said, "Thank you for not asking."

"Not asking what?"

"If I killed him." She hung up.

I knew she didn't kill him. At least I knew it until I remembered her telling me about whaling away with the pooper-scooper in a fit of anger. Could Giselle actually have killed Rasmussen? I flashed back to another time and realized that I had suspected Giselle of murder once before. But I barely knew her then, and she had changed so much since those days that I had almost forgotten. But do people really change that much? I had thought her capable of murder at one time, so why not now? Then again, I had been wrong that other time, and besides, what real motive did she have? She hadn't liked the way Rasmussen treated his wife, or my mother and her beau Anthony Marconi, but that hardly seemed cause to kill the man. She was certainly angry when he yelled at her and—worse—at her dog, Precious. Still, it was a huge leap from there to murder.

Besides, there were more practical issues. I wasn't sure Giselle could have managed it physically. Rasmussen had not been a small man, and he had the power of intimidation on his side. I just couldn't imagine Giselle mustering enough confidence to attack the man and do him in.

What if Goldie was onto something with her *Orient Express* comment? What if several people, all bubbling over with motives and emotions, had teamed up to do away with Charles Rasmussen and his belligerent, evil ways? I didn't imagine some grand conspiracy, mind you, just a perfect storm of proximity, opportunity, and righteous anger.

"Come on, Jay," I said, refilling my mug and padding off to the living room. My thick fluffy slipper socks made a satisfying *whoop whoop* on the carpet. I plumped a couple of pillows against one arm of the couch, stretch my legs out, and covered up with my old blue afghan. Jay didn't need a second invitation to hop up and sprawl with his chest on my thigh and the rest of him stretched toward my feet. I wriggled us both around until I was comfortable and picked up my phone.

Tom answered on the third ring. "Hi you."

"Hi yourself."

"Are you okay?"

*Aside from insane from trying to make myself ask what you're up to and furious that I even have to?* "What do you mean?"

"You sound like you're stuffed up."

"Oh." He was right. I felt a bit stuffy. "Hang on."

I tried to reach the box of tissues on the coffee table but they were just out of reach. "Jay, take it," I said, pointing at the box with my vertically flattened hand. He leaped up, shoving a front foot into my gut for his launch off the couch and over the table. "Oww!" Jay took no notice of my pain. He was intent on the job at hand. He grabbed the new copy of *Outdoor Photography* from the table and brought it to me. "Thanks, Bubby, but that's not it." He grinned, wriggled, and cocked his head. I pointed at the tissues again and said, "Take it."

Jay tried to grab the box from the side but it was too big for his mouth, and the harder he tried, the faster it slid until it fell off the table. He tried a couple more times, then looked at me for help. I knew he would figure it out, so I just waited while he stared at the box for a few seconds. Then he grabbed hold where the slit for tissues is and brought it to me. The black of his nose was pugged up against the edge of the cardboard slot and he sneezed when I took the box. "You want one, too?" I asked him as I pulled out a tissue and blew my nose. Jay hopped back onto the couch and curled himself around my feet.

"Okay, all clear," I said into the phone.

"What was all that?" asked Tom.

"Jay had a little trouble with the tissue retrieve."

Tom chuckled, then asked about my mother. I was just going to tell him about the vandalism of the feral cat colony when he said, "I'm in Indy."

*But we're going to Indianapolis tomorrow.* "You are?"

"Yeah, I tried to call you earlier to see if you could get away." He seemed to be waiting, but I couldn't think what to say. I was too busy trying to pick my heart up off the floor. "Tommy's flying in tomorrow afternoon. It was a lot cheaper to Indy, and since I was headed there anyway..." *You mean* we *were headed that way*, I thought.

"Okay," I said finally. "We can go see the puppies next week." I grabbed another tissue as my nose started to run.

He cleared his throat. "I, uh …"

"You're going to see them?" I worked at keeping my mixed emotions out of my voice. "That makes sense, I guess." I blew my nose as quietly as possible.

"I already did. This evening. Are you catching cold?"

I'm not sure which was more disappointing, this awkwardness with Tom or missing the chance to play with a bunch of baby Labs. "No, I just got a little chilled out there this afternoon."

He asked about both photo shoots, the woods and wetlands and the feral cats, and I gave him a very short synopsis, then asked, "So what did you think?"

Any other guy might think I was still talking about the afternoon's outing, but not Tom. He sounded like he could still feel those roly-poly little bodies all around him. "They were great. Barely six weeks old, nine little yellow girls. And I really like the bitch." Meaning the mother of the puppies.

"Who's the breeder?" I know a lot of the active dog people in Indiana, so there was a good chance I knew this one.

"Jill Peabody. She just moved here from North Dakota. She doesn't breed much, just a litter every three or four years so she can keep one for herself." I knew Tom had walked away from a number of breeders for a variety of reasons, including some who he thought had too many litters. "You should have seen them, Janet." I held the phone at arm's length and mouthed *seriously?* I missed a little of his tale, but he never noticed. Puppy talk does that to people. "Is your computer on? You have mail."

"Ohmagosh," I said. Each one was cuter than the next.

What I wanted to ask next was *Do you really think this is a good time to get a puppy, with your big sabbatical plans and all,* but what came out was, "I thought you were going to wait for a black male in the spring?" When he didn't say anything, I started to laugh.

"What?" he asked.

"About that list of possible names." Tom had been throwing out potential names for a month or so. Names like Jim and Gander and the like.

"Yeah," he said, and I could hear the smile that I knew was curling around the corners of his eyes. "Better start a new list."

# FORTY-NINE

My throat felt like there was a butterfly trapped in it. It wasn't sore, not yet, but the tickle spread from behind my tongue up into my ears. I got up and started to make coffee, then opted for tea with honey instead. Sunrise was an hour and a half off, but I wanted to be in place by first light. I just needed to pry my eyes open first. Between blowing my nose, trying to breathe, and wrestling with a crazy mélange of thoughts, I hadn't slept much. I let Jay out the back door, fed Leo, and had a sneezing fit. *Great, just what I need.* Jay came in and inhaled his kibble, and I gave him a big fat carrot to complete his breakfast.

"Looks like you're going to have a new little sister in a couple of weeks," I told him. I meant Tom's yellow puppy girl, but the image my mind latched onto was Gypsy's tabby daughter. *Oh, no,* I thought, pushing it away. *Where did that come from?* Jay rolled his eyes at me, wriggled, and bit off a hunk of carrot.

As I dressed, I went back over the previous night's conversations. I would check in with Norm at a decent hour and be sure he knew that Giselle was a friend. I made a mental note to ask him what kind of retainer she was looking at for a murder defense, if it really came to that. Tom and I had talked about Giselle's situation, and he didn't think it would go that far. I wasn't so sure. Maybe I could organize a crowd-sourced legal fund for her, I thought. If everyone who despised Rasmussen chipped in a few bucks, she should be in good shape.

Tom had also thought Goldie's *Orient Express* theory was hilarious. The creepy stalker was another matter. "Next time, take his picture and have them do something about it."

"I took a couple, but you can't see the face," I said. "I don't even know for sure that it's a guy."

"Just don't take any chances," he said. "Maybe you shouldn't go out there alone in the morning."

"That red-headed kid—what's his name? Jason? He's going to be there. Besides, stalkers don't stalk at dawn."

"I hope you're right," he said.

I hoped I was right, too. I stuffed a bundle of tissues into my jeans and checked the weather app on my phone. Thirty degrees, clear this morning, high in the mid-forties, then a cold front coming in. Rain, possible flurries late. *Perfect*, I thought. I drank my tea standing by the sink and watched Jay mark the fence line at the back of the yard. I sneezed. Again. Once more. *Terrific.* I resisted taking anything that might dull my senses, but I couldn't be out there with gloves, camera, and a snotty nose, so I rummaged around the drug stash in the cupboard. Heartworm prevention for Jay. Ibuprofen for me. I shook the bottle, and heard a lone pill rattling around. Two out-of-date prescriptions, one for each of us. A couple of packets of anti-flu drink mix with don't drive warnings.

A packet of Benadryl, left over from last summer when Jay's face swelled up from some kind of bug bite. That would dry me up, but put me to sleep. I decided I'd just stuff wads of tissue up my nose if necessary.

Lights were on in quite a few homes in The Rapids of Aspen Grove, including Alberta's. As I trudged across her lawn toward the woods, I glanced at her kitchen window and there she was, waving. I held up my camera and gestured toward the pond and woods, then went on. The sun had not appeared yet over the horizon, but the eastern sky was streaked in rainbow-sherbet colors. I sniffed, and felt ice crystals pinch my nostrils.

Something moved between me and the pond, and I stopped. It moved again, and I saw a shape in the advancing light. It was the size of a small dog. I stood very still, barely breathing, and waited, willing the sun to send more light into the world. The shape came closer, and I could hear, faintly, the crunch of paws on frozen grass. It stopped. The leading edge of the sun cut into the distant sky, and the edges of the animal seemed, for just a second, to glow.

Fox.

I smiled, waited, barely breathed. I could feel it watching me, deciding what to do. The light came on, and I could see more clearly. The animal's fur seemed in that light to be on fire, and something about the attitude, the posture, said *vixen*. She stared at me, and I slowly bent my knees and sank down, making myself smaller. She had something in her mouth, but I couldn't see what. Bird? Rodent, I thought. Slowly I brought my camera up. If she held for just another minute or two, I thought I could get the shot. She took a step to my right, looked over her shoulder at the woods, and back at me. I clicked the lens. She startled but didn't run. I clicked a series of shots and lowered my camera. "Thank you," I murmured. She turned away, stopped, and looked back at me. No doubt she wanted to be sure I wasn't chasing her, but I like to think she was saying so long. I watched until she disappeared into the trees.

Jason emerged from the woods when I was about ten yards out. He waved with one hand, signaling me not to speak with the other. When I reached him, he turned and led me through a stretch that would be pure muck if not for the overnight freeze. We stopped beside an enormous sycamore and he pointed toward a stand of bittersweet that straddled the wood and swamp. "Wood ducks," he whispered.

I could see movement, then the shapes of the ducks. My long lens, though, gave me a clear view, and I took one photo to test the birds' reaction. They paid no attention. I took a series of shots, zooming in close for some and making sure that others showed distant features that identified our location. "This is good, right?" I said. "For protecting this area?"

"I think so," said Jason. "I mean, they're not exactly spotted owls, but they are critically endangered, and they need habitat in the migratory flyway."

We left the birds in peace and walked deeper into the woods. Speaking softly, Jason said, "I saw a gorgeous fox a few minutes ago."

I pulled up the array of photos on my camera and showed him.

"Oh, wow," he said, a huge grin on his face.

My nose started to run and I felt a sneeze coming on. I ripped my glove off and pulled a tissue from my pocket and sneezed into it. And again. "Oh, boy," I said.

"You want to go back?"

I lasted another twenty minutes, but my throat was getting seriously sore, my sinuses were pressing into my nerve centers, and my nose was running like a washerless faucet. I told Jason to stay if he wanted, but he started to lead the way out of the woods, saying, "Nah. I have a test at 10:30. I better go review."

We left the woods and walked in their shadow. The back of Alberta's house was visible, but the cattails along the far edge of the pond blocked our view of the street and my van. The wind wasn't as bad as it had been the previous day, but it was still blowing down the grass slope toward us at a good clip.

Jason raised his nose into the air just as I caught an odd odor, at least odd for this time of day. "Do you smell something," he asked.

"Barely," I said. I blew my nose and tried again. "Charcoal starter?"

"Weird," he said.

We passed the cattail barrier and had a clear view up the slope. The odor was stronger. "I wonder if someone spilled it or dumped..."

A loud *whoosh* interrupted me, and flames leaped toward the sky. Jason grabbed my arm and said, "What the..."

"Ohmygod," I yelled, and started to run up the slope. Alberta ran out her front door as I reached her driveway. I wasn't thinking, just running toward my van. The driver's-side doors looked as if they had sprouted wild red hair that was dancing in the wind.

"Stop her," yelled Alberta.

"Stop! Janet," yelled Jason, and then he had his arms clinched around me. He whirled us around, held tight as we came to a stop.

"My van!"

Alberta ran from her front porch and screeched, "Jay! He isn't with you, in the van?" She started to hobble-run along the far side of the vehicle toward the back hatch.

The flames died as quickly as they had appeared. I tried to answer Alberta, but my voice wouldn't work. I managed to rasp out, "Tell her no," and Jason did. Alberta stopped, came back to us, wheezing. She patted my arm again and I realized she was wearing slippers and no coat. "Go inside. You'll catch pneumodia." *Aaackkk, stuffy head talk.*

She ran back to the house, and from the door she yelled, "I'm calling the police!"

# FIFTY

"Take this," said Alberta as she set a glass of orange juice and a bottle of pills in front of me.

Jason came into the room and placed a couple of bags on the far end of the table. They looked vaguely familiar but I couldn't place them. I couldn't think. I could barely breathe.

"They don't seem to be damaged," Jason said.

"What?"

"Your purse and camera bag."

*Oh, that's why they look familiar.*

"Thanks." I reached for the orange juice, but my hand was shaking so much that I was afraid to pick it up. I pressed my arm to the top of the table to steady it and nudged the little bottle with my index finger. The name on the label was turned the other way, and it seemed like too much effort to turn the thing around. "What's this?"

Alberta stuck a straw into the orange juice and held the glass for me to take a sip. She said, "Antihistamine, decongestant. Take one, you'll feel better in a jiffy."

The juice tasted like summer. I took another long mouthful and signaled enough for the moment. "Thanks."

Alberta opened the little bottle and put a pill on the napkin in front of me.

"No, I can't, I have to drive."

Jason sat across from me and said, "I can take you home." He looked at his watch.

"You have a test," I said. The sugar in the juice was starting to work its magic. I could almost think.

"Not until ten-thirty," he said.

Alberta set mugs of coffee in front of us both and said, "No, dear, you won't have time. I'll drive her home."

"But my van is here. I don't need a ride."

Alberta and Jason exchanged a look, and another piece of my mind fell back into place. "How bad is it?"

"Most of the damage is outside," said Jason. "But I don't think you'll be driving it."

I sneezed into my elbow and excused myself. My legs felt unsteady but workable as I walked to the bathroom. I blew my nose and looked in the mirror. My hair stuck out like insanity itself, and my nose and eyes were clashing shades of red. *Ohmygod.* I thought about Jay, how he had begged to come with me, how I had considered bringing him for a walk after my photo shoot. For a moment I wasn't sure whether to sit down on the toilet or kneel in front of it. The feeling passed.

My next thought was of the threats to both me and Alberta. *The fire next time.* Who writes such an odd threat, and who carries it out? I couldn't even figure out how I earned the honor. Alberta, sure, that made sense. She had no doubt made enemies over the feral cats and her opposition to the condo development. But what had I done? All this over a few photos?

I splashed my face with cold water, patted it dry, and used some of Alberta's rose-scented hand lotion to take the fire out of my desiccated cheeks. The fragrance felt as good as the cool moisture.

Jason's voice brought me back into the kitchen. "... over by that gray house."

"What are you talking about?" I asked.

No one spoke for a moment, and then Jason said, "I saw someone walking away, on the other side of the street, by the big gray colonial."

Alberta got up and let her dogs in from the yard. Indy, whose photo I had taken many times, hopped into my lap and licked my chin, and I almost felt a layer of stress peel off and blow away. "Come on, you scalawags, off to your room." She had her family room set up for the dogs, with beds and toys and chewies. With Gypsy and the kittens in the house, the terriers had been spending a little more time there than usual. Judging by the way they scampered off, though, I didn't think they minded much.

Jason spoke again. "I've seen that guy before, when we were here for the teach-in."

"Jeans and a hoody pulled up, no face?" I asked.

"That's him."

"Or her," I said. "If it's the person I've seen, it could be either."

Jason seemed to consider his response. "I think it's a guy. Young. Moves easily but bad posture." He closed his eyes as if bringing up a memory. "Wide shoulders, big feet. Big hands when they're out of his pockets." He opened his eyes and found me staring at him. He shrugged, half smiled, and said, "Field biology. I've learned to see."

Alberta came back to the kitchen doorway and said, "Police are here."

Two uniformed officers stood by my van. "Wow," said the one whose name tag said Jim Fong. I wondered whether he was related to Angela Fong, director of Felicity Feline Rescue, but I deferred the question.

"Ma'am," said Smith. "This your vehicle?" Smith was African-American, close to six feet tall. I bet she hated being asked if she played basketball.

I gave her my information and told her what had happened. I started to tell her that Jason had seen the hoody character, but when I looked away from Smith, I discovered that Officer Fong had led Jason to their cruiser and was talking to him there. I guessed they wanted to get our stories independently. Smith turned to join them, but I said, "By the way, the old guy across the street sees a lot of what habbens around here. His lights were on this morning, so it bight be worth a visit," I said. "Sorry. I have a code. By nodes is stuffed up." Smith, I discovered, did know how to smile.

Half an hour later they had wrapped it up and a tow truck had loaded up my poor singed van and hauled it off to the dealer to wait for the insurance adjuster, and Alberta and I were playing with the kittens while Gypsy watched and purred from a rocking chair.

"Just what I deeded," I said.

"What do you mean?" asked Alberta, teasing the kitties with a fabric mouse on a string.

"I deed my van," I said, and sniffed. "I don't deed it burned up."

She started to laugh. "I'm so wound up in this land thing, you know, the woods and wetlands, that I thought you were talking about the deed to your car." She put the teaser wand away and the kittens began to wrestle. "I heard 'deed,' but you meant 'need.'"

"That's what I said. Deed. Ndeed. Stupid code."

I felt tiny needles through my jeans, and then the little gray tabby was in my lap, looking at me. She climbed up my sweatshirt until she was right under my chin. I put a hand under her rear end, and stroke her little cheek. "Hello," I said. "I shouldn't tell you this, but I think about you a lot." I looked up and found Alberta watching us with a funny little half grin on her face. "Have you found homes for all of them?"

"Oh, I think so." The smile got even stranger.

"What?" I asked, pressing the kitten into my lips and feeling the little body relax in my hands.

"Homer is taking the little calico. You knew that." She shook her head, smiling. "He's completely bonkers about that little cat. You know he comes every day to see her?"

I tucked the kitten up under my throat and felt her breathe.

"You friend is taking the black one."

"What friend?"

"Goldie."

"Ha! So she listened to me for once," I said, and the tabby girl shifted. I tucked her into the crook of my elbow.

"I think that one has a home, although the person who wants her hasn't committed yet." The kitten sighed and I felt a little twist somewhere in my chest.

"I don't dough wy people can't cobbit," I said, and my eyes started to water at the sound of my own voice. I cupped my hand over the little gray body and felt her heart beat through my fingertips.

"It is a mystery," said Alberta.

"If that person doesn't want her, I do," I said, surprising myself but knowing immediately that it was true.

"About time you said something," said Alberta. I looked at her and we both started to laugh, which made my nose run. I grabbed a tissue from my pocket and managed to blow my nose one-handed. I looked at my sleeping kitten and said, "Well, Uncle Leo and Uncle Jay are in for a surprise."

Alberta's phone rang. I put the kitten on the cushion where her brother and sister had fallen asleep and followed Alberta to the kitchen. She looked at me and spoke into the phone. "No, she's fine... No, they towed it... I'm driving her home now... I'll tell her." She hung up and said, "Homer. He said to tell you he'll call you later. He has some news about the murder investigation."

*Great*, I thought, not sure I wanted any more news today.

# FIFTY-ONE

FRIDAY WAS A WASH, mostly. I never left the house except to pick up the backyard and throw the tennis ball for Jay a few times. I had planned to get groceries and run a few other errands, but I decided to be stingy and keep my cold all to myself. Tom called around ten and invited me to go to his place for lunch with him and Tommy, but I had to excuse myself every two minutes to sneeze or "blow by nodes" and we rescheduled for dinner on Sunday, after the cat show. Tom promised to be there to see Leo run. As the incidental teammate, I took no offense. "I just hope I can breathe to run," I had said, and Tom assured me that if I rested and took my Echinacea I'd be fine by morning. I told him about my van, and he offered to drive me and Leo to the show the next day, but I assured him that the rental car was adequate.

"So tell me about the puppies," I said. I knew he hadn't exhausted the topic the previous night. I hadn't heard him so excited since Drake finished his Master Hunter title. "Aqua," he said, calling one puppy not by a name, since she didn't have one yet, but by the color of her rickrack collar, "has a really nice shoulder and turn of stifle," meaning the angles formed by the bones in the shoulder and knee joints. Good structure goes a long way to keep a dog sound throughout its life, especially if it's jumping and retrieving. "But she's not as people-oriented as Pink. And Purple brought back every toy I threw, even the big duck she had to drag."

Tom waited while I sneezed. "Pink is really nice, too. Great structure." He paused, and I knew he was remembering every detail. "I'll send you the link to the latest pictures," he said, and then his tone became softer, less analytical. "Pink followed me all around the yard without even being coaxed." The smile in his voice told me that Pink was his puppy, but I didn't say a word. "It's going to be a tough choice, and of course they have to pass their eye exams in two weeks." They would be screened for inherited eye disease, and an issue that might not be a problem for a family pet would be a nonstarter for a competition dog. "So she can come home in mid-December."

"I'll mark my calendar." *If we're still speaking by then.*

We talked a few more minutes, but with Tommy there it wasn't the right time to ask about his travel plans. I was starting to wonder whether Goldie was right. Had I imagined something I hadn't actually heard? *No, I heard what I heard.* Right then I heard a man's voice in the background. I knew Tom wanted to spend time with his son, so I suggested we talk later. I didn't tell him about my kitten—my kitten! I didn't want to steal his thunder, but smiled at my little furry secret. I had a baby animal on the way, too.

After I hung up, I hauled out my makeshift feline agility obstacles. I dragged the coffee table into the kitchen and shoved the couch, chairs, and end tables back against the bookcases that lined the walls, and set up a course of sorts in the living room. After the fifth time I had to tell Jay to get out of the way, I shut him into the bedroom. Leo supervised from the top of a low bookcase, leaning toward me and talking the whole time.

"Mrrowwwwlllll!"

"Good thing I don't know what you're saying, Catman," I said, and he chirped.

We had a terrific session, and lack of practice time didn't seem to have hurt. I offered a final squeeze of fish paste, and while Leo attacked it with his quick little tongue, I said, "I hope you don't mind a little sister, Leo *mio*." I ran a hand from the top of his head to his tail, and said, "You'll always be my best boy cat."

I don't know whether it was the fish paste or the activity, but by the time I got the furniture back in place, I was done in. I let Jay out of the bedroom and sat down on the couch to regroup. "Should we go back to bed, or have some lunch?" I asked.

"Lunch, definitely." At least that's what I assume Jay would have said had he not already run into the kitchen. The back door banged open, and I shot up from the couch, thinking I hadn't closed it completely. Then a voice said, "Soup's on!"

"Wow, that was magical," I said.

Goldie was standing by my stove, a soup pot in her hands and a deep, zippered canvas tote dangling from her wrist. "I am magical," she laughed, setting the pot on the stove and turning the burner to medium.

"So I hear," I said. I lifted the lid and sniffed. "What is it?"

"What's it smell like?"

"Doe idea," I said, taking her coat from her.

"Poor baby," Goldie said when I got back from the closet. "Some soup and a fresh baguette will set you straight." Leo hopped onto the counter to inspect the canvas tote, and Goldie lifted him down and said, "Never you mind, Mr. Leo."

Leo licked his paw, flicked it, and strolled away, tail high, as if to say, "Eh, who cares?"

Jay, who had been watching the same canvas tote very carefully, as if it might open itself, spun around and knocked me sideways as he shot out of the kitchen. "Holy …," I said. The doorbell rang and I had a sneezing fit all at the same time. I grabbed a paper towel, wincing when it touched my sore nose and looking around for my box of tissue.

"I'll see who it is," said Goldie, already half way to the door.

No tissue. I scurried to the bedroom, grabbed the box from my night table, and ducked into the bathroom, where I splashed warm water on my face. It helped a little. I went back to the kitchen.

"Nice jammies," said Hutchinson. I'd forgotten what I was wearing, and anyway, I figured the bell was a delivery. "You look awful."

"Gee, thanks, Hutch. Anything else while you're on a roll?"

His mouth twitched, and he said, "Yeah. Congratulations." I raised my eyebrows at him. He looked at Goldie and back at me. "We could be the Three Little Kittens Club."

I laughed. "Sure. We could get t-shirts and everything."

"Wait. What?" said Goldie.

"Janet's adopting the little gray kitty," said Hutchinson.

"Oh, that's wonderful!" Goldie clapped her hands and laughed. "Why didn't you tell me?"

"I just found out myself," I said. "And by the way, why didn't you tell me about the black kitten?"

She dished up soup for all of us, set the thick crusty loaf on a plate, and poured olive oil and balsamic with herbs into three saucers.

"Wow," said Hutchinson. "What else do you have in that rucksack?"

"Just don't ask her about those herbs in the oil," I said, dipping a hunk of bread.

Hutchinson hesitated mid-dip, then said, "Oh, what the hell," and we all dipped and slurped without speaking for a couple of minutes. Then he wiped his mouth, patted his belly, and said, "So, I have some news." Goldie refilled his soup bowl while he spoke. "I told you they found blood on that table thing, right?"

"The pause table, yes."

"It's not canine. It was human, and the same blood type as Rasmussen. They're waiting for DNA, which will be a while. The lab is backed up."

"Okay." It didn't make sense. No one picked up the pause table to whack the guy. "So, did he fall?"

Hutchinson pursed his lips, nodded, and pointed at me. "He apparently suffered three blows to the head. Two of them were with a sharp instrument of some sort. And the blood on that broken scooper thing they found also matches his blood type."

I closed my eyes and mumbled, "Pooper scooper."

"Yeah, that thing."

*Oh, Giselle, what have you done*, I thought.

"So they found Giselle's prints on the scooper, but..." Hutchinson leaned on his arms on the table, "there were a lot of other prints, too, including..." He waited until I looked at him to finish. "...a match to whoever left that poster board on your car. They pulled a print from the duct tape."

"You saved that?" I hadn't thought about it at the time, or paid attention. I just wanted the crap off my windshield.

"Of course," said Hutchinson, and then he leaned back and grinned. "But the pooper-scooper injuries didn't kill him. They bled a lot, but that's about it."

"You said there was another weapon," said Goldie.

"Not exactly a weapon. A heavy, sharp edge. And they found tiny splinters in that wound. They match the plywood in the, what do you call it? The pause table. At least at first glance. And when that hit him, or he hit it, it fractured his skull."

"But how did he get inside the tunnel?" I asked.

"They said he could have walked or crawled a long way. He was probably disoriented, maybe scared. Maybe he crawled in there to hide."

My head felt like a cotton candy maker, spinning with light fluffy stuff for brains.

"Now we just have to figure out how it all happened," said Hutchinson. He pushed his chair back as if he might be leaving.

"And about your van," he said. "I checked on that. The old man across the street saw someone in front of Alberta's place just before the fire. Fong thinks the guy might know who it was, but he's scared to say."

"Can't say I blame him," I said, "especially if it's the same person who's been vandalizing Alberta's place." Which it had to be, since the message to her as well as to me was "the fire next time."

Hutchinson stood up. "Stay there. Get some rest." The front door opened, and he called, "Hey, I'm going to the cat show this weekend. See you there!"

# FIFTY-TWO

As Scarlett O'Hara knew very well, tomorrow is another day, and I was a new woman after sleeping the rest of Friday afternoon and, after a grilled cheese sandwich and more hot liquids, another ten hours before morning.

As an experienced obedience and agility dog, Jay knew something was afoot, and I felt guilty, knowing the rude awakening he was about to get. I bundled up and took him outdoors for a rousing game of tennis ball with some obedience commands thrown in for mental exercise. When we went in, I sat down with coffee and cereal and explained to him that this was Leo's weekend. I'm pretty sure he understood, and he wasn't buying it. I loaded Leo into his carrier, gave Jay an enormous carrot, and left.

Leo was scheduled for double duty. He would make his competitive debut in the agility arena, and spend some time greeting people at Alberta's TNR information booth. He wasn't feral and never had been, but he was very social, and, as a stray, he could easily have ended up homeless. Or worse. Besides, he was friendly.

Alberta had saved me a seat, and a spot under the table for Leo's carrier.

"The display looks terrific," I said, and it did. Sally Foster had set up a twenty-four-inch all-in-one computer to run a loop of informational videos interspersed with awww-inspiring photos and videos. Alberta had hung a beautiful new banner for "Save-the-Cats of Aspen Grove," and another volunteer had a give-away basket of kitty coloring and sticker books flanked by a stuffed cat wearing a "Help Yourself, Help Us" sign.

By the time I tucked Leo's carrier under the table, stowed my gear, and said my hellos, I had about half an hour until Leo's agility class. I peeked under the table to see if Leo was reacting at all to all the sensory input. He had his eyes closed and his paws tucked up under his chest.

"Is Leon doing okay?" Sally Foster whispered, leaning in beside me for a peek.

"Leo," I said. "He appears to be meditating."

Knowing my cat was relaxed, I walked to the far end of the arena to check out the agility enclosure. It was the same set up we had used for the demonstration at the Dog Dayz canine trial the week before, so no surprises there. A few competitors and spectators had already staked out their spots around the enclosure, but I didn't see anyone I knew at first. Then I noticed what appeared to be an enormous long-haired tabby standing on his hind legs and waving at me. For a split second I wondered whether the drugs I had taken to suppress my lingering cold symptoms were making me hallucinate. Or maybe Goldie really had put something in the soup? I leaned forward and squinted, and the waving cat morphed into Jared

Spenser and Moose, his huge Maine Coon. I waved back, checked in with the gate keeper, and made a pit stop.

When I got back to the TNR table, Hutchinson was there talking to Alberta, a big cardboard box in his arms, It was stuffed to the rim with, well, I wasn't sure what all was in it. "What's all that?"

"Kitten supplies."

Alberta smiled at me and winked, then asked Hutchinson to show us. Hutchinson emptied the box and then began to reload it, starting with the big items. "Here's her carrier. She'll need it to go to the vet and everything. And these are her beds."

"Three beds?"

He stared at Alberta as if she'd lost her mind. "Yeah. For the living room, bedroom, and my office." Alberta elbowed me. "Food and water bowls. This, just for now." He held up an elegant little beaded pink collar that must have cost a bundle and might fit her for a week. "Kitten food." He'd picked a top-of-the-line food, I'd give him that. He showed us a couple of books, and said "I'm reading *The Complete Idiot's Guide to Getting and Owning a Cat* on my e-reader right now, and that's helping me figure this out." He nodded at us, so I nodded back. Positive reinforcement is a good thing. "And a few toys." I counted seventeen of them as he dropped them into the box. "That's all I got. What else does she need?"

Alberta patted him on the arm and said, "Nothing, dear. You'll both do just fine."

Hutchinson wanted to watch Leo in agility, so we stashed the kitten's hope chest under the table. I opened my carrier and Leo stepped out and stretched, then stood while I slipped his harness on. I picked him up and he shoved his face into mine in a sort of combo nose-bump-and-cheek-rub maneuver. "You could maybe bring his carrier and my chair?" I pointed at my folding nylon chair, still in its sheath.

We found a good spot near the agility arena, and Hutchinson grabbed a chair for himself and sat next to me. "This is fun," he said. "I had no idea there even was such a thing as a cat show until last week. I watched some of the judging." He shook his head and laughed. "I can't believe the cats put up with all that lifting and stretching and stuff."

"People just don't give cats enough credit, and most cats aren't socialized like they could be," I said.

"Yeah. Look at that one," he said, pointing at Moose, who was draped over Jared's shoulder. "That's the biggest cat I've ever seen."

I couldn't argue with that.

Then Hutchinson changed subjects. "I talked to Fong this morning. He found that kid, the one that's been following you around."

"He did?" I blew my nose, hoping that Fong had shaken the snot out the kid when he found him.

"The neighbor, the old guy, finally said he thought it was a neighbor kid. Pointed them to the house."

"Did they find out why he's been watching me?"

"Claims he was just going for walks," said Hutchinson. "Just happened to see you around here and there. But," Hutchinson lowered his voice, "the kid's been in trouble before. Small stuff. Mostly."

"Mostly?" *Like what, other than stalking women?*

"He was accused of setting a fire in a neighbor's tool shed last year."

That made me stare at Hutchinson. "Did he torch my van?"

Hutchinson shrugged. "Fong said they didn't find any evidence. He's trying to get a search warrant for the kid's house, but they don't have a lot of cause, so I don't know."

"Well, who is he?"

"Name's Rudy Sweetwater."

I must have reacted without knowing it, because Hutchinson said, "You know him?"

"Not really," I said, "but I've seen him around. His mother does agility." I thought about sullen Rudy waiting for his mother at Dog Dayz and the agility trial and wondered whether she was keeping him close because he'd been in trouble. People were moving around in the arena and I didn't want to ruin the day with any more talk of ugly things, so I said, "They're starting."

# FIFTY-THREE

THE FIRST CLASS WAS for us beginners, and the first cat in was Sue O'Brien's Abyssinian, Dessie. I hoped for Sue's sake that they had a better run than they did at the demo the week before. Sue set the lithe little cat down and waved a pink feather teaser to get her attention, but Dessie's wide eyes were flicking up, left, down, left, right. Everywhere but at the teaser. Her tail lashed the start platform like a live electrical wire, and I held my breath, expecting her to run for it.

"She doesn't look very happy," said Hutchinson.

"Which one?" I asked, looking at Sue's tight lips and narrowed eyes.

Sue waved the teaser wand at her cat. The feathers flew back and forth at the end of the cord, and on the second swing they caught Dessie in the back of the head. I knew it was no more than a tickle, but the tawny little body flipped around and Dessie let out a scream that could clot blood. Leo stood up and stared toward the arena, and I hugged him to my body and whispered, "It's ok, she's just a little upset."

Dessie's screech turned into a low, rippling growl and she swiped at the feathers, catching them in her fist and ripping them apart. Dave O'Brien, Sue's husband, stepped up to the outside of the arena and yelled, "Just get her out of there!" and Sue screeched back, "I told you this would happen!" Dessie leaped into the air and caught the arena netting six inches in front of Dave's face. She laid her ears back and hissed at him.

One of the stewards appeared behind Sue. She was holding Dessie's carrier, and in a calm voice she said, "Everyone be quiet and back away from her." She pulled Sue backward a few steps and then signaled Dave to retreat. He did. The steward crept past Dessie, murmuring, "Good kitty, good girl, everything's fine, you don't have to do this if you don't want to." The cat, still clinging to the netting, grew quiet and turned her head to watch the woman. Leo snuggled into my lap but he was watching, too. The steward set Dessie's carrier on the floor and took a tiny can of cat food from her pocket. She popped the top off and showed it to Dessie. "Look what I have. Mmmm. Yummy." She set the can in the carrier, stepped back, and knelt, still talking softly. "Good kitty. Come on, kitty kitty kitty."

Dessie dropped to the floor. The arena skirting blocked her from our view until she approached the carrier. She stopped and looked at the steward, then disappeared inside. The steward latched the door and removed Dessie and her distraught owner from the ring.

"Wow, who's that, the cat whisperer?" asked Hutchinson.

"Just another crazy cat lady who knows what she's doing," I said, hoping that Sue and Dave would have the sense to realize that Dessie didn't want to be an agility cat, at least not at public events.

The rest of the class ran smoothly for the most part. Jared and Moose had another inspiring run, which finished Moose's title. Next up was a lovely little gray-and-white cat. Hutchinson said, "She's so cute!" and he was right. She had the face of an angel, albeit a playful angel. The announcer introduced her as Mackenzie. She was also full of p & v, and barely waited for Lisa Chin, her owner to get in position before she zoomed up and down the steps and over the first jump. Their run went off almost without a hitch, and would have been perfect if the little speed-demon hadn't caught the feathers being used to entice her onward. There was a short tug session, and she finished the course in style and well under time. Lisa's husband, Matt, was standing beside me and could hardly contain himself when she finished with a nearly perfect run.

Next up was a stunning marble Bengal named, appropriately, Shere Khan. "I think we're up soon," I told Hutchinson, and I carried Leo to the ready area. "Okay, Catman, we're just going for the fun, right?" We were in sooner than expected, as Shere Khan lay down after the second jump and refused to move.

Leo was relaxed in my arms, but was looking at something across the room. Tom. I turned to block Leo's view, but it was too late. "Mmrroowwlllll!" He squirmed until his front paws rested on my shoulder, and let out a series of rolling chirps. *Oh, boy,* I thought, *so much for a nice run.*

But Leo surprised me. As soon as I set him down at the start line, he gathered himself and watched me. As always, he "ran like a dog," as someone had said at the demonstration the previous week, meaning that he didn't need a lure. He ran clean and true and was just barely under Mackenzie's time. He got a big spoonful of stinky fish paste when we left the arena.

Hutchinson and Tom met us as we came back toward the spectator area. "Atta boy, Leo, my man," said Tom, leaning in to give Leo a kiss. Then he gave me one, and I said, "Your priorities are not lost on me, you know."

Tom winked at me.

"Wow, that was great," said Hutchinson. "You think I could do that with Amy?"

"Amy?" I asked.

"My kitty. That's her name."

"Good name, Hutch," I said, and it may have been the lighting, but I think the man blushed.

They called us back to the arena to announce the qualifiers, the cats who earned legs toward their titles, and the class placements. You would have thought I'd never competed in anything before, the way my leg muscles quivered. Third place! Leo got third place! Granted, there were only five entries and two didn't finish the course. *Details, details*, I thought, burying my nose in orange fur and chanting "Leo *mio*." Mackenzie came away with second place and her new title, and Moose took top honors, which included a big blue ribbon and a catnip mouse. Jared's face looked like mine felt, with its big goofy grin.

Tom walked me back to Alberta's display and then went off to find us some coffee, and I sat down and set Leo on the table, where I dished up another helping of fish paste. He stretched out to await his admirers, who didn't take long to arrive. He accepted petting from everyone, big and small, but was particularly lovely to the children who came to see him. Jay visits the library so that children can read to him once a week, and I wondered whether Leo might not like to be a library cat every once in a while.

"Here you go," said Tom, setting a little cardboard carrier in front of me. It held coffee, pretzels, and a donut. "They don't have much over there," he said.

I sipped the coffee, expecting it to be bitter or watery. "That's pretty good," I said, then, "I'm not going to stay too long. Maybe we could go grab a bite somewhere?" *Maybe we can finally have that little talk of ours?*

"I would, but I promised Tommy I'd help him with some shopping," he said. "Actually, he'd probably rather do it alone, but I don't get to spend much time with him and he's leaving Monday."

I nibbled the salt off a pretzel. I didn't want him to see my disappointment, which was a silly feeling that I attribute to cold medicine and stress. "No, you need to do that. We'll catch up later." A family with three little boys appeared at the table, and Leo greeted them with a loud "Meoww!"

"I'll call you later," said Tom, and poof! He was gone.

Leo finally seemed to have had enough about twenty minutes later when he climbed off the table and into my lap. I wondered whether he needed a litter box, but that didn't seem to be a pressing concern. It was past noon, though, and my head was beginning to go into a cold-and-meds-induced fog. "Time to go home, Catman," I said, and I set him in front of his carrier. He went straight in and curled into a ball on his fleece cushion. I lifted the whole shebang onto the table and went for my coat. I was just pulling my hat from the pocket when a shrill voice slammed into my ear drum.

"Why don't you show pictures of all the birds they kill?"

I turned to look at the other end of the table. A white-haired couple stood shoulder to shoulder across from Alberta and Sally.

They wore matching yellow jackets and sour pusses. The man, his silvery hair standing up like a cockscomb, waved a scolding finger in Alberta's general direction.

"Sir, studies show . . ."

"Cats are an invasive species," screeched the woman. "They kill a lot of wildlife."

"They do kill a lot of rodents, it's true. Sometimes they kill birds, although not as often as people think." I marveled at Sally's calm voice, and thought *she's had this conversation before.* "We would prefer that cats live indoors, but many feral cats won't live indoors, and in any case, there just aren't homes for them all. Trap-neuter-release is a humane alternative."

"Humane? *Humane?*" bellowed the man. He turned slightly toward me and I saw the writing on his t-shirt. 'Callaway' over a stylized V. That was the brand of golf ball that broke Alberta's window.

"So you think killing the cats would be the more humane solution?" asked Alberta, and I half expected her to leap over the table and sock him one.

"Oh, no, no, of course not," said the woman. "We love all ani . . ."

"Yes, if necessary! They don't belong in the wild, killing songbirds," said the man.

"By that reasoning we should also eliminate hawks and owls and a whole slew of other birds, don't you think?"

"You're just trying to confuse the issue!" The hand and arm attached to the man's accusing finger were expanding their range, and getting dangerously close to the computer screen on which the offending cat videos were playing.

Sally gripped the top of the computer with one hand and held the other palm-out toward the couple. "Please be careful. This is an expensive ..."

"Expensive be damned!" he yelled. His hand moved to his left and started to swing backhanded toward the screen.

# FIFTY-FOUR

THE ANGRY BIRDER SEEMED bent on smashing the back of his fist into the computer. I set my teeth and waited for the crash, too far away and too surprised to try to stop it. As I watched, long fingers landed like talons, closing over the man's wrist and spinning him away from the electronics. Sally wrapped her arms protectively around the back of the computer and glared at the man.

"Let's all calm down here, shall we?" Hutchinson still had a grip on the man's wrist, but his voice was calm. "Sir, I'd like to release your arm but I want to know that you have control of yourself."

The older man sputtered and shook himself, but nodded. "Yeah, yeah, okay. I was just..."

"Harry, let's just go now." Harry's wife had backed away from the table and her husband and stood slightly hunched, working her purse strap through her fingers and back again.

Harry rubbed his wrist where Hutchinson had grabbed it and glanced at his wife, then turned and looked at Sally. "I just don't like those cats," he said.

"Yes, I get that," said Sally. She had stopped hugging the computer, but still had her hand on the top edge.

Harry puffed out his chest, patted down his white cockscomb, said, "Let's go, Rita," and marched off. Rita hugged her purse to her chest and fell into step behind him.

"You know them?" I asked Sally.

"They live in The Rapids," she said. "Hard to take their concern for the birds seriously. Last year they wanted to poison the pigeons that were pooping on the copper cupola on the clubhouse."

"Where's Alberta?" asked Hutchinson.

"I don't …," I turned away from Sally and looked at Hutchinson. "Why? What's happened?"

"Little problem at her place," he said.

"What?" It came out like a croak. "Her dogs! Gypsy and the kittens!"

Hutchinson shook his head and said, "No, no, sorry, not her house. The cat place. Officers are on the scene." I grabbed the back of the chair for balance, and Hutchinson said, "Really. Fong is there. It's just … more vandalism …" He stopped as Alberta walked up.

"What's going on?" she asked.

"Someone went after the cat stuff again."

"What stuff?" I asked. "They already trashed it. What's left to damage?"

"Oh, no," said Sally. "We had new wood delivered this morning."

"And straw," said Alberta. "I ordered straw, too." She smiled uncertainly at a couple of women who had stopped to look at her display, and spoke to Hutchinson. "Do I need to go now? Is there anything … We're planning to shut down in another hour or … By the time I'd get there …"

There wasn't anything I could do to help there, so I interrupted and told Alberta to call me when she knew more. I tucked Leo's ribbons into my tote, picked up his carrier, and headed home. Ninety minutes later some hot soup and grilled cheese had worked their magic, and I was bundled up in sweats and my blue afghan with Jay tucked in between me and the back of the couch. Sleep crooked her finger at me, but the telephones said no.

First, my cell phone. It was brother Bill, calling from Shadetree Retirement. He didn't even complain about having to assume Mom duty. In fact, he had been the one to insist that I not take my cold to share with the residents. "She's doing pretty well," he said. "They're trying to keep a handle on her water intake so we don't have a repeat."

"That's good," I said. The land line rang and I got up to look at the caller ID. Alberta. I went back to Bill. "And how is she, you know..."

"Lucid, but, wait a second while I find a more private... okay, so, Janet, have you talked to her or her friend Anthony lately?"

"I saw them at the hospital. Why?"

"Well, they're engaged."

"In what?"

"To be married!" Bill laughed, and said, "They just told me. Norm already knew, but they asked him to keep quiet."

"Wow." That was about as far as I could wrap my brain around the news.

"I think it's great. What the hell. Who am I to stand in the way of anyone's marriage?" He had a point, especially considering that he and Norm couldn't marry in their state of residence. Yet.

When we had wrapped that up, I called Alberta. She said the police had finished and she and a couple of people were starting to salvage what they could and clean up the rest. "At least the wind has died down," she said. I ignored her protests and said I'd be there shortly to help. I put my two small pet carriers in the car in case they needed them for kitty shelters, added a layer under my sweat-shirt, and cranked up my rental car.

Alberta was alone when I got there, dragging broken two-by-fours into piles arranged by length. "I think we'll be able to use most of the wood," she said.

"Where are your volunteers?" I asked. "And I thought you said you got more straw?" I had envisioned another scene of broken bales and straw blown hither and yon.

She gestured toward maybe twenty straw bales stacked against the back of the club house and said, "You know, people have things to do." She smiled. "A couple of people were here for a little while." *Must have been a minuscule while*, I thought, knowing that Alberta couldn't have been home very long. "And here comes someone now," she added, pointing past me with her chin.

Hutchinson was pulling on work gloves as he came around the corner of the building and surveyed the latest damage. He glowered at the smashed boards, growled something I couldn't make out, and began grabbing, swinging, and pitching boards with a bit more emotion than the job really warranted. Alberta and I exchanged raised-eyebrow looks and stayed out of his way. Finally, he stopped, slapped his gloved palms together and said, "Okay, who do you think is doing this?"

Alberta took a step back from him and said, "For heaven's sake, I don't know!"

Hutchinson softened. "No, I know, I didn't mean you did. I'm just … if I catch the a …, er, jerk who's doing this …"

We all went back to gathering the final lengths of wood, and Alberta suggested we go warm up for a few minutes and come back with a couple of rakes to finish up. She got no argument from me. I wasn't really cold, but I could stand to visit the bathroom after all that liquid lunch and time out here. As we walked toward the slope to Alberta's driveway, we saw someone dragging a little red wagon loaded with bags of something. Cat food?

"I haven't seen a sign of a cat since we got here," I said.

Hutchinson said, "They hid in the bushes by the building, and in the plants along the fence, last time. And I guess under people's decks and sheds."

"They'll come out for dinner," said Alberta.

The approaching wagon squeaked and clanked over the ground, uneven now from heaving after a few nights of freezing temperatures, and the figure pulling it looked up. "Giselle," I said.

Alberta suggested she leave the wagon and join us for a few minutes, so she fell into step with the group. "I didn't do it, you know." Her lower lip stuck out and her arms folded across her chest. She glanced at Hutchinson. He nodded at her but didn't say anything, so Giselle said, "A lot of people touched that pooper-scooper."

A police cruiser drove slowly by, and Hutchinson waved. "They're still looking for that kid, that Rudy Sweetwater."

Hutchinson's words registered as if in the background. I was remembering again Giselle's story about hitting something with the pooper-scooper, hitting over and over and over. What was it she had said? "It was like a red veil fell over me." I had to ask.

"Giselle, do you remember telling me about hitting something, not being able to stop?" She stared at me. "What were you hitting?"

Her eyes went wide and she seemed to have trouble finding her voice. Finally she said, "The ground. I was picking up after Precious, and I was so angry, and I called him a piece of shit, I mean, Rasmussen, not Precious, and then instead of picking up the poop I hit it, and then I just kept hitting it, and first I heard the handle crack and my arms were tingling and I just..." She took a long breath, and her voice was closer to a normal tone when she spoke again. "I felt a lot better then."

"So you threw it away?"

"Huh? No, it was just cracked. I figured Jorge would fix it when he found it. I just leaned it against the garbage can."

I believed her. I had no idea whether Hutchinson did, but he was kind enough to say, "Keep the faith. We'll figure it out."

We spent about ten minutes warming up with coffee and chocolate chip cookies. My sinuses felt a lot better after I blew my nose. We all had a quick peek at the kittens, and promised to come back for a little playtime before we left. I stepped out onto Alberta's deck to wait for the others. I pulled my phone out and stared at it, burning to hear Tom's voice, but he needed this time with his son and he had said he would call later. I put it back in my pocket.

A light breeze was breaking through the earlier stillness, and with it came the faint scent of something burning. Probably leaves, although it was late in the season and I wasn't sure a neighborhood like The Rapids of Aspen Grove would allow burning. Maybe a fireplace, or drift from beyond the subdivision. I thought I saw something moving near the clubhouse. A large black dog, maybe? I got just a glimpse before it disappeared behind the building.

Another thread of air brought a stronger trace of smoke and a hint of charcoal starter. For a split second I didn't think much of it, but smells are memory triggers and my memory jumped to the image of flames leaping over the top of my van, and I suddenly felt very cold in spite of my many layers.

I went back inside to see if they were about ready. We were, as my film professor used to say, burning daylight. Hutchinson was on the phone and mouthed, "Just a minute." Alberta said Giselle was in the bathroom and she'd wait for her. I went out the back door and stepped off the deck. A flock of perhaps thirty starlings flushed from a pair of pin oaks off to my right, and I heard an oddly familiar sound that I couldn't place. A sort of *whoosh*.

# FIFTY-FIVE

THE GATE AT THE side of Alberta's house was shaded by an arbor and the latch had never thawed from the overnight freeze. I kicked the gate free, and had to clear the ice that dropped into the latch mechanism before I could re-latch it. I hadn't noticed how slick the downward slope was earlier. The grass crunched beneath my boots, and the inside of my nose pinched. *Getting colder*, I thought. The breeze was mostly not there, just a whisper now and then from somewhere just left of my trajectory. A thin gray line rose from the back of the clubhouse, as if someone had run a giant pencil through the steely sky.

For a moment I wondered whether I could sneak into the club house and sit by the fireplace for a few minutes. I pictured myself ensconced in a large leather club chair, feet on a matching hassock, a book in one hand and hot brandy in the other. *You gotta lay off those cold pills,* my little voice said. I walked a tad faster, gloved hand in my pockets and shoulders hunched. It was definitely getting colder.

As I passed the sprawl of shrubbery at the end of the clubhouse, the breeze caught me full in the face and the dual scents it carried nearly bowled me over. Smoke. The throat-clutch of petroleum distillates. As I rounded the clubhouse, a wave of heat hit my face and I jittered to a stop. I sensed movement to my right, but the scene to my left had my full attention. The straw bales along the back of the clubhouse were topped by a thin line of flames that grew taller as I watched, rising like living things from the dry line of fuel beneath them.

The stink of charcoal lighter fluid hit me with the double whammy of instant migraine and wrenching nausea. At first I thought it came from the straw bales, but knew it shouldn't be so strong since it was already burning. Then I heard another *whoosh*, closer and louder this time, followed by a long wail that sent a needle of fear straight to my heart. I spun around.

Two more fires. The broken two-by-fours we had stacked earlier were blanketed by a sheet of blue and orange flame. Just beyond them another fire seemed to dance on the air a few feet above the ground. It moved this way, then the other, so bright against the background of dark, distant trees that at first I couldn't make out anything but the fire itself.

And then it started to scream.

Someone—or something—was on fire. I started to run, pulling my coat off and screaming, "Lie down! Lie down and roll!" The screaming figure spun around, and I saw that for the moment it was just a sleeve on fire. "Lie down!" I was almost there, my coat held in front of me to wrap around that terrible arm and smother the fire. Thirty feet and closing.

Suddenly there were voices everywhere. The screaming figure in front of me. Voices behind me yelling, "Don't run!" and "Roll on the ground!" and "Oh my God!" A police cruiser slammed over the curb and onto the far end of the wide stretch of lawn behind the clubhouse. It spun sideways into a stop and two officers jumped out and ran. One of them carried a blanket, the other something red. *Fire extinguisher.*

"Get it off me!" The voice came out like a rusted hinge. Its owner dropped to the grass, pulling the zipper open on the burning jacket. The first cop arrived, his own jacket in his hands. He used it to smother the flames, and the screaming turned into a moan. The police officer pulled his own jacket away, looked at the charred sleeve, and asked, "Are you burned?"

"It hurts!" said a voice I thought I knew, although the police officer blocked my view of its owner.

"Help us here!" I spun toward the voice and froze for a moment. The straw bales were engulfed in flames, and burning bits of straw rose here and there on the breeze. Then a few more, and the whole thing seemed to take on a life of its own. The flames changed shape, growing longer, hungrier. They found no fuel in the limestone wall of the clubhouse, so they reached for the roof. More burning bits rose and landed like so many matches. Tiny flames began to appear here and there on the roof.

New screeching spun me back around. The sounds coming from the figure on the ground had changed. The pure terror was gone, replaced by raw rage and something like despair. Someone else was screaming, too, off to the side. Then I realized I knew those faces, the screaming woman and the one holding her back. Candace

Sweetwater, her face twisted and wet, trying to free herself from Sally Foster's embrace.

Sally let her go, and Candace ran to the little group on the ground. Behind me, I heard more yelling, and turned to see a crowd of people emerging around the side of the clubhouse. They must be evacuating the place through the front door, and the more curious members came to see what was happening. Hutchinson sprayed the straw bales with an extinguisher. It helped for a moment, but ran out of juice before the fire was out.

"Get back!" I yelled, and when he looked at me I pointed to the roof. The near edge was on fire now, and burning leaves were beginning to rain down from the gutters.

Sirens. Lots of them. A fire truck screeched to a stop by the hydrant at the street and a half-dozen firefighters got to work. Two more police cruisers arrived, and an ambulance.

I stepped closer to the group. Candace Sweetwater knelt beside Jim Fong, the police officer who had rolled her son in a blanket. Someone had pulled the boy's ever-present hoody partway off, exposing his face, which seemed to be cycling through a kaleidoscope of emotions. Candace reached to touch him, and Rudy Sweetwater screamed again.

"Don't you touch me!"

"But why? Why, Rudy?" Candace's voice was thin, as if the life had been pinched out of it.

"You know why!" Rudy let out another scream as Jim Fong's partner made room for the EMT, then glared at his mother, the look made demonic by the flames reflected in his eyes.

Candace sobbed.

The EMT tried to open Rudy's mouth to check his airways, but the boy waved him off. "It's just my arm!" Then he looked at his mother and screeched, "I hate you! You should have taken his money when you had the cha..." His words ended in a stream of four-letter words as the EMTs unwrapped the jacket to see Rudy's arm.

Alberta pressed up against me and we turned to watch the firefighters. They had all but extinguished the fire, and I heard the guy who seemed to be in charge tell a couple of them to go inside and check for hot spots. "Unbelievable," said Alberta.

"All you care...about is...your damn...dog...those stupid cats," Rudy said, flinching as the EMT cut the sleeve off the boy's hoody. "And...that horrible...man!" He seemed to rally on the last part. Rage is a powerful painkiller.

"What are you talking about?" asked his mother.

He stopped speaking as the EMTs shifted him onto the gurney, and my thoughts leaped to what Marietta had said about what Jorge had seen. Rasmussen on the agility course in the dark. Rasmussen talking to someone out there. Someone running in the dark a few minutes later. Had that been Rudy Sweetwater? Was he the killer?

I stepped closer to the gurney. "Rudy, did you kill Charles Rasmussen?"

The EMTs and Officer Fong all stared at me, and Candace wheeled and said, "How dare you!"

"Shut up, Mom," Rudy screeched, his voice like an open wound. "I didn't mean to. I told him he should think about the things he does to people. He wrecked my life." Tears popped out of his eyes, but his voice got stronger. "He stole my mom's business and she lost all that money and ..." He gasped as the EMT strapped him in. "He was a bad man. They tell us to stop bullies in school. Well, he was a bully. He was chasing a little cat out there, chasing her and yelling at her, when I first saw him." He stopped and his whole face seemed to clench. Then he went on. "I told him to stop that, and he shoved me. He shoved me and called me a little shit."

The EMTs started to wheel the gurney toward the ambulance, but Rudy stopped them. "The second time he shoved me, I tripped and fell, and he laughed." Rudy was starting to cry. "He laughed and said some things about you ..." He looked at his mother, and I could only imagine what Rasmussen must have said about her. "I was leaving, but I saw a scoop by a garbage can outside the ring, and I just ... I picked it up and I ran up behind him and I hit him." Tears were running down his cheeks now. I felt Hutchinson move in next to me, but kept my eyes on Rudy. "He sort of stumbled when I hit him, and he started to bleed, and I hit him again. But," he said, "I didn't mean to kill him. I just wanted to hurt him." Rudy got control of himself, but his face was pale and pinched. "He turned around and said he was going to 'skin me alive,' and I ran."

"So he was on his feet? You didn't knock him down?" I asked.

Rudy shook his head. "But that really made me mad," he said, glancing at the ashy mess he had created, and with a chilling calm that belied his emotional story.

"And he was okay when you left?" asked Hutchinson, his voice calm.

Rudy laughed, then moaned. "No. I ran, but then I heard a noise behind me and heard him make this weird *oomph* sound, and I turned to see. That little cat was there, off to the side, and the douchebag was on the ground next to the pause table," said Rudy.

Hadn't Hutchinson said they'd found cat hair on Rasmussen's pants?

"He tried to get up, but I guess he hit his head." He laughed again, and said, "It was funny. The cat sort of looked at him and looked at me and then meowed and left."

"We need to go," said the EMT at the back of the gurney, and they began to roll it toward the ambulance.

Rudy was still talking, and Hutchinson and I followed, along with Candace. "He got to his hands and knees, and just sort of stayed there, swaying around. So I left."

I said, "Rudy, the pooper-scooper....You hurt him, but those blows didn't kill him."

"Jeez," said Hutchinson, very softly so that only I heard him. "The cat killed him."

We both stopped walking and stared at each other. But I had a couple more questions, and ran to catch up. "Rudy, did you send the fake bomb to Alberta's house?"

He tried to grin, but the pain on his face created a creepy smirk. "Yeah. Wish I could have seen her face when she opened it."

"Why threaten Alberta?"

He shrugged. "Lots of people were mad at her, so I figured it would be fun."

"But why wreck the cat shelters?" I asked.

"I didn't do that," he said.

"But then why set them on fire?"

His whole face relaxed and his expression went blank. He looked at his mother, and at Alberta, and back at me. He shrugged and said, "Why not?"

# FIFTY-SIX

Tom had left a message on my cell phone sometime during the melee at the clubhouse, but I didn't see it until I emptied my pockets pre-shower at home. By then, I had just over an hour to make myself presentable and meet him and Tommy at Paula's on Main. I had no idea what dinner would be, but I had half a mind to order the key lime pie for an appetizer. That and tee martunis should fix me right up.

Goldie had come running over the moment I pulled into my driveway, and I'd given her the synopsis. When I told her I had more on my evening agenda, she pushed me toward the bathroom and said, "Go, go. I'll feed the boys." And, once I gave them a group hug, she had done just that. She'd been sitting at the kitchen table when I re-emerged, Jay's head on her lap and Leo on the table, his leg dangling and, every few seconds, tickling Jay's ear.

"Hey, you still know how to clean up good," she said, looking me up and down. "I haven't see you in a skirt since … since …"

I fastened the second silver hoop into my ear and said, "My hair okay?"

"Everything's gorgeous," she said. "But don't let me be the judge of that. Get going!"

It wasn't quite raining, but a fine mist called for the wipers, and it took me a minute to find the switch in the rental. I was getting a little tired of being without my own van, scratches, pet fur, coffee stains, and all.

The host was checking names to find the table when I felt an arm around me. "I'll take it from here," said Tom. He wrapped me up in a hug and whispered, "You really have to stop getting into these situations, Janet." He backed off and looked into my eyes, and I thought my heart might stop. "I don't know what I'd do ..."

The host was gaping at us, but I didn't care. "It wasn't, I mean, I wasn't in any danger," I said. *Unless you call proximity to a firebug with accelerants a danger.*

"Liar," he said. "Come on." He took my hand and led me to a table at the back of the restaurant.

"Janet," said the young man, rising. He was a good three inches taller than his father, and had the same warm, firm way of folding my hand into his. His coloring was entirely different—blonde, blue eyes—but he had Tom's grin that suggested trouble on the way. "I'm so glad to finally get to meet you." Whatever jitters I'd had about meeting the family, which consisted of this one young man, dissolved.

Conversation worked its way backward in time, beginning with the afternoon's fiery events. "He's not badly burned," I said. "I guess he managed to pull his hand up into the sleeve. He needed treatment, but it could have been much worse."

"So if that Rudy kid didn't break Alberta's window, who did?" asked Tommy.

"Harry, the cranky birder who created a scene at Alberta's TNR booth," I said. "He was wearing a Callaway t-shirt, and the ball that broke the window was a Callaway. I told Hutchinson about the shirt, and the police followed up."

"That's pretty extreme," said Tommy.

"I guess he caved in when they showed up at his house. He admitted to hitting the ball through the window and to dismantling the cat shelter and breaking up the wood."

"Crazy," said Tom. He changed the subject then to a recap of Leo's competitive debut, and I could tell two things about Tommy. First, he'd already heard it at least once, and second, he didn't mind at all. "I hope I get to meet Leo and Jay before I leave," he said.

"You're about to start your dissertation research?" I shifted my gaze and found Tom watching me with a look I wanted to dive into. I had missed that look, and I knew I would miss it even more when he left. I swallowed the urge to knock the table aside and throw myself at him, and instead I said, "I know you told me, what, somewhere out west?"

Tommy laughed. "Right. West of Spain." He explained that he had been planning to do his research in northern California and Nevada, but at the last minute a grant had come through, and he was off to Spain at the end of the week.

"Getting everything arranged at the last minute has been a bit of a nightmare," he said, and raised his glass and waited for us to follow his lead. "Here's to dads who know how to make travel arrangements." I almost choked on my martini when he followed up with, "Especially for dogs."

Tom patted my back. "Are you okay?"

"Wrong pipe," I managed to squeak out.

When it was clear I'd survive, Tom said, "Tommy adopted a really neat little dog a few months ago. Probably part Aussie." I dared to look at him, and knew immediately that he had figured out my error. The crinkles around his eyes deepened as he grinned at me. "He's taking her along, of course. That's why I moved the Indy trip up. Had to see about her travel documents."

As we finished dinner and coffee—I was too stuffed for the key lime pie—we circled back to the situation at The Rapids of Aspen Grove. "Have you spoken to Goldie this afternoon?" asked Tom.

"What? No, just on the fly." I realized as I thought back that she had run over in quite the rush when I got home. Apparently she had news but had shelved it in favor of my rendezvous.

"Seems Goldie has arranged a meeting between proponents of the TNR program and resident cat colony and some of the birders who oppose it," said Tom.

"That's great," I said, puzzled. "She called you?"

"No. I stopped by, thinking you might be there." He reached under the table and squeezed my hand, setting off a familiar tingle somewhere low and deep. *Slow down there, missy*, warned my ever-watchful guardian voice. *You still have a few snarls to tease out of this relationship.* Tom spoke again. "There's more."

"What?"

"Louise says she's going to dissolve her husband's development company and use whatever money is available to purchase the pond, woods, and wetlands," he said. "She plans to establish a trust, allow limited access to researchers and artists. Big plans, from what

318

I hear. Alberta's involved, and they've hired Giselle to handle their online presence."

"Wow. They have an online presence." I grinned. "I guess they're going to need digital images."

Tommy seemed restless, so I told Tom, "Maybe Tommy has things he needs to do?" I expected him to say he'd see me the next day, or the day after.

Tom pulled his keys from his jacket pocket and handed them to Tommy. "I'll see you in the morning," he said, and Tommy said goodnight and was gone.

"What about the puppy?" I asked.

"She can come home at nine weeks," he said. "Mid-December. Whichever one 'she' is."

I knew he'd already chosen, even if he didn't know it.

"It's going to be a full house," I said, and told him I was adopting Gypsy's tabby daughter. "Well, you know, two houses." *Tell him you want to live together.*

"About that..."

The server interrupted with the check. Tom told her to wait while he signed the slip and sent her on her way. Then he said he had something to ask me, and claimed to have asked me before, in the car, but I had ignored him. I thought back and remembered a time when I had missed what he was saying as my mind wandered.

He took my hands and started to speak, but I also started to speak, and when the laughter and kissing had stopped, all I could remember was that we had both come up with the same proposal. The devil, as they say, would be in the details.

**THE END**

### ABOUT THE AUTHOR

Sheila Webster Boneham writes fiction and nonfiction, much of it focused on animals, nature, and travel. Her first Animals in Focus mystery, *Drop Dead on Recall*, won the 2013 Maxwell Award for Best Fiction Book from the Dog Writers Association of American (DWAA) and was named a Top Ten Dog Book of 2012 by NBC Petside. Six of Sheila's nonfiction books have been named best in their categories in the DWAA and the Cat Writers Association (CWA) annual competitions, and her book *Rescue Matters! How to Find, Foster, and Rehome Companion Animals* (Alpine, 2009) has been called a "must read" for anyone involved with animal rescue. Sheila has a PhD in folklore and MFA in creative writing, and frequently teaches writing classes and workshops. She enjoys talking to groups of all kinds about writing and animals. You can reach her through her website at www.sheilaboneham.com or her Facebook page at www.facebook.com/sheilawrites.

# www.MIDNIGHTINKBOOKS.COM

From the gritty streets of New York City to sacred tombs in the Middle East, it's always midnight somewhere. Join us online at any hour for fresh new voices in mystery fiction.

At midnightinkbooks.com you'll also find our author blog, new and upcoming books, events, book club questions, excerpts, mystery resources, and more.

## MIDNIGHT INK ORDERING INFORMATION

 ### Order Online:
- Visit our website www.midnightinkbooks.com, select your books, and order them on our secure server.

 ### Order by Phone:
- Call toll-free within the U.S. and Canada at 1-888-NITE-INK (1-888-648-3465)
- We accept VISA, MasterCard, and American Express

 ### Order by Mail:
Send the full price of your order (MN residents add 6.875% sales tax) in U.S. funds, plus postage & handling to:

> Midnight Ink
> 2143 Wooddale Drive
> Woodbury, MN  55125-2989

### Postage & Handling:

Standard (U.S. & Canada). If your order is:
> $25.00 and under, add $4.00
> $25.01 and over, FREE STANDARD SHIPPING

AK, HI, PR: $16.00 for one book plus $2.00 for each additional book.

International Orders (airmail only):
> $16.00 for one book plus $3.00 for each additional book

Orders are processed within 12 business days. Please allow for normal shipping time.
Postage and handling rates subject to change.

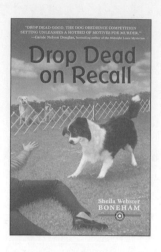

## Drop Dead on Recall

### SHEILA WEBSTER BONEHAM

When a top-ranked competitor keels over at a dog obedience trial, photographer Janet MacPhail is swept up in a maelstrom of suspicion, jealousy, cut-throat competition, death threats, pet-napping, and murder. She becomes a "person of interest" to the police, and apparently to major hunk Tom Saunders as well. As if murder and the threat of impending romance aren't enough to drive her bonkers, Janet has to move her mother into a nursing home, and the old lady isn't going quietly. Janet finds solace in her Australian Shepherd, Jay, her tabby cat, Leo, and her eccentric neighbor, Goldie Sunshine. Then two other "persons of interest" die, Jay's life is threatened, Leo disappears, and Janet's search for the truth threatens to leave her own life underdeveloped—for good.

**978-0-7387-3306-7, 408pp., 5³⁄₁₆ x 8**                    **$14.99**

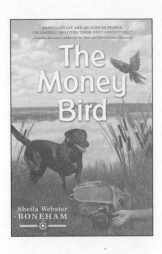

# The Money Bird

SHEILA WEBSTER BONEHAM

Animal photographer Janet MacPhail knows that trouble is in the air when Labrador Retriever Drake fetches a blood-soaked bag holding an exotic feather and a torn one-hundred-dollar bill during a photo shoot at Twisted Lake. One of Janet's photography students reports seeing a strange bird at the lake, but he turns up dead before Janet can talk to him. When she learns that the mysterious retreat center near the lake is housing large numbers of tropical birds, Janet is sure there's a connection and decides to investigate between dog-training classes, photo assignments, and visits to her mom at Shadetree Retirement. With help from her Australian Shepherd Jay and her quirky friend Goldie, Janet is determined to get to the bottom of things before another victim's wings are clipped for good.

**978-0-7387-3487-3, 336pp., 5³⁄₁₆ x 8**                    **$14.99**